Praise for *Mary McGreevy*

"You have to love the title character of Walter Keady's second novel, who suffuses the whole book with her graceful charm and feisty humor....Keady, who grew up on a farm in the west of Ireland, clearly knows the territory. Both his plot and his prose are as down-to-earth as the parish he creates."

—*The New York Times*

"Walter Keady tells a moral tale without moralizing, daring to make gentle fun of the Irish Catholic Church, writing a sweet love letter to Irish Catholics themselves."

—Carolyn See, *The Washington Post*

"To Keady's credit, Mary is ever asking the large [spiritual questions]...the great strength of this novel is that it is not afraid to ask big questions that probe the soul, and the heart."

—*The Philadelphia Inquirer*

"Written with charm and humor and massive doses of Gaelic atmosphere, *Mary McGreevy* is a heartwarming, evocative story of a strong and willful woman."

—Ann LaFarge, *The Constant Reader*

"*Mary McGreevy* is one of the those novels that within the space of the first chapter it's clear you have to find a way to continue reading uninterrupted by any means possible....Any sleep missed while reading *Mary McGreevy* is well exchanged for the energy, humor and lives explored by Walter Keady. A very good story indeed."

—*New Visions*

Praise for *Celibates and Other Lovers*

"Writers who find their calling later in life are rare enough. Walter Keady not only did just that, but leaves readers wondering what took him so long."

—*The Austin-American Statesman*

"[Keady's] affection for these characters—in combination with lively, funny dialogue, a sympathetic hero and the often hilarious capers perpetrated by his comrades—lend this debut a great deal of charm."

—*Publishers Weekly*

"Keady tells this story with great skill, style, and warmth—and with a great deal of gentle humor as well."

—*Library Journal*

"Sometimes a book comes along that just makes you feel good....It's as fresh and breezy as a perfect spring day. As playful and innocently sensuous as young love. There's no doubt that Keady is enormously fond of his characters—but he is also clear-sighted enough to recognize their foibles."

—*The Orlando Sentinel*

"Realistic people and elegant prose...Keady...has written of human beings, their wants and needs and sorrows and joys, in a manner that is universal."

—*Irish Echo*

"Walter Keady paints an entertaining portrait of life, love and Catholic guilt in a post-Word War II...fishing village in Western Ireland....Keady has cleverly, subtly captured the warm, nostalgic spirit of rural Ireland in the 1950s."

—*The Boston Sunday Herald*

"Keady's novel is written with simple grace and charming turns of phrase. The novel's core is bittersweet, and the sense of chances missed and love lost lingers all the more strongly for the author's light touch."

—Lynn Harnett, *Herald Sunday*

THE ALTRUIST
a novel by Walter Keady

MacAdam/Cage
155 Sansome Street, Suite 550
San Francisco, CA 94104
www.macadamcage.com

Library of Congress Cataloging-in-Publication Data

Keady, Walter, 1934 —
The altruist / by Walter Keady.
p. cm.
ISBN 1-931561-39-7 (alk. paper)
1. Young women—Fiction. 2. Pregnant women—Fiction.
3. Unmarried mothers—Fiction. 4. Illegitimate children—Fiction.
5. Ireland—Fiction I. Title.
PS3561.E16A48 2002
813'.54—dc21

2002156264

Manufactured in the United States of America
10 9 8 7 6 5 4 3 2 1

Book design by Dorothy Carico Smith.

THE ALTRUIST
a novel by Walter Keady

MacAdam/Cage

To Patricia, Veronica, Virginia

I. COMMITMENT

The lorry barreled through Kildawree, ignoring the slow-through-the-village warning sign. The driver was in a hurry to get to Castlebar so as not to miss what his girlfriend called their window of opportunity while her husband was at work. On the long slow incline known as the Mile Hill he dropped into low gear, for his load was heavy. At the crest he moved into top again, letting the behemoth roll headlong down the slope. The road was narrow, bare width for oncoming cars, though not lorries, to pass without slowing and pulling off on the margin. About a mile from Ballinamore he saw the red car coming, weaving along the thin white center line. He maintained speed, keeping as close to the margin as safety permitted; it was the other driver's responsibility to straighten. But the car curved farther into his path. He braked hard, too late. The unfortunate Honda swung away just as he was about to plow into it, so that the driver got the full brunt of his thirty-five tons. The scream of brakes jarred against the crunch of metal and the shatter of glass. Then all was silent, except for the bleat of a sheep in a nearby field.

A tragic accident occurred outside Ballinamore early this afternoon, Aisling Banaghan heard on the radio as she was getting the dinner ready. She stopped to listen. *Mary*

McGreevy, the former Minister of State for Agriculture, was killed when the car she was riding in was struck by an articulated lorry just outside the town.

"Eugene!" Aisling shouted at her husband who was washing his hands in the scullery sink. "Come and listen to this."

Her companion, Kitty Tarragh, the driver of the car, was also pronounced dead at the scene of the accident. A hospital spokesman said she had apparently suffered a stroke while driving.

"Good God Almighty!" Eugene stood in the doorway drying his hands.

"Poor Eilis," Aisling said. "She and Gran are so close."

It was one of the biggest funerals ever seen in Kildawree. The two coffins lay side by side in the parish church for the Mass of the Resurrection. Though there were those who said the pair shouldn't have been allowed inside the sacred walls in death since neither had appeared there alive for the past forty years. But Mary McGreevy had been a Minister of State and there would have been a terrible hullabaloo in the media if she were denied Christian burial. Besides, wasn't her daughter Bridget one of the most devout Catholics in the parish? And anyway, Father Heaney was a fierce liberal altogether who'd bury a stray dog in consecrated ground if someone asked him.

The metamorphosis of once holy Ireland was made even more manifest when the Taoiseach delivered the eulogy at the mass and spoke about Mary McGreevy's exemplary life of public service, as County Councilor, Teachta Dala, and Minister of State for Agriculture. One of the finest women

Ireland had produced in this century, he said, citing her devotion to her constituents and her bold policy-making in one of the most difficult departments of government. Not a word about the scandals of earlier years: her illegitimate child, apostasy from the faith, facing down the archbishop of Tulach here in this very church. For which omissions and many others that same child, now Mrs. Bridget O'Connor, felt guilty but grateful, knowing well that it was only the decadence of the seventies and the power of a liberal and godless media that had enabled her mother to be voted into office by a generation of tepid Catholics. The present archbishop of Tulach, Most Reverend Dr. Thomas Whelan, was not among those present: he had a prior engagement, he told Father Heaney when the latter phoned to tell him about the dignitaries of state who planned to be there, and to inquire if his Grace would like to preside.

When the clay struck the coffins, Eilis O'Connor wept some more and left the graveyard abruptly, without waiting for parents or siblings or anyone else, and without a thought to the post-funeral reception in the parish hall that she would be expected to attend. She was more than halfway back the road to Kilduff, half walking, half running, as if burning energy might assuage her grief, when Aisling and Eugene Banaghan caught up with her. "Can we give you a lift?" Eugene rolled down the window of the Opel.

"I'd rather walk, thanks." But then she changed her mind and got into the backseat.

"We'll miss her. We'll miss them both," Eugene said.

"Don't," Eilis said. "Don't say a word." When they came to the boreen leading to her house she said, "Don't turn in;

I'd like to go home with you."

They drove in silence to the Banaghan house. "I'll say this for her, she lived life to the full," Eugene remarked going in the door. "She was one great woman, your grandmother."

"Can we go for a walk?" Eilis asked her cousin later, after Eugene had gone down the yard. She and Aisling walked back the narrow road between grassy banks alive with flowers. Eilis felt the summer heat come through her black dress. "I don't know what I'll do without her." She choked and stopped and began to cry.

Aisling put an arm around her shoulder. "We're all going to miss her."

"No warning, no preparation. I was down last week to see her and she was running around as if she were twenty-one instead of eighty-one." Eilis held a hanky to her nose.

"We were lucky to have her so long."

"I wouldn't be here if it weren't for her." Eilis had to smile through her tears. "I mean having Mammy the way she did." She took Aisling's hand and squeezed it. "Of course we wouldn't be cousins if she hadn't seduced our grandfather Feerick." They both laughed at the merry wickedness of the late Mary McGreevy who deliberately had a child—Eilis's mother—out of wedlock back in the days when such conduct was not only mortally sinful but socially proscribed. And chose a married man with six children as the father.

"At least she was lucky enough to have a child," Aisling said. "More than some of us can do."

Their conversations always came round to this, the perennial anguish of her barren cousin. For the past ten years Aisling and Eugene had labored in vain to make a baby. Trying simple lust first of course, expecting nature to take care of the rest. When after a year of exuberant effort no progeny germinated, they had prayerful recourse to the supernatural, for they were devout Catholics and believed in benevolent divine intervention. When heaven paid no heed, they sought out Catholic doctors in Dublin who prescribed reinforcements approved by the Church. When those didn't work they sneaked off to England to non-Catholic physicians, whose medicine was said to be more potent, though their ethics might not be Vatican-approved. When even modern technology with all its powers was of no avail, they patronized a woman in Connemara who was said to induce fertility with *pisreogs*, a form of traditional Celtic medicine that in the New Age was again gaining credence. That, too, failed.

"I want my baby." Aisling was a good three inches taller than Eilis, with the dark hair and eyes of her grandmother, Rita Feerick. "I'll die without children, Eilis; I know it. It's not fair." Sitting on the side of the road to the possible ruination of her good frock, she put her hands to her face and cried.

When they got back to the house she made scones and they ate them hot with jam and herbal tea, sitting in the parlor. All the while she talked of her need for a child. And grumped at God and nature and genes and chromosomes and organs and spermatozoa and ova and gametes and zygotes or whatever it was that was keeping herself and Eugene from creating new life. Eilis nodded and nodded till her eyelids began to droop. The sadness of the day had made her tired.

"Have you given any more thought to adopting?" They had discussed that possibility many times in the past couple of years.

"We're still afraid. It's very risky. You hear so many stories."

"You have to take *some* chances in life."

"Actually, I'd be willing to take a stab at it. But Eugene says no. He'll only adopt if he knows who the parents are."

"Gran used to say that Grandfather Feerick set great store by good blood in a family. It seems Eugene feels the same way."

"He's afraid, too, that if we adopted, the mother might come looking to take the child back. That has happened, you know. And mothers have won their cases in court, too."

It was just about then that Eilis nodded off to sleep.

The ache was deep, penetrating, like the damp chill of a winter evening; but, unlike the cold, there was no warmth into which she could escape. It stayed with her throughout the days as she went about her library duties, it settled into her body as she tried to sleep each night. *Gran, how could you die on me?* They were so close, the two of them—thick as thieves her mother often said, sometimes a bit sourly—that life without her was unimaginable. Gran had always been there, and so *would* always be there, Eilis had implicitly expected.

The letter arrived just a week after the funeral. When she got home to her flat on Saint Mary's Road in Galway city it lay on the landing where the landlord had left it. The sender's address said *Lavelle & Lavelle, Solrs., Castlebar.* Inside was a brief note folded around another envelope.

Our recently deceased client, Ms. Mary McGreevy, instructed us to deliver the enclosed to you after her death.

We tender our most sincere...

She tore open the envelope.

> *My dearest Eilis,*
> *You will read this shortly after I die, whenever that will be. In case I don't have the chance to say a proper goodbye to you— and, given the vagaries of life, who knows if I will—I want to tell you one last time how much I love you, and have always loved you. And although I don't believe in mother church's heaven, I still have hope that we shall meet again. As you and I have discussed many times, I do think reincarnation is a distinct possibility, and our best hope of survival.*
> *Which brings me to my last request. I ask you most earnestly to conceive a baby as soon as possible. This child, with my blood and Wattie's and yours coursing in its veins, will be the vehicle of my return to you, and the means of keeping us close. And then I in my new incarnation, or one of my children, will bring you back in a similar manner when your time comes. Perhaps we can perpetuate each other off into the distant future by such an unending cycle. So please, conceive me as soon as you can.*
> *With much affection until we meet again,*
> *Gran*

Eilis stood there, mouth open, staring at the paper in utter disbelief. Not even death could stem Gran's penchant for demanding the impossible, from herself and from others. The woman who had faced down a hostile electorate in her last campaign because she had introduced tough new regulations to prevent the possible spread of foot-and-mouth disease, and had won, was now demanding, from beyond the grave if you don't mind, nothing less than her own return to earth.

Conceive a baby as soon as possible. Eilis perched on the edge of the sofa. Apart from any other consideration—and there would be so many things to take into account here— she was ambivalent about *ever* having children because of her concern with world overpopulation. She rang her friend Mairead and they met later at O'Brien's pub.

"I loved your granny *because* she was a bit loony," Mairead said over a pint. "But I do think this time she went over the brink." Mairead was drop-dead gorgeous, with jet-black hair and a smooth olive complexion.

"But I'll have to do it, somehow or other. I know it's daft, I know it'll ruin me, but I couldn't live with myself if I didn't. Just the thought that if I refused her last request I might— even just might, mind you—keep Gran from coming back and being near would haunt me for the rest of my life. So the only question is how."

It took them three pints and more than two hours of discussion to reach a possible solution.

Friday evening she went home to Kilduff, and after dinner walked back to visit the Banaghans. They sat outside in the long summer twilight, watching the colors slowly fade from the garden flowers.

"Are you still thinking of going to America?" Eugene asked.

"Will you not be putting ideas into her head," Aisling said. "What would she want to go to America for?"

"Well, I hope not. 'Twould be fierce lonely here without you."

Eilis hoped Aisling wouldn't notice her blushing. She was very fond of Eugene. "I don't know what I want to do." And she didn't. Five years out of University and still slipping and sliding in the mud of indecision. Yes, of course, she wanted to do something worthwhile. Yes indeed, she was a feminist, like Gran and Mairead, who believed that women were entitled to the same opportunities as men. But she lacked the ambition to prove that belief in the dirty arena of male-dominated business—or of politics, where Gran had excelled. She wasn't competitive, that was her problem. No hurry, Gran would say whenever they discussed the matter: she herself had been thirty-four when she came out of her shell and left the convent. Eilis had thought once that she'd like to become a priest. That was when she was bursting with idealism at the end of secondary school and there was a lot of talk about Rome relenting and ordaining women. Gran had looked strangely at her when she confided that desire, though she made no comment: she'd never discourage you from doing anything you thought was worthwhile. Then came University and the asphyxiation of her faith in the maelstrom of new ideas and the scandals of old clergy. Though much of her idealism survived, it was now divorced from religion. So while she still had a vague longing to do something remarkable, she wasn't able to decide what that something should be. She volunteered at the hostel that sheltered the homeless, but that was just a once-a-week effort. After President Robinson's visit to Somalia she almost volunteered for relief work there, and regretted afterwards not having done so. She *had* talked about going to America, but that would be just a cop-out, as Mairead said: there were plenty of job opportunities here at home in Ireland at the present time.

"Why don't you go for teaching?" Aisling suggested now. "You're still young enough. And it's great fun. I love it. Especially the small children." Even in the dim light Eilis detected a glistening in her cousin's eyes.

She came back to visit again on Saturday morning. "Eugene is out the land looking at the cattle," Aisling answered her question.

"Good. I wanted to talk to you on your own. Would you mind sitting down." They were standing by the kitchen sink, Aisling washing the breakfast dishes.

"What's this all about?" Aisling dried her hands and sat with Eilis at the table.

"Would you be willing to adopt if *I* had a baby?"

Aisling stared, her face a melange of incomprehension, interrogation and bewilderment. She made several efforts to respond, her lips moving but no words coming. Finally she managed, "You're not pregnant, are you?"

"No. Not yet, anyway. What I was thinking was this: in America they have surrogate mothers for women who can't have babies themselves. I thought maybe *I* could be a surrogate for *you*."

Silence for a minute. Then Aisling said, in a dry tight voice, "I don't know what you're talking about."

Eilis explained. She had read a lot about the subject on the Internet after she and Mairead came up with the idea as a solution to Gran's request for a baby. But her cousin only said, "You're insane, Eilis O'Connor. I never heard such a daft idea in my whole life."

"What's wrong with it?"

"Well, it seems so obvious that I don't know how to put

it into words: you can't go around having babies for other people."

"Why not? You said Eugene would be willing to adopt if he knew who the parents were. Well, here's the mother. And there isn't anyone you know better, is there?"

Aisling was still holding her head in her hands when Eugene walked in the door. "What's the matter?" He looked from one to the other. "You both look awful serious."

"This one," Aisling said, "has come up with a notion so cracked it has my head spinning."

"Aisling!" Eilis wasn't ready yet to discuss the matter with Eugene.

"Well, you might as well tell him about it. He'd have to know, wouldn't he?" Aisling returned to the sink and began to scrub the porridge pot with an excess of vigor.

"Tell me what?" Eugene sat and took off his cap. "'Tis warm out there." He wiped the sweat off his forehead with his sleeve. Eilis thought she'd die of embarrassment, but she told him anyway. When she finished he looked over at Aisling. "And what's so cracked about that?"

"Eugene! Do I have *two* daft people on my hands now?"

"Just a minute, woman! Let's look at the whole thing without preconceived notions." He smiled at Eilis. "No pun intended. But I need a cup of tea first."

Practice

After Eilis left, the Banaghans sat in their kitchen looking quizzically at each other. "It's a terribly daft idea," Aisling said. But the excitement in her eyes now suggested it was the kind of daftness that appealed to her. "My daughter would be my cousin."

Eugene scratched his head with both hands. "What bothers me, now that I think more about it, is this: is it right?"

"What do you mean, is it right?"

"Well, you know…She's not married and all that."

"After all the things we've done ourselves, you're worried about *that* in this day and age?"

"Well now, we can't ignore it."

"*We* ignored the church's law against artificial insemination when we went to England, didn't we? Anyway, the Blessed Virgin herself wasn't married when she conceived Jesus."

"Ah now, you can't use arguments like that. Almighty God doesn't have to follow His own rules if He doesn't want to. But we do."

"Listen, *a stor*, let Eilis decide how she wants to handle it. After all, it's her decision."

"But we're involved. We gave our consent to her offer, didn't we? So we can't say the sin is hers alone: aren't we the ones inciting her to commit it?"

"Arrah, who says there's sin in it anyway?"

"What are you talking about? Of course there's sin in it."

"Didn't a priest say on Gay Byrne not long ago that young people are more and more making their own moral decisions, without reference to the Church? And about time, too, if you ask me. A lot of things they told us were mortal sins when we were young we now know aren't sins at all."

"Well, is that a fact? Such as?"

"A great deal of the stuff they told us about sex for one thing. Even Father Heaney himself admits that now. When he was over at the school last week and we were discussing catechism lessons, he said he considered that some of the prohibitions still in the new catechism relating to the sixth and ninth commandments are totally out of date."

"I don't believe what I'm hearing. Like what?"

"He gave the example of impure thoughts. They're only natural, he says. Everybody has them and we can't help them and they're part of our biology, he says. Yet we terrorize our children—and grown-ups, too, for that matter—into thinking they'll wind up in hell if they enjoy them."

"That man will get himself into trouble one of these days, between the queer things he says and the drink."

"Anyway, we should let Eilis work things out with her own conscience. I'm sure she's well able to do that."

"I suppose. The world *has* changed, no doubt about that." Eugene went to the door and stared out at the sky for a long time. "It takes two to make a babby—have you thought about that? She didn't say how she was going to go about getting...And we have a stake in knowing who it will be, since it's going to be *our* babby."

"I expect it will be her friend Joe. Anyway, whoever she chooses will be a man of good character. You can be sure of that. She wouldn't go for anyone else."

Pregnant. *Have to get preg. Have to get preg.* The phrase kept twittering in Eilis's head, to the tune of Beethoven's Fifth opening bars. *And do it soon*, came Gran's counterpoint. *Remember what I said: I'll be waiting.* She was committed to having a baby in the near future, and she berated herself daily for doing nothing about it. But how to get pregnant with no man in her life, other than Joe Mahony who was gay?

She had long since lost her virginity, thanks to the quietly persuasive Professor O'Flaherty. All through her first year at University she had fantasized about her initiation to sex, though she never actually sought to convert daydream to reality. She had dates, of course, but not too many: while pretty enough to attract boys' attention, her combination of brains and feminist rhetoric—which she had learned from Gran, of course—kept most of them from seeking her out. Among those who did, there were none with charm or grace enough to coax her knickers off. It was the professors, both married and unattached, who made the most serious advances. Two in particular were utterly stricken and must have her, they declared. Art Ryan, a poet with wild hair and huge glasses, she found absurd, even repulsive. But she rather liked Mairtin O'Flaherty, psychology professor, a tall, thin man with friendly eyes and a sense of humor. He would stop her in hallways for chats and find her at lunch in the cafeteria. At Christmas he invited her to a party he gave at his house for College faculty. Had he not been married she might have allowed him, if anyone, the privilege of devirgination. At that time it was the *anyone* that preoccupied her. Despite the fact that the majority of her friends—and most of the student body, according to campus myth—had long since entered the active sexual arena, she still clung to her monthly confession. Which practice was incompatible with fornication. But the professor's persistence eventually got her into his bed—or rather the borrowed bed of a junior colleague, a single fellow with a flat—at the beginning of her final year, and for the next eight months they trysted discreetly. Mairtin taught her the techniques of lovemaking and, if his cries of pleasure were any indication, she was quite an apt pupil. Not coincidentally, his philosophy of sex, expounded *post coitum*, to the effect that all erotic activity was moral as long as no one was harmed, weakened her religious faith till she dropped both her monthly confession and her objections to adulterous intercourse.

Was it possible that Joe might father her child? They were great friends, she and Joseph Kieran Mahony, ever since they met in a third-year English class and naively, importantly, discussed the future of Irish literature. He confided in her his sexual orientation a few months after graduation when, her pride smarting from dismissal by O'Flaherty, who bedded only students, she hinted that maybe she and he could be more than just friends. They did in fact become more than just friends, but not in the way she had hoped: he asked if she might pretend to his family that she was his girlfriend. The parents were fierce-to-the-world traditional Catholics, he said, who would die of shame at the very thought of his homosexuality. But at least they lived far enough away, down the country below Castlebar; more serious danger stemmed from Uncle Denis, in whose travel agency he worked. That man was holier than the Pope himself, Joe said, and more vigilant of deviation than the Roman Curia. He had just founded a far-out Catholic organization that he called *The Society for the Promotion of Christian Marriage.* "To help Christian families live better is its objective, he says, but his real purpose is to get people to renounce extramarital sex. In this day and age. Can you believe it?" Uncle Denis had pressured Joe into joining the Society, hinting that his job might be at stake if he refused.

So to oblige Joe, Eilis visited his family as the girlfriend, and enjoyed the experience so much that she introduced him to her own family and friends as her boyfriend. She had maintained that pretense for the past couple of years in spite of a number of romantic, if short-term, relationships with other men. At the moment she was in recovery from the souring of one such liaison.

"I'd love to help you," Joe said when she made her diffident proposal, after explaining her commitment to Aisling and Eugene, though not her promise to Gran. "I truly would if it was possible." She had met him in Salthill after work. He was a tall slender lad with blond hair, cut so short that not even the stiff Atlantic breeze could ruffle it, and an artless smile that stirred deep biological urges within her. They walked the promenade and clambered over rocks till they found a place to sit that was sheltered from the wind.

"It's all right. I understand. I just thought I'd ask."

"I love you like a sister, Eilis. You're so bloody good to me that I'd do anything for you, I think you know that. However, let me put it this way: physically I probably wouldn't be *able* to help you." He stood and stretched and gazed out to sea. "Anyway, Ger and I are now officially a couple, and I wouldn't want to be unfaithful to him so early on."

She cheered up when Eugene Banaghan dropped by her flat later in the evening. "What brings you to town?" He looked awfully dapper in a tweed jacket and tie. It wasn't often she saw him dressed up.

"Just a bit of shopping. Farm stuff and the like. Herself told me to be sure to take you out to dinner."

"I ate already. But I'll cook something for you."

"Ah, not at all. I'll get a bit in a pub." He got to his feet in a dejected sort of way. "Would you come for a drink anyway?"

They walked to a pub on Bridge Street. Eugene had bacon and cabbage and a pint of Guinness. Eilis asked for a lemonade. "No booze," she said when he pressed her to have something stronger. "I had too much wine last night." Mairead had cooked dinner and between them they had polished off a bottle of Cabernet.

"Carousing with the boyfriend, I suppose."

"No." She might as well tell him. "My friend Joe won't do it."

"You asked him already?"

"Yes."

"I hope you won't mind my asking." He took a swig of stout. "But did he ever...I mean, did you two..." He waved his fork. "Before this came up?"

"Curiosity killed the cat." She punched him lightly on the shoulder. "No, we didn't."

"Well, that's it then. He might never in his whole life

have…"

"There's no might about it. He never has."

"Ah!" Then with his mouth full, as if mumbling into his plate, he said, "And how about yourself?"

"Is everything all right?" The waitress stopped on her way to the bar.

"Grand." To Eilis he said, "Sorry. I shouldn't have asked that. It's none of my bloody business, is it?"

"As a matter of fact, I haven't." There had been three others since the Professor, whose moral code said that a white lie was permissible in answer to an impertinent question.

Eugene continued eating. "Getting started is the hardest. Aisling told me the first couple of times weren't much fun for her. 'Twas my fault, I suppose. I was a rough young country lad, and I didn't know what I was doing."

"One has to learn, I suppose." She remembered the expert fingers of Mairtin O'Flaherty.

"They say that in the old days it was the custom for uncles to start the business for girls. And the aunts would train the lads. 'Twas a good system, I suppose. And there was no sin in it, my father claimed."

"Well, Uncle Harry is not teaching *me*, I can tell you." The idea of that gross man's unwashed body and porter breath being even close to her was revolting.

After dinner he walked back to the flat with her. She made a pot of tea and opened the tin of biscuits Aisling had given her when she was home. They talked about Kildawree and the neighbors until Eugene said casually, "Do you think you'd like to get a bit of that training from *me*?"

It was so out of context, and she was beginning to get

sleepy, that she looked at him without comprehension. "What was that?"

"Nothing."

"You said something."

"It was nothing. I shouldn't have said it."

"Said what?" The look on his face—a mixture of embarrassment and devilment—was intriguing.

"Never mind. It was nothing at all."

"It *was* something at all. You asked me a question. Now what was it?"

"Oh cripes. I'm embarrassed now." He covered his face with his hands.

"Well, say it anyway. Go on."

"I only said would you like to try a bit of that training with me? But I shouldn't have. Sorry. Very sorry." Hands still covering his face.

She might have been shocked, or angry, or both, but she was neither. She had gotten used to the pleasures of sex with Mairtin, and had felt deprived when the affair ended. Now, though her more recent experiences had been dismal, she was almost savagely anticipating the carnal thrills that would induce her pregnancy. Besides, she liked Eugene an awful lot. She smiled at him. "It mightn't be such a bad idea at all."

"I wasn't codding, you know."

She had to be dumb not to have thought of it before. "Of course! Why can't *you* be your baby's father?" She jumped up off the sofa and looked down at him. "It's the obvious solution." Wouldn't Gran be pleased as punch with this mix of blood? The family story had it that she almost chose Eugene's uncle, Jack Banaghan—whom she later married anyway—to be the father of *her* child, Eilis's mother.

But Eugene was shaking his head. "It wouldn't work, I'm afraid. I'm part of the problem, you see, according to the doctors." His face reddened like a turkey cock's wattle.

However, she was excited now by the thought of sex with him, the fulfillment of a nocturnal fantasy. "Well, anyway, maybe you can give me some of that training you talked about." Then she thought of her cousin. "Oh bollocks." She plopped back onto the sofa.

Eugene looked puzzled. "What's the matter?"

"What about Aisling?"

"Aisling?"

"I don't expect your wife would approve of your giving me that kind of lesson."

"I suppose not. On the other hand, since it's for...Well, maybe it'd be all right."

"I can just see me trying to explain to Aisling..."

"Right. Of course, there would be no need to tell her."

"I'm awfully fond of Aisling. I'd never do anything to hurt her."

"I understand." Disappointment writ large on his face.

She changed the subject. They talked of Kildawree and the neighbors and inevitably of Gran and Kitty and their sudden demise. She made more tea; they ate more biscuits. It was almost midnight when he rose to go. "Where are you staying?" she asked.

"Jack Conroy."

"Isn't it a bit late to crash in on him now? You can sleep here on the sofa."

"Would it be all right?" He seemed pleased at the idea.

"Everyone else who comes to town does." She fetched

sheets and blankets and made up a bed for him. Then she went to her room. But she couldn't sleep. The possibility of erotic renewal, images of Eugene's strong body and hairy arms wrapped around her, kept her aroused. Should she have accepted his offer? What about Aisling? The evil of adultery stemmed only from injury to the adulterer's spouse, said Professor O'Flaherty. Which evil wouldn't occur if the spouse didn't know about it. Too bad she hadn't worked this out earlier. Too late now. At least for tonight. Or was it? It was. It wasn't. Was it right? Terrible not to be able to decide. She gave up from mental exhaustion and was beginning to doze when her legs of their own accord swung over the side of the bed. She sat up and threw back the blankets. Onto the floor and out the door. Into the parlor. Turned on the light, which made her squint. Eugene shot up on the sofa.

"What's the matter? Are you all right?"

"I'm ready for my lesson." She raised her short nightgown over her head.

Eilis's father and two of her brothers finished tying down the tarpaulin over the lorry load of hay. "Can I go with you, Dad?" fourteen-year-old Ciaran asked.

Frank O'Connor had anticipated the request. "I'd like if you'd take a look at the tractor this afternoon; the timing is off, I'd say." Ciaran loved to tinker with any kind of engine.

"But I want to go with you."

"Tell you what." His father climbed into the cab. "I'll take you to Westport tomorrow." He started the engine before the lad could argue further. Terry, the older boy, looked on silently. Glad to see his father go; in a few minutes he'd be stretched out in a corner of the barn, his head buried in a book. Ciaran shambled down the yard, frustration in every step. Frank swung the lorry out onto the road. It was good to have a customer for hay so early, barely into September. Cash flow! That was the name of the game; you had to keep the money coming in. However, it wasn't just the anticipation of payment that kept his grin hovering all the way to Loughrea with the hay, and then on to Galway. A little after three he parked the lorry outside a semidetached on Shantalla Road.

"Your timing was good." Julia let him in. "I just got home a few minutes ago." She was still in her nurse's white, cheeks flushed after cycling from the Regional Hospital.

"You look gorgeous as usual." He pulled her into his arms and kissed her fiercely on the lips, the nose, the nape, and then the lips again. He bit her left ear lobe before holding her at arm's length.

"Aren't you the hungry man, Mister O'Connor." Without giving him time to catch his breath she went at him, licking and biting and tonguing, breasts crushed against him, pelvis rotating, hands massaging.

"The boys. Where are they?"

"Danny is playing football. Tommy is swimming. We have the place to ourselves."

He carried her upstairs into her bedroom, set her down on the duvet, pulled off her shoes, slid his hands beneath her skirt, and tugged at her white hose. Their love-making was energetic, because he liked it that way; and prolonged because her needs so required. Afterwards, snuggled under the duvet, she talked about her job and how her boys were doing and how she missed him every day. "I hate having to share you."

"I'll always be here when you need me."

"Indeed you won't. But that's all right."

Later, they showered and dressed and climbed into the cab of his lorry and headed for a restaurant out on the Spiddal road, where nobody would know him. They were holding hands, following the hostess to their table, when he spotted a familiar face. At the precise moment that she looked up at him.

When she saw her father coming towards her in the restaurant, holding hands with a strange woman, Eilis thought she was hallucinating. Daddy didn't do things like that. He was a traditional farmer who worked hard every day of his life and took care of his family and went to mass on Sundays and confession for the men's sodality and he was much too old for that kind of thing—and it really was him standing there in front of her with a lopsided grin on his face.

"How are you, Frank?" Eugene said.

"What are you two doing here?"

"I suppose I could ask you the same thing," Eilis said, glancing from Daddy to the woman to let him know she was expecting an introduction.

"I'll talk to ye again. The waitress is calling us." Off the two of them went, no longer holding hands.

Eilis looked at Eugene. "Now what do you suppose that's all about?" Hoping desperately that somehow he could come up with a simple innocent explanation.

"I'd say now that you're not the only one who's taking lessons."

"Eugene! That's my Daddy, for God's sake. It's not possible."

"Many's the good tune in an old fiddle."

"Jesus, Mary and Joseph. Daddy can't be…" She thought she was going to cry. Mairtin O'Flaherty might engage in extramarital affairs—he was, after all, a professor and a romantic—but Frank O'Connor was a stolid farmer who, Mammy once told her, hadn't a romantic bone in his body.

"Anyway, he's not that old."

"He is so. He's forty-nine. And he's got six children." *Her* father couldn't be doing this. *She* might do what she had done last night, because she was young and foolish. But Daddy was old and wise and he was her anchor to reality and rightness. Mammy had instilled religion into her, but it was Daddy who had most often talked about honesty and truthfulness and loyalty.

"*I'm* thirty-four. Do you think I'm old?"

"No. Not really. Anyway, you were just showing me how. Like an uncle."

"Was I a good teacher?"

He was much more vigorous than Mairtin, which she had found exciting. "You were great." She couldn't imagine Daddy…blushed at the very thought. "Can you see them? What are they doing?" She pushed away her plate. "I can't eat any more."

"He has his back to us. But I caught *her* looking this way a couple of times. He's getting up now. Oh cripes! I think he's coming over. Don't look around, for God's sake."

Daddy's hand on her shoulder. "Listen. This is not what you might be inclined to think. But it might be just as well if you didn't mention anything about it to your mother. Let sleeping dogs lie, as it were. It would only get her upset. You know how your mother is?"

"Arrah, why would we say anything?" Eugene said. "It's none of our business anyway."

"And ye can count on me, of course, not to tell anyone that I saw the two of you here."

"Sorra bit of harm is in what *we're* doing," Eugene said. "I was just up for the day doing a bit of business and Aisling asked me to take your daughter out to dinner."

"Well, that's it then." Daddy squeezed her shoulder again. "I'll be seeing you all."

"Can we go now?" she asked Eugene as soon as Daddy left. "I can't stay another minute in this place." She refused to let him into the flat when they got back.

PREGNANCY

Eilis woke at three in the morning and couldn't get back to sleep. The enormity of the commitment she had made to Aisling and Eugene came home to her as if she were seeing it for the very first time. She could still go back on it, couldn't she? They'd surely understand. But of course she couldn't go back: her real commitment was to Gran. Her dear adorable impossible grandmother had asked her for a baby and she must not refuse. On the other hand, maybe Gran had changed her mind after she wrote the letter but had never gotten round to withdrawing it from the solicitors? The last time Eilis had talked to her she gave no hint that she was expecting such a sacrifice from her granddaughter. So just maybe...

It was then she heard Gran's voice, as plain as if she were in the room. *I didn't change my mind, a gradh. You do understand why I want this baby, don't you? I'm waiting to come back. So have it soon.* The experience was bewildering, though Eilis felt no fear at the sound of her grandmother's voice: it was so natural, matter-of-fact, Gran-like in its utterance. She reminded herself that Gran was dead and couldn't possibly be talking to her, but that thought in no way lessened the reality of the voice.

So Gran wanted her baby. Whatever the cost, then, Eilis would have it. All day at work she reiterated this commitment to herself, while she catalogued books and advised her patrons. She had been closer to her grandmother than to anyone else in the world, and ached every waking hour from the pain of her loss. She could not fail her now. Gran was going to come back in her child. Eilis would give her new life; in a sense she'd become the mother of her beloved grandmother.

But that evening her resolve faltered again. What about her own life? Surely it would be ruinous for her to go ahead with this promise. Her parents would feel disgraced. Even in the crass Irish world of today where unwed pregnancy had ceased to shock by becoming commonplace, it was still unthinkable for an O'Connor of Kilduff. High-minded motives notwithstanding, sin was still sin, Mammy would shout. And scandal was still scandal, Daddy would say. She'd never be able to explain her reasons to them. They'd believe that Gran had asked her all right: nothing was ever too farfetched in granny lore—Mammy's own birth was living proof of that. However, Eilis would never be able to go home again.

She argued and waffled and listened in vain for further encouragement from Gran. The next day she talked with Mairead over lunch. "Where will I find someone to father my child? I haven't had a date in months."

"Arrah, why would you need a man? Go for artificial insemination."

"Mairead! I'm not one of Frank O'Connor's heifers." They were in Ellie's café, amid the chatter of diners and the incessant beat of rock music.

"In the States, artificial insemination is the father of choice for surrogate mothers."

"Will you stop. It makes me think of a vet and a cow's

back-end and a big long... Ugh! No, thank you. Anyway, I'm
sure the bishops wouldn't condone it, and in this one
instance I'd be in full agreement with them."

Mairead sipped her third cup of tea. "Their lordships
don't approve of fornication or adultery either, and these are
your other choices."

"Don't you have any handsome swains on your current
string?" Mairead always had fellows hanging around, but
while she let the occasional lad into her bed, she never went
steady with any of them.

"Nobody you'd want to father your child, that's for sure.
Why do I always attract the creepy ones, will you tell me
that?"

Eilis was a week late before it crossed her mind that she
might no longer need a man. "Oh God, Mairead," she told
her friend the moment they sat down to lunch, "I think I'm
pregnant."

"How could you be pregnant? You haven't got laid
forever, unless you've been hiding things from me."

Eilis told her about Eugene, which she had been embarrassed to do heretofore. "But *he* couldn't have done it. He
told me he's sterile."

Mairead spat hamburger with laughing so hard. "Christ
Almighty, Eilis, aren't you the innocent one. They all tell
that cock-and-bull story because they hate wearing condoms.
Anyway, what's your problem? You wanted to get pregnant,
didn't you?"

"I'm not sure anymore." Now that vacillation might no
longer be an option, she was terrified.

"Well, go find out if sterile Eugene has snagged you."

On Thursday morning the doctor's office called her at the library. She was pregnant, the female voice at the other end assured her. And she distinctly heard Gran chortle *isn't that wonderful*. But her own dominant emotion was fear. She barely dragged herself back to the flat in the evening, what with the imagined weight of the new creature inside her and the terrible prospect of unmarried motherhood. For a couple of hours she cursed Eugene, swore at her stupid self, bemoaned Aisling's failure to reproduce, and railed generally at fate, God, and in particular her wicked grandmother. To all of which Gran remained discreetly silent. Eventually Eilis made herself an omelette and rang Mairead.

Her friend was terse. "Go to England and get an abortion if you don't want to go through with it."

"Mairead! This is my granny's second life. I can't just get rid of her like that. And besides, it's Aisling and Eugene's baby that they've been waiting for for years."

"It's your baby, too, Eilis. Don't forget that. The decision about having it or not is yours. Besides, Eugene sneaked it in on you, the bugger."

A woman's rights over her own body. Reproductive control. Issues she and Mairead had discussed endlessly in the abstract. And in the abstract she had asserted those rights. But this new life inside her wasn't abstract. It was a human being who would one day walk and talk and look like her. And Gran said she'd return to earth in this human being. So Eilis would go home this weekend and tell Aisling and Eugene that their baby was on the way.

First she must talk with Joe. She met him after work on Friday, in Eyre Square by the statue of Padraig O'Conaire. A dark November evening with cold damp air and an occasional sprinkle. "I don't have too long," he said. "Ger's expecting me home for dinner; it's his night to cook." He did have time for a cup of something at Ellie's.

"I need a favor," she said when the pot of tea arrived. "No, not that." Placing her hand on his arm when he looked startled. "I'm already pregnant."

"Go on out of that. You're not serious?"

She poured the tea for both of them. "I am."

"Jeez! You're one fast worker, Eilis, I'll say that for you."

"Gran was in a hurry."

"How was that?"

"I didn't tell you the whole story before because I didn't want you to think I was a head case, but the reason I wanted to have a baby was that Gran asked me to."

"I'm lost."

She told him everything. He listened in silence. "You don't believe me?"

He sipped his tea and sat back in his chair. "You have to admit it's a bit weird."

"Anyway, I have a favor to ask."

"You know I'd do anything for you."

"Aisling will want to know who the father is—I mean Aisling and Eugene of course. And I can't tell them the truth, for a very special reason."

"I think I can guess why."

"Why?"

"Because it's Eugene?"

"Now why would you say that?" Was it so obvious? Would the whole world guess the truth that easily?

"Because you told me once how much you liked him."

"Promise you won't tell anyone."

"They don't call me Joseph the confessor for nothing."

"Anyway, with regard to the favor, do you think...What I was wondering was if you'd be willing to pretend *you're* the father?" She put her head down, not daring to look at him. His silence gave answer. When she looked up he looked down, his eyes not meeting hers. "I was afraid you wouldn't go for it."

It was a while before he responded. "You ask me the damndest things, Eilis. I keep saying I'd do anything for you and then you ask me to do the impossible. Shit!"

"Ger, I suppose."

"I couldn't do it to him."

"You don't have to take responsibility for the child, or anything of the sort. That's a given."

"Even so. Ger would hit the roof when he found out. I don't want to lose him."

"He doesn't have to find out, of course."

"Once it becomes generally known he's bound to hear. Galway is a very small town when it comes to gossip. You know that."

"Yes, but..." Inspiration came, born of desperation. "*Everyone* doesn't need to know, do they? In fact, the only person I want to believe that you're the father is Aisling Banaghan."

"So how do you keep the rest from hearing?"

"Because we won't tell them. I can tell Aisling that you're the father but that you don't want anyone to know because you don't want to take responsibility for the baby. I'll swear *her* to secrecy and refuse to tell anyone else who the father is. What do you say?"

He hmmm'd, he maybe'd, he scratched his head some more, and finally said all right.

Eugene was out the land when she came by on Saturday morning. Aisling, standing in the middle of the kitchen floor, shut her eyes and observed a moment of silence. Then she grabbed Eilis in a smothering hug. "Oh God! I don't believe it. Aren't you a marvel. How did you do it?" Radiant, bursting with *joie de vivre*, as if she herself had just been told she was a mother. "Tell me about the father. Was it Joe?"

"Who else?" As if answering with a question might exculpate the lie.

"Well, I'm very happy. I like Joe. Is he pleased at being a father?"

"He's sort of pleased, yes. There's just one thing: he's not taking any responsibility for the baby. That was understood from the beginning. So he wants his part kept absolutely secret. I promised him it would be."

"Of course. It's better for us that way. I mean there's no danger of him interfering when it comes to the adoption." She wrapped herself around Eilis again. "You're so great. A real altruist." There were tears in her eyes. "I was recently reading a book where the author claimed there was no such thing as true altruism, that there were always selfish motives lurking somewhere. Well, now I know he was wrong."

Eilis had supper with her family. It was an event she usually enjoyed—the banter and gossip and sometimes serious conversation. She was fond of her siblings and had even grown to like her mother again, now that Mammy no longer tried to run her life for her. But tonight Eilis felt estranged, as if she no longer belonged with them. It was also her first time home since she met Daddy in the restaurant with the strange woman. So she took little part in the teasing and storytelling, and even resented Mammy's casual questions about her job and her friends and her social life in Galway. It was time to start getting some distance from them all: soon enough they wouldn't want to see her.

After the washup she took a flashlight and left the house to visit the Banaghans again. Her father was standing by the yard gate in the dark. "Listen. Don't mind your mother; she's too damn inquisitive at times."

"Right." She kept on walking.

"Eilis!" He followed her through the gate. "Listen. You'll be sure not to say anything to anyone about...you know?"

"Certainly not, Daddy. You can trust me." How was *he* going to react when she sprang *her* news?

"It was all perfectly innocent anyway."

"Of course."

"I'll see you later, then." He walked back to the house whistling "The Gypsy Rover".

As she turned onto the Kildawree road, a car came towards her, headlights blinding. It stopped. "Where are you off to now?" Eugene rolled down the window.

"Back to visit you. Where else?"

"I'm going into town to a meeting. But herself is at home."

"Can I come with you?"

"Hop in." He drove in silence till after they passed Kildawree. "I hear you and Joe have been together," he said as they sped down the long Mile Hill slope. "You used your charms, I suppose, to change his mind?"

"It wasn't Joe I was with."

"Oh! Someone else again?" Savagely, traveling too fast for comfort now.

"You." Eilis was acutely aware that they were hurtling past the scene of Gran and Aunt Kitty's accident. "I mean *you* are the father, Eugene. And will you slow down, for God's sake. You're scaring the life out of me."

He slammed on the brakes and pulled off the road by the front gate of a house. "What was that you said?"

"I said that you are the father of my baby—the biological father."

"Ah no, no. That can't be." Arms waving in all directions. "I've been tested. I told you all about it."

"Listen, Eugene. I've only had sex with one man in my entire life." Oh, the liar she had become; but there was no need for him to know about her other lovers. "Now I'm pregnant. So who do you think is the father? Unless it was a virginal conception?"

"Jesus God! I don't believe it." He grabbed her shoulder. "I do believe you, of course. It's just that I gave up thinking it could ever happen to me." He took several deep breaths, as though he was winded. "Christ! I feel this minute like I was just run over by a bullock. But you know something?" The look on his face was of a child caught stealing sweets—guilty as charged but, oh, what pleasure. "I might as well tell you the God's honest truth now. When I told you the story about the uncles that evening, I had something of this sort in the back of my mind. A kind of a hope, if you know what I mean. I prayed to God afterwards that something *would* come of it." He pounded the dashboard with his fist. "And by heaven He made it happen." He grabbed her face with both hands and kissed her hard on the mouth. "I could float up into the wild blue yonder this very minute." Then the grin faded and his look turned apprehensive. "Aisling mustn't ever know, of course. She'd kill me stone dead, so she would."

"You didn't tell her about Joe refusing me, did you?"

"No. Though I almost did. Something stopped me. Cripes almighty! Eugene Banaghan, father. That has a great ring to it, so it has."

She leaned over and kissed him, briefly, softly, on the lips. "Listen. Whatever you do, don't tell my parents. Tell Aisling not to, either. I want to keep it from them as long as possible."

Nevertheless, two weeks later the news reached Bridget O'Connor's furious ears.

DISCOVERY

A fine-looking woman, Bridget O'Connor. Many a younger man still looked at her with interest. Forty-five years old and not a single gray strand in her dark red hair, and her lightly freckled skin as clear as her daughters'. If her figure was not as slender, it was still a lot better than her age and motherhood of six might lead one to expect.

When the rumor first reached her, by way of her youngest son who was thrown the taunt by a sneering classmate, Bridget wailed what terrible liars people were nowadays spreading calumnies like that and she hoped he, Ciaran, had told the wretched boy so in no uncertain terms. But she knew deep down, immediately and with the infallibility of the born pessimist, that the rumor had to be true. So she was prepared for tragedy when she heard the story again a few evenings later, this time in a most kind and delicate way from Maeve Flannery, who helped her arrange the altar flowers. Maeve had been told it by her own daughter, who worked in Galway and was friends with a girl employed by a doctor there.

It would be true, but not the whole truth, to say Bridget was furious. Fury was indeed the principal ingredient in her stew of emotions that Friday evening coming home from the church. But it was mixed in with all the other feelings and prejudices and practical considerations of a devoutly

Catholic mother faced with the public sin of an unmarried daughter. It was further laced with the bitter remembrance of her own unhallowed birth.

She had a visceral urge to drive straight to Galway that night and challenge Eilis. But twenty-six years' experience of her eldest's quiet intractability in matters she had decided on, told Bridget that confrontation would serve no purpose. Everyone said Eilis took after her father, but you had only to look at her red hair and green eyes and feel the brunt of her stubborn temper to know she was made in the image of her granny McGreevy. So Bridget submerged her anger in prayer and waited till morning, when she rang Eilis.

"Let's do lunch." Her daughter had a prior commitment, so Bridget said she'd drop by the flat as soon as she reached the city. "I have something for you," she said, holding back the bile that threatened to show her hand too soon.

Eilis was on her way out the door just then, she said, and wouldn't be back until late. "I'll be down for Christmas, Mammy. You can give it to me then. I have to go now."

She arrived late on Christmas Eve, so there was no opportunity for private conversation before Bridget and her three daughters headed off for church. They had started the practice when the children were very young—Bridget taking the girls to midnight mass and Frank the boys to the morning one—and now it was a family tradition. Bridget noted that Eilis spoke little on the way and seemed withdrawn. Only ten-year-old Marie, the youngest, who adored her big sister and kept up an endless stream of chatter to impress her, seemed able to get more than a few words out of her. Bridget was quite put out when Eilis stayed in her seat during Communion while practically the entire congregation went to the altar. She would say nothing about this afterwards, of course—what went on between Eilis and her God was her own affair—but at the same time it was a bit odd, to say the least.

It wasn't until morning, when the male contingent was at mass and she had assigned Niamh and Marie to peel potatoes, that Bridget was able to create an opportunity to talk privately with her eldest. "Let's go for a walk," she suggested, since Marie was a noted sneak and eavesdropper. It was a crisp day after a hard-frost night. They put on their coats and gloves. "You look tired," she told her daughter as they walked briskly up the boreen.

"I'm all right."

"You're sure?"

"As a matter of fact, I'm not."

"What's the matter?"

"I'm pregnant, Mammy. That's what's the matter."

"I know." Bridget heard herself say the words as if from a distance. Calmly, when she should be screaming *How could you do this, you trollop?*

Eilis stood perfectly still in the middle of the road. "You *know*, Mammy! How do you know? You couldn't know. Nobody knows."

"Why do you think I asked you to come for a walk? The question is—"

"Doesn't anybody know how to keep a confidence anymore? I only told three people."

"What happened?" Keeping her voice level. Reminding herself she was dealing with an adult daughter who was responsible for her own life, and not to fly off the handle and yell at her as if she were a naughty child.

"What can I tell you? It happened."

"Is this Joe's doing?" She'd never have thought Joe Mahony would be guilty of such a thing. But nowadays one never knew: young people's standards were so different.

"No, Mammy, it's not. And I don't want to say any more on the matter."

"Well, if it wasn't Joe, then who was it?"

"I can take care of my problem, Mammy. So let's not talk about it any more."

"For God's sake, Eilis, you're not planning to…You can't do that, you know. That would be cold-blooded murder. Whatever else—"

"Mammy, calm down will you. I'm not planning to have an abortion, if that's what you're worried about."

"Well, thank God for that much. So when are you going to get married?" Time for her, anyway, Bridget had said more than once to Frank. They were married themselves and had three children by the time *she* was twenty-six.

"I'm not getting married, Mammy. Can we turn back now, I'm getting cold?"

"Well, I can tell you being a single mother is no joke these days. There are a couple of them in Ballinamore, and they're working day and night to keep body and soul together, and they hardly ever see their children. If you want to rear a child, get married. That's my advice to you now. It's the only decent thing to do."

"Does Daddy know?"

"Not yet."

"Then don't tell him till after dinner. We wouldn't want to spoil his appetite. Don't worry, Mammy. I know what I'm doing."

They were in the middle of the cleanup after the Christmas dinner—Niamh washing, Marie drying, Ciaran picking the remaining flesh off the turkey carcass, Bridget putting away the leftover food—when Frank came into the kitchen. "We have to talk." He grabbed Bridget by the arm and led her out the back door.

"What in God's name has got into you?" His eyes were wild with confusion and anger.

"She told me. She said you already knew. What the bloody hell is going on here, Bridget?"

"If she told you, then you know just as much as I do. So calm down now and we'll talk about it afterwards." Bridget marched back into the kitchen. Later, when the boys had gone for a walk and the younger girls were in their room playing with their presents, she lured Eilis into the parlor where Frank was sitting by the fire.

"I'm just letting you know," Eilis said before she sat down, "I won't stay if you start lecturing."

"Nobody is going to lecture you," Bridget said. "You're old enough to be responsible for what you do. All we want to know is what are your plans? I don't think that's too much for your parents to ask."

"You know very well what my plans are. I'm going to have a baby."

"We do know that. But what are you going to do then? How are you going to support it? Where are you going to live? How are you going to manage?"

"I'll manage." After a pause Eilis said, "I was going to tell you later, but it might as well be now. I'm giving the baby up for adoption."

"Christ Almighty," her father moaned.

"Just like that?" Depths of horror in Bridget's tone.

"Like you'd sell a bloody calf," Frank said.

"Well, I thought you might at least be pleased about *that*," Eilis shouted. "I didn't think you'd appreciate having the little bastard running round *this* holy house of Nazareth."

"Stop it this minute, Eilis." Bridget folded her arms. "There's no call for that kind of irreverence."

"Look," Frank said. "Regardless of who its father is, this baby will be my grandchild. And I don't want any grandchild of mine being given away like a puppy dog to anyone who'll take it."

"Daddy!"

"Your father is quite right. The way they do adoptions nowadays you wouldn't even know where the child was going or who its parents might be. It could wind up in a house where it was badly treated or beaten or neglected. You read about those cases in the paper every day. Now you wouldn't want that to happen to your child, would you?"

"I *know* where my baby is going. And I know who its parents will be."

Frank and Bridget stared at each other. "Well," Bridget said, "now we're getting somewhere. Are they good people?"

"The very best. Relations of your own, no less."

"Relations? Who?"

"Your cousin Aisling. And Eugene, of course."

"Oh dearest God in heaven, no. Let it not be." Bridget joined her hands in prayer.

"Christ Almighty, Eilis," Frank shouted. "Your mother doesn't even like those people."

"Well, I do and they're a lovely couple and they'll give my child a good home and I'll be able to watch it growing up." Then she put on the pleading look that her father could never resist. "They need a baby so much, Daddy. They're never going to have one of their own. This way, too, *you'll* be able to see your grandchild any time you want."

"Tell me, Lord, that I'm not hearing this," Bridget prayed.

"I knew it was a waste of time talking to you." Eilis swept out of the house and walked back the road to visit Aisling and Eugene.

At about nine o'clock, as Eilis and the Banaghans were having tea, there was a knock at the back door. Ciaran, grumpy, mumbled that he had been sent to tell Eilis to come home: the priest was visiting and had asked for her. Eilis, sensing a trap, was of two minds about going, but in the end she agreed because Father Michael Heaney was the kind of man you could talk to. He always made you feel that he was listening to you and sympathized with your position. And he had a sense of humor: there were always a couple of laughs in his Sunday sermons.

"Tell them I'll be home in a few minutes." But she waited another half hour before returning. Her parents and Father Heaney were in the parlor. The priest was on his feet. "It's time for me to go," he was saying as she walked in the door. He was smiling and dripping good cheer; she had an immediate feeling he had drink on him.

"Arrah, not at all, Father," Frank said. "Sure it's early yet." He, too, had obviously been drinking. "Anyway, now that Eilis is here I'm sure you'll want to talk to her."

"Father Heaney would like to have a chat with you, Eilis," Bridget said.

Eilis plopped into an armchair by the fire. "What did you want to talk about, Father?" Though it was well she knew; no doubt they had invited him back for this very purpose.

"Ah, yes, yes!" The priest dropped onto the sofa next to Bridget, then squinted at Eilis as if trying to spot a bug under a microscope. "We did have something to talk about, didn't we?"

"Children and marriage, Father," Bridget whispered.

"Certainly. Yes, to be sure. Marriage, as you know, is a most solemn state. Very solemn indeed in the eyes of God. As a matter of fact, just down the line after the priesthood and virginity, to be precise. Not to be undertaken lightly. Not at all. As a matter of fact, better not at all than lightly. So you can see from this how solemn it is." He stopped, joined his hands in his lap, and stared at the ceiling.

"The bit about children, Father," Bridget whispered. "Don't forget that."

"Oh, absolutely. Yes. In fact, practically the only excuse for marriage, according to holy mother church. The only one. Almost anyway. Children. No question about it, one of God's greatest blessings to mankind. Isn't that right, Mrs. O'Connor? Sure where would we all be without them? The primary purpose of marriage, they tell us, is the procreation and rearing of offspring. Never forget that, my boy." He peered across at Eilis. "You're a girl, aren't you? Have I been giving the wrong sermon? I'm so sorry. I thought you were a boy." He turned to Bridget. "Was she always a girl?"

"Yes, Father. If she wasn't she wouldn't be in the kind of trouble she's in." Bridget glared at Frank. "Shame on you, anyway, for giving him all that brandy."

"Trouble?" The priest stared glassy-eyed at Bridget. "Who's in trouble? Can I be of assistance?"

Bridget, pointing at Eilis, said, "*She's* in trouble, Father," her tone indicating that her patience was near breaking point.

"She is? Such a nice young girl, too. What seems to be the problem? Mary, isn't it?"

"It's Eilis," Bridget said. "And she's in *trouble*."

"Trouble."

"*Trouble* trouble, if you know what I mean, Father."

The priest continued to stare at Bridget, as if trying to penetrate her mind. Then, like a pot coming to boil, understanding bubbled. "Oh! Trouble." He waved one arm in a tiny circular motion. "You mean that kind of trouble?"

"Precisely, Father."

"Do I have to sit and listen to this gibberish?" Eilis turned and faced the fire.

"And you want me to talk to her?"

"He's in no condition right now to talk to the cat," Eilis muttered.

Frank, who had begun to doze, shook himself awake again. "You're all fierce quiet. What you need is a good drink. How about it, Father?" Raising a questioning eyebrow at the priest. "I have a little more of the Hennessy left." He weaved unsteadily to the sideboard.

"Frank, please don't," Bridget pleaded.

"Well, maybe just a small one then," Father Heaney said.

"Good man yourself." Frank retrieved a bottle from the cabinet, poured a stiff brandy into a snifter and brought it over.

"God bless you." Father Heaney raised the glass and waved it around. "*Slainte go bhaile libh.*"

Frank had an equally generous drink himself. Then Father Heaney accepted his offer of another, drained it quickly and promptly passed out. Bridget sat rigid, face frozen, eyes shut, silent. Not even when the priest's head slid gently onto her shoulder did she move. Frank blathered on, talking to Eilis about the weather, arguing that since we had such a fine summer we were bound to have a wet and cold winter. Suddenly Bridget opened her eyes and glared at her husband. "*You* can get him home now; I'm going to bed." She leaned the priest's head back against the sofa before getting up and leaving the room with all the dignity of an unjustly treated wife and mother.

It was Bridget O'Connor's stated contention to her husband that, despite Eilis's denial, Joe Mahony *was* the father of their grandchild. Wish made a strong contribution to this belief because, while she infinitely regretted the fact of her daughter's pregnancy, nevertheless, since it *had* happened and there must of necessity be a male involved, better that it should be Joe than anyone else she could think of. A fine lad otherwise and from a good family, he would without doubt fulfill his duty to provide for the child. So although Frank was against the proposal—for reasons of his own that he couldn't share with his wife, he didn't believe Joe to be the culprit—Bridget decided that an honest discussion with young Mr. Mahony was in order. Two days after Christmas, therefore, just after Eilis left for Galway, she rang Joe—she had his telephone number because she was a mother who believed in the virtue of rummaging through her children's belongings. He was home, surprised indeed to hear from her, and yes, though sounding a bit puzzled, would be happy to meet her for lunch at Talbot's near Eyre Square on Saturday at one o'clock. And no, of course not, though seeming even more puzzled about this, he wouldn't say a word to Eilis about her ringing him, or about their luncheon arrangement.

They both arrived punctually. Bridget ordered the lamb, Joe the fish and chips. When the waitress took away the menus, Joe said, "I suppose this has something to do with Eilis?"

"I'm sure you know what it's about, Joe." Bridget had rehearsed the scene many times over the past few days and was determined there would be no acrimony, just a calm and fearless acceptance of reality.

"I do?" Puzzlement all over the young man's face.

"Eilis has told us about her condition, so there's no call for subterfuge. What we need to talk about now is what to do next."

"What to do about what?"

"Well, if you want to be that way. Mind you, she has always said you were a decent young man, so I'm sure you won't deny your responsibility now for her predicament."

He looked straight at her with those innocent eyes that she found so attractive. "Mrs. O'Connor, I don't have the faintest idea what you're talking about."

"Do you mean to tell me she hasn't told you?"

"Told me what?" Again that innocent puzzled look.

"That she's pregnant."

"You can't be serious? Not Eilis."

"So she didn't tell you?"

"Mrs. O'Connor, you're not by any chance—I most sincerely hope—suggesting that I...? That is, of course, if she really is...? Because if you are you couldn't be more wrong."

How could she doubt such transparent honesty? Yet where did that leave her? "Well, if it wasn't you, who could it be? She hasn't had any other recent boyfriend that I know of."

"All I can tell you is that it wasn't me. I'm a member of *The Society for the Promotion of Christian Marriage*. You may have heard of it? A Catholic organization dedicated to stamping out extramarital sex."

Lunch arrived. They ate in silence for a while. "The lamb is quite good," Bridget said eventually.

"The fish isn't bad either. But the chips aren't as crisp as they might be."

"You'll help me find out who it was, won't you?"

"I will indeed, Mrs. O'Connor."

"Good man yourself. Don't worry now." She reached out and touched his arm. "We'll straighten things out yet."

When they left the restaurant he walked up to the Cathedral with her in the rain to pray for her daughter.

PERSUASION

Marie ran back in the rain to the Banaghans after first mass on Sunday morning. "Mammy is in a terrible temper," she panted as she removed her jacket and Wellingtons. "She'd bite your nose off if you so much as looked at her." Marie sneaked her visits to Aisling when her mother wasn't noticing.

"What's the matter with her?" The cousin was preparing a chicken for the oven.

"I don't know. I just left a few crumbs on the table after breakfast and you'd think I had destroyed the house the way she carried on." Marie shook the rain out of her hair and sidled up to the range to warm herself. "She's been in bad humor ever since Christmas when Father Heaney came to visit. He was very funny that night, Father Heaney. Do you know what he did? He came in and he looked at Niamh and said are you Eilis and aren't you very young for your age? Imagine thinking Niamh was Eilis. Sure they don't look a bit alike and anyway Eilis is ten years older. He's been in the parish long enough now to know everyone wouldn't you think? But he was real funny. Daddy gave him a glass of brandy and he gulped it down on the spot like he had a terrible thirst and then he said to Daddy 'sure the occasional glass doesn't do a man a bit of harm.' I think brandy smells awful. Do you know what?" She pushed a strand of wet hair back from her forehead.

"What?" Aisling was smiling as she tied the chicken's legs: when Marie got going there was no stopping her.

"Terry says Father Heaney drinks like a fish. I didn't know priests were allowed to drink. Are they do you think? Or is he doing it on the sly? I wonder if priests do things on the sly too? I was afraid to ask Mammy in case she'd get mad at me. I think she likes Father Heaney. Are women allowed to like priests do you think? Niamh said it would be a sin for a girl to like a priest. They were told that in Christian doctrine class. Supposedly. But I don't believe her. Aren't you supposed to like everybody? I don't like Jason Reilly in my class; he's always mean to girls. Do you think Mammy likes Father Heaney more than she likes Daddy? Sometimes I think she doesn't like Daddy at all. I like Daddy. He's nice. I think he's nicer than Mammy. Sometimes anyway. But I like Mammy too. Except when she's being mean like today. I don't…"

Bridget O'Connor did like Father Heaney—she even acknowledged the fact to herself. But only in the chaste way a pious woman might safely be fond of her parish priest. Her devotion would never exceed the bounds of celibate propriety. He was a kind, thoughtful, serious man who was always most courteous to her, never arrogant or distant, as his predecessor had been. She had taken care of washing and ironing the altar linens for the past ten years and never once during the eight years Father Colleran was parish priest had he ever said a public thank you; he hardly even said a private one. In contrast, Father Heaney in his very first year had thanked and praised her from the altar, not once but twice. He would most likely do it again at mass on New Year's Day, just as he had last year. Not that she needed to be thanked for what she did for the Lord, of course; but it was nice to know her work was appreciated.

She told herself that she cared enough about Father Heaney to be seriously annoyed at him for drinking. And she was going to let him know her mind on the subject. Getting into an irritable bed on Christmas night, she decided to go back and read the riot act to him next day. Morning reflection in a cooler temper, however, suggested she let him deal with his scandalous behavior himself. Besides, she needed his sober assistance in dealing with Eilis and her appalling adoption plan. So she waited till Monday afternoon, then told Frank she was going back to Garveys for groceries; no need to let him know more, since he had several times commented snidely that she seemed to visit the parish priest a lot. She did buy a box of tea bags, then crossed the street from the grocery shop to the priest's house.

Father Heaney himself answered the door. "Come in, Bridget, come in. They say we'll have more rain." He ushered her into the parlor. "Can I make you a cup of tea? The housekeeper doesn't come in today."

"No, not at all, Father. I won't take much of your time now because I'm sure you're busy."

"There's no hurry at all. Sit down for a bit, anyway. For yourself I'll always have plenty of time."

"It's about Eilis again. I still don't know what to do with her."

"Ah yes. I'm sorry about that. I'm afraid I overstepped the bounds." He bowed his head. "I'll come out and talk to her again, if you think it'll do any good."

"She went back to Galway on Friday. But she'll probably be home again in a few weeks." Bridget was looking into the fire till the priest's silence made her glance up. His lips were formulating words but no sound was emerging. "What's the matter, Father? Are you all right?"

He tried a half-smile that came out as a grimace. "A few weeks might be a little bit late for me. He took a deep breath. "I haven't told a living soul yet, Bridget, but I'm sure I can tell *you* since I may rely on your discretion?"

"Certainly, whatever it is."

"I'm going to be leaving very shortly."

"Well, for heaven's sake! And you only here a couple of years. I'm terribly sorry to hear that. You'll be going to a bigger parish, I suppose?"

"No, no. I'm *leaving*. Leaving the priesthood."

It wasn't possible. Not Father Heaney. Sure, she knew all about the exodus of the clergy. Who alive didn't know that priests and nuns the world over, including once holy Ireland, were resigning and getting married and becoming atheists and agnostics—like her own mother, the Lord have mercy on her, did forty-five years ago. An exodus that was the single worst crisis for the church in the past twenty-five years. But it couldn't be happening to her Father Heaney. "You're joking, Father."

"No joke, Bridget, I'm afraid. I've been thinking about it for a couple of years now but haven't mentioned it to a soul yet. I'll be telling His Grace in a few days. In the meantime I'd appreciate if you'd keep it under your hat."

"But why? If you don't mind my asking."

"I'm fifty years of age, Bridget. I'm tired of battling the flesh. I'm tired of being alone. I have given the best years of my life to God. And now I hope He won't begrudge me taking my declining days to find a bit of peace and love and contentment for myself. Does that make any sense at all?" At which point Father Heaney choked up and covered his face with his hands.

The mother in her wanted to comfort him, the woman wanted to hold him, the Catholic wanted to urge him to be strong. She threw off her coat and knelt beside him. "It'll be all right. It'll be all right." She placed her hands over his, shaking with him as the sobs racked his body. "God will understand." When his convulsions increased she knelt closer, wrapped her arms about his shoulders and nestled her head in his neck. "Everything is going to work out for the best."

"Sorry," he murmured eventually. "I didn't mean to break down." He made no effort at release from her embrace, so she stayed where she was, feeling his body relax. Never had she held a man, except her husband, this close for so long. So different from Frank in smell and touch. Pleasantly different. Then she felt the pity in her give slow way to even more tender response, an arousal that made her suddenly release Father Heaney and retreat to her chair.

"I don't know what to say. I mean, about your leaving. Are you sure you're doing the right thing?"

"Of course I'm not. I only know I have to do it."

She knew she should encourage him not to abandon his vocation, to fight the good fight and gain the crown, to stay the course and persevere to the end. All the powerful admonitions she had ever learned from classroom and pulpit she now ought to pour out on this poor lost priest who was so sadly giving up. But she couldn't do it. As in a dream when legs won't run, her tongue wouldn't utter what her mind made ready. In the end, after a long silence, all she could manage was, "So when are you planning to leave?"

"Whenever His Grace tells me I should go." He was gazing at the fire, as if trying to see the future in the flames. "I hope the people of the parish won't be too mad at me."

"Indeed they won't. And since I'm on the Parish Committee I'll make certain that you get a decent send-off." There was silence then, the comfortable quiet that falls between friends who have for now resolved their differences and are loath to dispel the glow of peace. "One last thing," she said eventually. "If you don't mind my raising the matter again: have you any thoughts on what I should do about Eilis?"

"If my twenty-five years of dealing with young people have taught me anything, it is that you get nowhere fighting with them. The best you can do is listen and advise and then leave them to God and the wisdom that may come to them from their own mistakes."

"I can't wait that long," Bridget said. "The future of my grandchild is at stake."

That night she talked it over again with Frank: he agreed with her in the matter of adoption. "Tell you what," he said, "I'll go up to Galway during the week and have a chat with her on my own. She mightn't be so stubborn if you're not there." Bridget agreed, though without much expectation of success, knowing how adroit Eilis was in bringing her father around to her own way of thinking.

So Frank went to Galway on Thursday and took Eilis to lunch in the Claddagh Room at the Great Southern—a bit extravagant, but worth the money if it would soften her up. "This is very *flaithiul* of you, Daddy," she said over the soup.

"What are you up to?"

"I'm a generous man, and I'm very fond of my daughter." He unleashed his innocent grin that even he knew wouldn't fool her for a moment. But he didn't broach the subject until they had done with the sweet and were having their tea. "You're not serious about giving your babby to the Banaghans, are you?"

"I knew it!" She shouted the words, startling an elderly woman at the next table into turning her head. "I knew the minute I saw you walk in the door of the library that that was what you were up to. Well, thanks very much for the lunch, Daddy, but it won't work."

"Whoa, *a chailín*! This is not your mother screaming at you now. It's only the poor old Dad asking a favor."

"That soft soap will get you nowhere this time, so you might as well give up before you start."

"Have it your way. But let's talk about it for a minute anyway. Try to see my side of the story, even if you don't agree with it."

She looked at him the way you'd stare down a jovial trickster. "Go on if you want, but it's not going to do you a bit of good."

"Put yourself in my shoes. You're about to become a grandmother and your daughter says she's going to give away your grandchild. Now how would you feel?"

"Not fair, Daddy. It's not as simple as that and you know it."

"What are people going to say? The likes of Joan Garvey, for instance. That old biddy has a tongue on her as long as the Shannon river and 'tis she knows how to use it. She'll make me and your Mammy the cod of the parish. Is that what you want to happen to your poor old mother and father?"

"Nobody is going to make a cod of you, Daddy, because nobody is going to know. Do you think for one minute that I'm going to let the morons of Kildawree know what's going on with us? They've seen the last of Eilis O'Connor until her baby is born and given over to its adoptive parents. And Aisling and Eugene are telling no one where they got it from. *You*'ll know it's your grandchild and Mammy will know it's her grandchild, but you're the only ones who will."

"That's what I'm getting at. It's *our* grandchild. So you have to keep it in the family."

She bowed her head and remained perfectly still, so that he began to hope she might be changing her mind. Then she looked up. "Daddy, there's a lot more to this than you know. I wish I could tell you all, but I can't. Just trust me that I'm doing the right thing." She put out her hand to touch him. "Please, Daddy."

He ever after regretted that he pulled his arm away in anger. "I want my grandchild and I'm going to have it. So you can go back to work now. I'll wait and pay the bill."

Such was his depression that even two hours later he could muster no passion for Julia. "It's all right," she said. "I'm not in great form myself, either." She snuggled up to him. "Tell me about it, whatever it is that's bothering you."

"Eilis is pregnant." He hadn't been able to tell her on his previous visit. In the back of his mind was a lurking fear that she might think a grandfather too old for her.

All she said was, "Out-of-wedlock pregnancies are not at all uncommon these days." He told her the rest of the story, including the fiasco at the Great Southern. "Is it that important to you that the baby not leave the family?" she asked.

"It is."

"How far are you willing to take the issue?"

"As far as needs be."

"Would you be willing to go to court?"

"You're on to something, aren't you?"

"We have lots of illegitimate births at the hospital, and a fair number of them involve adoptions. So I've learned a bit about the law on that subject."

"And…"

"I just remembered that grandparents can adopt."

"You mean their own grandchild? She wouldn't give it to us: she promised it to the Banaghans."

"I seem to recollect a case where the grandparents got custody of a grandchild *without* the consent of the mother."

"Well, is that a fact? It could only be a last resort, mind you. It isn't something you want to do—bring your own flesh and blood into court."

"I think you should ask her first if she would let you adopt."

Eilis was on her way out the door when he arrived. "No, Daddy," she said and ran.

"Tell them we're on our way to bed, whoever they are," Aisling told Eugene when the doorbell chimed a bit after eight. Neighbors sometimes dropped in for a chat in the evening. She heard the murmur of voices down the hall but couldn't identify them till the parlor door opened and in walked Bridget and Frank O'Connor.

"I hope we're not disturbing you." Bridget took off her coat.

"You're always welcome." What was this all about? Bridget O'Connor's visits to their house were like snow in April: they *could* happen, but they rarely did.

"Sit up by the fire," Eugene said. "It's a cold night out there."

"You'll have a cup of tea?" Aisling asked, strictly out of politeness.

"No tea now, thanks," Bridget said.

"A glass of sherry, maybe? Or a Paddy?" Eugene looked at Frank.

"Maybe a small one."

Bridget glared at her husband. "Nothing for me, thanks."

Frank sat in Eugene's armchair by the fire. Bridget perched on the edge of the sofa. Eugene poured two whiskeys at the sideboard. "Will you have something yourself?" he asked Aisling.

"I'll make some tea. You'll have a cup, won't you?" She tried Bridget again.

"Just a cup in the hand, then."

From the kitchen Aisling heard murmurs of conversation between Eugene and Frank. Farm talk, from the occasional word she could decipher. Not a sound out of Bridget. She was here to talk about the baby for sure. Probably annoyed that they were adopting it. The woman never did like her: Aisling still remembered her animosity when as a child she, Aisling, would visit Granny McGreevy's house with Grandpa Feerick. She mentioned the matter once to her grandfather and he said Bridget resented *his* being her father and, because of that, disliked all his family.

Aisling got down her china cups and teapot from the top of a kitchen cabinet and put them on her silver tray, the latter a wedding present from Grandpa Feerick the year before he died. She had adored her grandpa and the tray always reminded her of him. Wasn't it funny that he was Bridget's father and now she was going to adopt Bridget's grandchild. So her baby would be Grandpa's great-grandchild after all, just as if she were giving birth to it herself. Grandpa would be pleased up in heaven; he always set such store by blood.

"That's a nice piece of plate." Frank pointed his whiskey glass at the silver tray. "It must have cost a bit."

"A present from old Wattie Feerick himself," Eugene said. Aisling blanched, but the moment passed without comment.

"I suppose you're wondering what brings us here at this time of night?" Bridget drained her cup and put it back on the tray.

"Sure you're always welcome," Eugene said. "We're relations and neighbors and we hardly ever see each other."

"We're all too busy, I suppose," Frank murmured.

"We came tonight for a particular reason." Bridget joined her hands in her lap and looked at the fire.

"Well, you're surely welcome anytime, with or without a reason." One glass of whiskey and Eugene was effusive.

"It's our understanding that you know about Eilis being pregnant," Bridget said.

"We do." Aisling glanced at Eugene. His mouth opened a couple of times, like a fish gasping for life, but no sound came out.

"We've heard that you'd like to adopt our grandchild."
Bridget spoke with as little emotion as if she were
speculating about the price of ducks.

"I can't tell you how much it will mean to us," Aisling
gushed, hoping her enthusiasm would diminish Bridget's
natural resentment.

"Frank and I are not in favor of that idea." Bridget's tone
was like the first drop of rain that precedes a downpour.

"We can understand that," Eugene said. "'Tis only to be
expected. But sure we're all relations, aren't we? Isn't it
better than having the babby going to strangers?"

"'Tis *my* grandchild," Frank said. "And it won't be going
to any strangers, I can tell you."

"There you are then. We'll take awfully good care of your
grandchild, I guarantee you that."

"What Frank means," Bridget said, "is that we intend to
adopt the baby ourselves." For the first time since she came
in she looked Aisling in the eye. "We thought we should let
you both know before you start getting your hopes up."

Aisling's brother had once hit her unexpectedly from
behind with a sack of hay, completely disorienting her. She
had that same feeling now. "Eilis promised *us* the baby." She
tried to keep her tone as calm as Bridget's, though her
inclination was to scream *you bloody bitch get out of my house*.

"Unfortunately, we can't allow her to do that."

"She has *no* right to give our grandchild away like a pup."
Frank was almost shouting.

"I understand your feelings, of course." Aisling was
recovering and her dander was up. "However, it's your
daughter's baby, not yours, so *she* gets to decide who will
adopt it. And she has decided that Eugene and I should be its

parents. I don't think there's any more to be said on the subject." She folded her arms and stared at the ceiling.

"We'll see about that, faith," Frank said.

"Eilis does *not* have the last word on it, you see," Bridget added. "Fortunately."

"What do you mean?" Aisling was getting exasperated at Bridget's composure. "Of course she does. She's the mother, isn't she? And the mother always has the final say on those matters."

"I wouldn't be too sure of that now if I were you," Frank said.

"Arrah, go on out of that, Frank." Eugene's eyes had acquired that vacant whiskey look. "Sure you don't know what you're talking about." He looked at his empty glass and got to his feet. "Here, have another one and we'll drink to the babby's health." He reached for Frank's glass.

"Eugene! No." Aisling was mortified. What kind of father image was this, just when they were trying to show the O'Connors what good parents they'd be?

"Right." Eugene subsided into his chair.

"In certain situations," Bridget spoke as if explaining a catechism lesson to children, "the rights of the grandparents come before those of the mother. We paid a visit to Mr. O'Malley, the solicitor, and he explained it to us."

"I don't believe you." Aisling was aware she was shouting, losing control. "I know for a fact that nothing can be done in the way of adoption without the consent of the mother. And Eilis wants us to have her baby. So there." She wanted to stick her tongue out at this ogre who was wearing an expression as smug as a cat after milk.

"Well, I suppose there's no point in arguing any further

then, is there?" Bridget stood. Frank followed suit. "We'll have to discuss it in court and let the judge decide." They both headed for the door.

Frank put a hand on Eugene's shoulder in passing. "Sorry about all this, my friend. I wish we didn't have to do it."

When they were gone Aisling said, "I wish you wouldn't drink whiskey."

"I only had the one glass to be sociable. What harm is there in that?"

"It turns your brain into porridge, that's what." She went to bed straight away but couldn't sleep for hours. In the morning she asked him, over breakfast, "Do you think she's right?"

"We better find out."

"We need a solicitor."

"Con Branagh. They say in at the cattle mart that he's the man to have in your corner when you wrestle with the law."

Mr. Branagh would see them first thing tomorrow morning, the receptionist said when Eugene rang. A big heavy middle-aged man with a whiskey nose and an island of hair on the top of his head. "I believe they're wrong," he said after Aisling explained the promise Eilis made them and related the O'Connors' proposed action. "But you never can tell with judges." He wagged a cautionary finger. "That's why you need a sly fellow like me around." He winked at Aisling and nodded to Eugene.

"So what should we do?" Aisling didn't like men who winked at her.

"Nothing." Mr. Branagh sat back in his chair and

allowed his paunch to rest against the desk. "You have the presumption of law on your side. If they want to do anything, they have to prove their case. Who's their solicitor?"

"O'Malley," the Banaghans chorused.

"Not a bad fellow, mind you. A bit inexperienced, in my opinion. Jamesie knows the theory of the law quite well, but I don't think he entirely understands yet the way judges and juries think. Or *don't* think, as the case may be. And let me tell you when it comes down to winning your case, which is all that counts in the end, it's more important to know the mind and heart and guts and balls—sorry, Mrs. Banaghan—of the fellow perched up there on the bench, or the citizens sitting in the jury box, than it is to know all that's contained in all the law books that ever were written. Especially in a case like yours, which has more emotion than statute behind it."

"So we wait for *them* to go to court?" Eugene said.

"If they want to proceed they'll have to petition the High Court in Dublin." The solicitor leaned even farther back in his chair and his stomach loomed like a giant half-moon over the top of the desk. "In which case Mr. O'Malley will have to brief Counsel."

"What does that mean?" Aisling could feel the knot tightening in her intestines. She just wanted her baby, not this legal morass of solicitors and counsel and briefs and courts and judges.

"It means a lot of money." Mr. Branagh wrote something on his legal pad.

"Well, you can be sure then that Frank O'Connor won't go for it," Eugene said.

Mr. Branagh looked at him. "Just keep in mind that I

would have to brief Counsel for you as well. Have you told me everything that's relevant to your story?"

"We have." Though Aisling was well aware that they were holding back the bit about Eilis getting pregnant deliberately to provide them with a baby. Her instincts told her this information could get them in trouble if the case went to court. She'd have to raise the matter with Eugene and Eilis so neither of them would let the cat out of the bag.

"You mentioned that you are giving the young lady some financial support?"

"Is that all right?"

"Certainly. My recommendation is to continue giving it. That way you can show in court, if the case goes to court, that you had a clear agreement with the mother well in advance. And pay her by check so you'll have a record."

"A fine man," Eugene said on the way home. "We'll have no bother winning with him behind us."

Father Heaney almost didn't turn up for the party in his honor. He sat in his parlor the whole afternoon in a blue funk. Was he doing the right thing? Had he gone mad? Wouldn't everyone in the parish be laughing at him behind his back? Not to mention his fellow priests. He saw his leaving anew in a momentary return to the old light of faith, the faith that had taken him from farm to seminary to ordination, and to what he had expected would be his whole life's work. What in God's name had got into him to even contemplate giving it up?

He could still withdraw his resignation, was the notion that kept running through his mind as he huddled closer to the fire. The Archbishop had strongly suggested a month of retreat in a monastery before he took the final step. "Get away from this giddy world for a bit, Michael. Where you can be alone with God and your own soul. Then see how you feel."

Father Heaney had refused. "It's no use, Tom. I've thought it all out." He still called the Archbishop Tom because they were classmates in Maynooth and had remained friends over the years. Now, alone in his parlor, with the January rain beating hard on the window, Tom's idea appealed briefly. Had he really thought it all out? Maybe he *should* go to a monastery. No, he shouldn't. Of course not.

What good would it do? He had lost his faith. It was as simple and as complex as that. *This Is My Body* no longer resonated because its theology no longer made sense to him. Too much reading and thinking over the years, about evolution and biology and quantum mechanics and astronomy and anything else that might shed light on the mysteries of past, present, and future. Too much meditating on the flimsy theological underpinnings of his faith. Too much wrestling with the reasons why nature must be denied. Not to mention too much battling the awful cravings of sex. All leading to vast intellectual, spiritual, and emotional confusion. Till mind and body, if indeed these could be separated, eventually coalesced in a fierce revulsion against all he had been trained to accept. He had to get away.

He'd miss his parishioners, that was for sure. They were kind and friendly and sociable and they genuinely cared about him. He'd miss the camaraderie of the Parish Committee and the visits to people's homes and the presidency of the football club and the gatherings with his fellow priests. But what other choice was there for him? He couldn't stand at the altar anymore and perform a liturgical service that was now meaningless to him. Nor mount the pulpit and tell his congregation to lead good Christian lives when he himself no longer understood what that meant. Nor tell them to pray for guidance and each other and the sick and the dead when he was unable to pray for even himself. Or urge them to frequent sacraments in which he, minister of those sacraments, did not believe. Nor caution them against sins of the flesh that he now thought integral to nature itself.

At seven o'clock on Friday evening, the 26th of January, there will be a farewell party for Father Heaney in the Parish Hall. All parishioners are cordially invited to attend.

The notice was carried in the Parish Bulletin, which was distributed at both masses on Sunday. Bridget and Frank O'Connor were the chief instigators, he guessed. He had stayed away from committee meetings ever since Bridget had mentioned the possibility of a party, knowing they'd prefer to discuss the matter in his absence. He wondered who might have opposed the event. Surely some of the committee must have, even though Catholic Ireland had become a lot more broad-minded in the past twenty-five years. He remembered that when Father Joe Tierney left his parish in the late sixties it was a scandal scarcely to be talked about in public; Joe had to slink away to England to find himself any kind of a job. Now they were giving him, Michael Heaney, a formal parish send-off.

At a minute to seven he threw water on his face and head, and brushed the little graying hair that was left to him. Then he sat on the bed and debated what to wear. Full clerical garb would seem hypocritical. He had a pair of blue jeans and a plaid shirt and an Aran sweater that he wore on holidays last year, but such a casual get-up might appear disrespectful. That left the gray suit he had bought a few weeks ago in Galway, his sober gateway to lay existence. It took fifteen frustrating minutes to knot the dark blue tie the shop assistant had picked out for him. Even then he wasn't sure it was on right: the last time he had knotted a tie was before his subdiaconate ordination twenty-six years ago.

Jacketed, he surveyed the stranger in the mirror. Was this

balding, late-middle-aged man in suit, white shirt, and tie really Father Heaney? Who he was, his self-image, his appearance to the world, were all swept away by this new outfit. The moment he stepped away from the shelter of his church he'd no longer be the reverend parish priest of Kildawree. He'd be Mr. Michael Heaney, nobody. With no real plan to become anybody. Jumping off to get away from the present, not running forward to embrace the future. A flat in Galway City, already rented. Just over two thousand pounds in the bank. The vague possibility of a secondary school job, teaching English at Colaiste Eanna. Some relations and old friends, but who knew how they might react? Ungrounded hopes of finding new companionship. Female, of course: celibate fantasies impatient for conversion to warm flesh. Oh God! He was safer where he was this minute. He retreated to the bed and sat. Courage. He had thought it out before, a hundred times. It would be all right. But it was all theory until now, when he must walk out the door and across the street and into the hall where his parishioners awaited him. No, not his parishioners any more: his friends maybe? Who were going to say goodbye and send him on his way. Wasn't that what dying was about: leaving everyone and everything you loved?

He needed a drink. A couple of whiskeys would make this dying bearable. He was reaching for the bottle when from somewhere within his once-disciplined will the command to say *no* came through. No. For too long it had been his escape. He would die sober. Maybe even rise again, sober. If he was to have a life after the priesthood, he wanted to be in control of it. He touched his tie, buttoned his jacket, marched out the front door and down the dark driveway.

The rain had stopped for the time being.

Father Heaney was half-right: Bridget O'Connor—though not Frank—was the instigator of his farewell party. Frank came round to the idea only much later, after he almost caused his wife to abandon the project. "It's the kind of thing that's best done quietly," he had said when she first broached the idea. They had just gotten into bed. She was reading a magazine, he was lying on his side facing away from her. "The less said the better. Let the man slip away in silence, I'd say, with the minimum of fuss. I'm sure that's the way he'd like it, too."

"Don't be such an old stick-in-the-mud, Frank."

"Well, it's true for me. What's there to celebrate? It's like a fellow walking out on his wife. I mean, would you have a party for me if I said I was leaving you?"

She put down her magazine. "I'm just as aware as you are that it's not a cause for celebration. And it's not a celebration I'm talking about. More like a wake, I'd say. At any rate a sad event. But we might as well face up to it and make the best of it, instead of shoving our heads in the sand and pretending it isn't happening."

"Cripes! What's got into you, anyway?" He turned over in the bed and looked at her. "You're the last person in the world I'd expect to condone that kind of behavior. Aren't you the one who was totally scandalized when Bishop Casey took off? Didn't I hear you say there must surely be a special place in hell for the likes of him? So what's different about Father Heaney running away?"

She felt like slapping him. "There's a world of difference. First of all, Father Heaney isn't running away. He hasn't done a thing wrong. He just wants to do something else with his life. Which I think he has a right to." She picked up the magazine again and turned the pages slowly so he wouldn't see how mad she was.

"You're only justifying him because you're keen on him. Maybe if you knew Eamonn Casey as well you'd forgive him, too."

She hurled the magazine to the floor. "That's a mean rotten thing to say, Frank O'Connor." There was no comparison at all between what Father Heaney was doing and what Eamon Casey did—a bishop who had fathered a child, for God's sake!

In the morning she refused to talk to Frank. All day and into the next she gave him the silent treatment, outwardly calm but inwardly oscillating between anger and self-pity and prayerful resignation. After supper the second evening, when the children were either in their rooms or gone out and she was reading a book by the parlor fire, he said, "If it'll make you happy I'll help with the shindig for Father Heaney."

She looked at him as if he were cold potatoes. "I don't know if I want to go through with it anymore."

"Oh, come on. You can't back out now. Everybody is talking about it."

She glared at him over her half-glasses, but curiosity overcame her. "Who's talking about it?"

"Oh, a lot of people have mentioned it to me. I met Jack Shaughnessy in Ballinamore today and he asked how the preparations were coming. 'Your missus is running it, I hear,' he said. So what can I do to help?"

She stared at him till some of the annoyance drained out of her. "You can get a few of the lads together if you want and give the hall a good scrubbing down. I was in there Sunday and the place is filthy."

So Frank and his helpers readied the hall and Bridget put the announcement in the bulletin and wondered if anyone would turn up. She needn't have worried: the parishioners came—over a hundred of them, by Frank's count. And they brought so much food that the late arrivals could scarcely find room on the tables to put down their dishes. They milled about, talking and drinking and eyeing the edibles, too polite to take any till the priest should arrive. Until at twenty past seven when he hadn't yet put in an appearance Bridget announced, "We might as well start eating before the food goes cold; he'll be here any minute."

"A terrific do, altogether," Jack Shaughnessy remarked to Frank O'Connor, stuffing his gob with half a chicken leg. "Your missus did a great job organizing it all."

"She had help," Frank said. The committee had nominated him to make the farewell speech. All the members, including himself, said they'd rather not give it. Very difficult and delicate, they agreed, sitting round the table in this very hall, speaking softly, not looking at each other. In the end, as chairman, Frank accepted the onerous task. He had in the back of his mind an idea of running for the County Council at the next election, and if he did it wouldn't hurt to have been heard speaking at a public gathering like this.

"Well, haven't the times changed?" Shaughnessy ran freckled-backed fingers through his carrot-red hair before biting into a chicken wing. "Me father wouldn't be found dead here if he was alive, the Lord have mercy on him." He sucked the meat loudly off the bone.

"The older generation had different standards." Frank sipped his Harp, wishing it were Jameson: the committee had decided that the only booze served would be wine and beer.

"They had indeed. The priest was God Almighty to them. Now we know they're no better than ourselves." Shaughnessy licked the tips of his fingers. "Sometimes not even as good, maybe."

"They have a hard life in some ways, though. It's not natural for a man to be without a woman all his life." Frank was looking over Shaughnessy's shoulder, watching his wife down by the door beaming at a man in a gray suit till it seemed her face was going to burst. It took him a minute to realized the fellow she was smiling at was Father Heaney.

"Is that why your man is leaving, do you think?"

"Why else? In all other respects doesn't he have a cushy job? A good house and a nice car and no shortage of money in his pocket and half the women in the parish looking ga-ga at him. But he can't touch them where he is now." Frank tapped Shaughnessy on the chest with two fingers. "There's the rub, you see."

"You think, then, we better lock up our wives the minute he's let loose?"

Shaughnessy, the sly old bugger, winked at him, but Frank wasn't about to take the bait. "I'm sure you'll be able to restrain your missus," was all he said before moving off to greet the priest.

"I was just saying to Bridget that it was awfully good of you to go to all this trouble." Father Heaney looked so different in a collar and tie.

"No trouble at all. 'Twas the least we could do for you."
He definitely would not like the idea of this man being
intimate with his wife. *The way you are with Julia*, a snide
voice echoed back at him. That was different, though he
couldn't for the life of him say how.

"It means a lot to me. I'll be very sad leaving you all, but
this farewell will ease the pain a bit."

"Sure you won't be going too far, Father." Bridget gazing
at him like a woman in love. "We'll expect to see plenty of
you in the future. He'll be living in Galway city," she told her
husband. As if she hadn't told him a hundred times already.

Frank dug his hands into his trouser pockets and stared
at the floor. "If you don't mind my asking, what will you be
doing up there to pay the rent?"

"Don't be so inquisitive, Frank."

"Not at all, not at all. It's a reasonable question, Frank.
The answer, I'm afraid, is that I'm not quite sure yet. I do as
a matter of fact have a couple of tentative offers of jobs, but
nothing is settled or committed for the moment. As you
might guess, twenty-five-year-old degrees in philosophy and
theology are not exactly the kind of stuff the business
community is screaming for."

"Can't His Grace do something for you?" Bridget
sounded almost indignant.

"He's trying. But, as he said to me, bishops no longer
have the kind of pull they used to have in the old days."

"A little drop of something for you, Father?" A woman
from the Ladies' Altar Society reached a plastic glass of
white wine in between Frank and his wife.

Father Heaney hesitated. You could almost hear the

argument going on inside him. Then he held out his hand. "Thanks, Rose." The glass went straight to his mouth.

Eugene Banaghan very nearly didn't go to the party either. What made him hesitate was Aisling's absence—up in Galway visiting with Eilis: he wasn't a man for social gatherings without the support of his wife. What tempted him to go was the thought that he might be able to talk to Frank on his own and persuade him not to interfere with the adoption. Sometimes a good man-to-man chat could resolve differences that the presence of the women made irreconcilable.

He arrived late at the parish hall so as to minimize the amount of time he'd have to spend there. He couldn't have known, of course, that the chairman of the parish committee would be so preoccupied with his public duties as not to have time for private conversations. So Eugene had to hang around, engaging in small talk with people he had little interest in, and trying not to drink more Guinness than was good for him, while he waited for the formal events of the evening to be gone through.

"It's both a sad occasion and a happy one for us all here tonight," Frank shouted from the stage after he managed to silence the din. "Sad because we're losing our parish priest, a man who has served us extraordinarily well here in Kildawree for the past two years. Happy because a good man has had the courage to take his life in his own hands and do what he believes is right for him to do." Frank paused, expecting enthusiastic approval, but had to wait for a hesitant handclap. "The world has changed and it's time for us here in holy Ireland to wake up to the fact. Gone are the days when a young man or a young woman had to make a decision and be bound to it for the rest of their lives, no matter what the consequences."

"Does that mean we can get rid of the missus now, too?" someone yelled from the rear. Nervous laughter erupted briefly.

"Furthermore," Frank continued, "we have in the past placed too much responsibility on our priests. We have demanded that they be as holy as Almighty God himself, instead of recognizing that they are the same flesh as the rest of us and that we shouldn't expect them to be any better."

Eugene, standing near the door, felt the shuffling discomfort of his fellow listeners. Frank was talking as if he were someone important on the Late Late Show, instead of being just one of their own. People in Kildawree didn't blather pieties like that. They might be religious in private, but they didn't talk about their religion in public. Even Father Heaney himself had always confined his preaching to the pulpit. You wouldn't hear him spouting about God or matters holy at football meetings. It must have been Bridget put her husband up to saying those things, Eugene decided.

"Even an Irish bishop," Frank declaimed, warming to his subject, "has said in the past few months that it's time to ask the question whether our priests shouldn't be allowed to get married."

"Hear! Hear!" someone shouted from the left side. But a fellow standing near Eugene muttered, "Mind your own bloody business, Frank O'Connor."

Eugene slipped out the door and sat in his car across the road till he heard the applause at the end of Father Heaney's response to Frank's speech. "Begob, you have the gift of the gab," he said later to Frank.

"Was it all right?" Frank was looking pleased as a cat with a mouse: several people had congratulated him on his fine oratory.

"Why wouldn't it." Then, "Can we talk for a bit?"

"What about?" Frank was instantly wary.

"You know what about. Just the two of us."

"Ah now...If herself sees us talking together there'll be hell to pay."

"We can talk in my car. Bridget's over there now chatting with her departing priest; she won't notice us leaving."

Frank followed him reluctantly. "Turn on the engine and warm her up a bit." It had turned sharply colder since the rain stopped.

"Aisling is devastated. As you know, she wants a babby something fierce."

"She would, to be sure. Quite understandable. Why wouldn't she." Frank looked towards the hall. "If herself comes out that door now I'm in deep dung."

"You had six yourself."

"Six? I had two Harps, that's all."

"Babbies. We're talking about babbies, Frank. You had six of your own. Surely you wouldn't begrudge Aisling and me just the one?"

"Ah now, that's not the issue." Frank blew on his hands. "'Tis got fierce cold in the past couple of hours. I'd say we could have snow."

"Then what is the issue?" Arguing with Frank was like flocking sheep without a dog.

"The issue is that the unfortunate babby is our grandchild, Bridget's and mine. If our daughter isn't able or willing to take care of it, then the duty falls to us. You can see that now, can't you?"

"What I see is a couple of very selfish people who would deprive a poor woman of her right to a bit of happiness."

"Hold on now. Insults will get us nowhere. We have to discuss the situation calmly."

"What's there left to discuss?" A dull anger was burning inside Eugene. "You have made up your mind, haven't you? Well, I can tell you this, Frank: you won't get away with it so easy. We're prepared to fight all the way to the Supreme Court in Dublin."

Frank stared at him as if he thought Eugene had suddenly gone daft. "Ah, sure that wouldn't be to anyone's benefit, except the solicitors and the barristers who'd take all our money from the both of us." He blew on his hands again. "I'm not saying, mind you, that the matter is completely closed yet. I believe there's still room for some reasonable discussion." He glanced across at the hall again. "But on no account are you to tell Bridget I said that."

"For feck's sake, Frank, why can't you talk straight for once in your life? Either you're willing to leave us the babby in peace or you're not. Which is it to be?"

"If it was up to me, Eugene…" Frank extended palm-upward hands, like Father Heaney imploring heaven at mass. "But you know how herself is?"

"So you're telling me *you're* willing to let the matter be?" But Eugene was suspicious: there was a streak of the dodger in Frank O'Connor that made him run with the hare and hunt with the hounds. "That wasn't the impression I had the night you were both back at the house."

"Politics, Eugene. Politics. And survival. A man has to

gallop alongside his wife when she's on the warpath. Maybe when she calms down a bit and the temper subsides we can…Mind you, I can't exactly promise you anything at this stage."

"So what are you saying then? That you'll talk her out of going to court?"

"We'll see, Eugene; we'll see. I'll talk to her for sure. Now I better get back over there before she discovers I'm gone." Frank O'Connor swung out of the car and hurried across the road into the hall, leaving Eugene Banaghan to wonder whether he had actually got somewhere or was merely the victim of a conjurer's illusion.

Bridget did see them leave, and full well she guessed what Eugene Banaghan was up to. She surmised, too, the hedged concessions her slippery spouse was apt to make. So as she bantered with Father Heaney she was contemplating how she'd deal with her husband. When she saw him return to the hall by himself she took advantage of an interruption by a couple of old biddies who wanted to talk to the priest, and took Frank by surprise just as he was about to join a group of his drinking friends. "What was that all about?" As ominous as the calm before thunder.

"What was what all about?" His stalling told her he had conceded something.

"What did you tell him?"

"Tell who?"

"I saw you leave with Eugene. And I know you weren't discussing the price of sheep. You told him you'd think about it, didn't you?"

"I did no such thing. He said Aisling is devastated; those

were his very words."

"We can't help that. She has no right whatever to covet our grandchild. I really hope, Frank, that you didn't leave Eugene with any false expectations."

"Now, Bridget! You know me better than that."

"So what did you tell him?"

Frank put on the face of a child before castor oil. "You know, I've been thinking about it." Arms folded, staring in agony at the ceiling that needed a new coat of paint. "Mind you, I didn't say this to Eugene, of course, but it has crossed my mind a few times lately, that after rearing six of our own maybe we shouldn't interfere if Eilis wants to—"

"Frank!" The bleat of a ewe that has just lost her lamb. "How could you? After all we talked about this. Families belong together, remember? We keep saying that. Our children are ours, and that includes our grandchildren. They have to grow up knowing who they belong to. If Eilis refuses to be a mother, at least her baby is going to know who its family is, who its grandparents are, and—"

"I'll say good night to you now," Father Heaney interrupted.

"But not goodbye, of course, Father." Bridget's tone was ever so tender. "We'll be seeing you again before you go."

"Sunday mass will be my last public function. I'll be moving Monday."

"Will you need a hand with the packing?"

"Ah, no, thanks, Bridget. There isn't much." Tears glistened in his eyes. "Oh, and from now on you might as well call me Michael."

"Poor devil," Frank said after he was gone. "I wouldn't want to be in his shoes for all the tea in China." But later that night in bed he allowed himself to speculate on what it would be like to be suddenly single. Would he head straight for Julia? Or would he survey the field? He fell asleep without reaching a conclusion.

Bridget was doing laundry on Friday afternoon when Marie came dashing in with the letter. "It's from Eilis, Mammy; there's no mistaking that terrible scrawl of hers. Do you want me to read it for you?"

"Leave it on the table." So Marie sat by the stove for the next ten minutes, waiting, watching, biting her nails, while her mother sorted dirty clothes and loaded the washer and then made herself a cup of tea before tearing open the envelope.

I have decided to terminate my pregnancy. Aisling told me you won't let me give the child to her and Eugene without taking us all to court. And since I don't want the whole thing dragged out in public, this is the only solution left to me. I'm going off to England in a few days to get the matter taken care of.

If her youngest hadn't been sitting there looking at her with expectant eyes, panting for the latest tidbit that she could run and report to her siblings, Bridget would have screamed. As it was she had to bite down hard on her tongue to keep from registering emotion. "Go away and play," she growled at Marie, then hurried down the yard. Frank was tinkering with the tractor engine. He said nothing, though in an ominous sort of way, when she finished reading the letter. "What are we going to do?" she demanded.

The signs of anger were visible in his reddening cheeks.

"Grandmother's blood!" He kicked the tractor tire savagely.

"That's uncalled-for, Frank. Mammy would never have done a thing like that. Anyway, we'll have to go up first thing tomorrow." She rang their former parish priest four times without success. The following morning, ready to leave for Galway, she tried again after sending Frank back to the bedroom to put on a tie. "Father Heaney? It's me, Bridget O'Connor. I've been trying to reach you since yesterday. Oh, of course, yes, Michael it is. It's just that it's hard to get used to. How are you keeping at all? How is the flat?" They talked generalities for a minute before she told him why she rang. Would he be willing to help her out with a very delicate matter? She'd explain all about it when she saw him. When? Today. Yes, today, this morning in fact. He could? He would. Grand. Then, listen, they were leaving right now. Yes, this very minute. Oh, of course, Frank was coming, too. Would he meet them in Kenny's Bookshop in, say, an hour and a quarter. Yes, half past ten would be fine.

He was there before them. She didn't recognize the man in the gray tweed hat and beige raincoat browsing the Irish History stack until he turned and smiled at her. "Bedad, it's you that's looking dapper," Frank said. "He's not wearing a tie, either," he jabbed at his wife.

"We'll go and have a cup of tea," Bridget said, "and I'll tell you what it's all about."

"I'd ask you back to my flat only I'm afraid it's still a bit of a mess." Michael Heaney turned up the collar of his raincoat against the biting wind.

"Not at all, Michael. Let's go round to the GBC." Over a pot of tea and in the presence of an assortment of cream buns, she explained to the ex-priest the latest developments in what she called "the soap-opera saga" of her wayward daughter. He nodded and yessed gravely and often, though he didn't offer any opinion or suggestion until she finished.

"She has to be stopped," Frank said. "This is a terrible thing altogether." He bit savagely into an eclair.

"What is it exactly that you'd like *me* to do?" Michael Heaney poured himself a second cup. "I don't have that sort of authority anymore. You know, the kind my Roman collar used to give me." His wistful expression almost side-tracked Bridget from her mission.

"Oh indeed you have. Why wouldn't you, collar or no collar. And you have a way of putting an argument that's so convincing. I have no doubt that Eilis will listen to you where she mightn't pay any attention at all to us."

"I'll do my best so. Mind you, it's a delicate matter. A very touchy one. The young people nowadays have a different way of looking at things than we had at their age. They don't see morality in the same black-and-white color scheme. Everything seems to be on a spectrum for them, shaded and qualified. Of course, when you think about it, who's to say they're altogether wrong. We were too easily persuaded in our day."

Frank's "huh" was noncommittal, whether out of incomprehension or disagreement it was hard to say.

Not so Bridget. "*We* learned the commandments, Michael. We learned what was right and what was wrong and when we did wrong we were *told* it was wrong and there were no two ways about it." She tapped her teaspoon on the table for emphasis. "The trouble with the young people of today is that no one is willing to lay down the law to them.

Everybody is so afraid of hurting their feelings or damaging their psyches or interfering with their liberty that the poor kids don't know what's right or wrong anymore. Not to mind know what's good for them."

"You have a point there, Bridget. It's a topsy-turvy world we live in. So much ambivalence…"

"Well, there's nothing ambivalent about abortion, is there?"

"There certainly is not," Frank said. "The people of Ireland were very definite about that when we had the referendum a few years back. *The right to life of the unborn*, if I remember rightly, was how they put it."

"It was," Michael agreed. "Those were the exact words of the Amendment."

"Let's go then and talk to the girl before she disappears." Bridget was up and off as if her life depended on it, leaving Frank to pay the bill.

It took several hard knuckle-knocks on the upstairs door of her flat to rouse Eilis out of bed. "Oh, God." Tousled, sleepy-eyed, dressed in a flannel nightgown, and barefoot, she stared at her mother as if only half-comprehending who she was. "Couldn't you at least wait until a civilized hour before barging in on a person."

"It's twenty to twelve already." Frank was standing two steps down because the landing could accommodate only one person.

"You, too? What's this, anyway? An army invasion?"

"Michael Heaney is with us as well," Frank said.

"Hello, Eilis," said the man behind him. "We're sorry to disturb you so early."

Eilis fled. Bridget entered. Frank followed. Michael

Heaney stood hesitantly in the doorway. "Come in, Michael," Bridget said. "She'll be ready in a minute." But they sat for almost fifteen minutes in the chilly parlor in their coats and hats before Eilis reappeared.

"So to what do I owe the pleasure?" She stood in the kitchen doorway, dressed in a long flowered skirt and oversized Aran sweater, hair neatly brushed and tied back in a ponytail, without lipstick or rouge—she never used make-up. Her expression was wary.

"We're sorry for intruding so early," Michael Heaney said again.

"You look great in civvies, Father. I love that tweed hat."

"Michael. From now on it's Michael." The grin was shy, embarrassed, boyish. "But not Mick, mind you. I was called Mick at school and I never liked it."

"I like the name Michael." She smiled back at him, ignoring her parents.

"What's all this nonsense you wrote about?" Bridget's tone as sharp as the raw air of the room.

"It's not nonsense, Mammy. It's what I'm going to do."

"Come and sit down and talk to us about it."

"There's nothing to talk about."

"Why don't you sit anyway, and we can have a little social conversation," Frank suggested. "We did come all the way up to see you, after all. And this man here who was out carousing all night dragged himself out of bed just to meet you."

"Frank!" Bridget's tone suggested her husband had just lost whatever wits he possessed.

"True for him." Michael Heaney grinned: you could see he was pleased to be branded a libertine. "You know what

Galway is like for us single fellows."

"Would you like a cup of tea, Michael?" Eilis asked. "Or is coffee better for a hangover?"

"Tea would be grand. If it's not too much trouble."

"I'll have a cup, too," Frank said.

"Mammy?"

Bridget hesitated. "Yes, please."

There was banal chatter while Eilis made kitchen noises. Eventually she reappeared with a large plastic tray that held a stainless steel teapot, a jug of milk, a bowl of sugar, mugs, spoons, and a plate of biscuits. "Aren't you great," said Michael Heaney as she put the tray down on a small table next the sofa. "That's a lot more than I could rustle up."

"You'll soon get the knack of it," Frank said.

"Will you listen to him." Eilis put milk and sugar in a mug, poured tea, stirred, handed it to Michael Heaney. "Coming from a man who wouldn't know which end of the teapot the handle was on." She poured for her parents and herself, then sat in the other armchair. "So how do you like Galway, Michael?"

"Ah, sure it's not too bad, you know. The flat is a bit on the small side, and, no more than your own, it's inclined to be cold and damp. I haven't yet got into the habit of fending for myself in the way of meals and things, but otherwise I'm surviving."

"Before you know it you'll find yourself a good woman to look after you," Frank said. "Then you'll develop a big belly like me and—"

"And *she'll* develop a big belly like me," Eilis said. "Sorry."

"Which is what we came to talk about," Bridget said.

"I told you there's nothing to talk about, Mammy."

"You're going to kill your own child? What do you mean there's nothing to talk about?" The edge of anger harshened Frank O'Connor's voice.

"If that's the tone you're going to take, I'm leaving right now this minute." Eilis got to her feet, put her mug back on the tray, and disappeared through the kitchen door.

"Eilis!" Bridget shouted after her.

"Ah shite," Frank muttered. "Excuse the language, Father."

"Goodbye." Eilis returned, struggling into a winter jacket. "There's plenty more tea in the pot." She went briskly through the outside door.

"Michael!" Bridget looked in anguish at the former priest.

"I'll see what I can do." Michael Heaney put down his mug and followed Eilis.

"It was the wrong thing to say," Bridget told Frank.

"It was the truth, wasn't it? Since when is it wrong to speak the truth?" Frank poured himself more tea. "There are times when you have to call a spade a spade. It's no use—"

"Hold it." Bridget waved her mug at him. "Just stop for a minute and think what it is we came to do."

"We came to keep her from murdering her child, that's what we came for."

"Well, you're not going to get anywhere with that tone of voice, let me tell you. Listen. We may have lost our chance already. But if—"

"We can call the guards and have her arrested." Frank was red in the face and breathing heavily.

"We can do no such thing. Not after that case a couple of

years ago." Bridget put her mug on the tray. "Remember the fourteen-year-old girl in Dublin who was raped and the guards wouldn't let her go to England for an abortion? And then the Supreme Court said she could go. So Eilis can legally go to England and get rid of her child and there isn't a thing we can do to stop her. If we're to prevent her going it'll have to be by *plamas* and not by roaring like a bull."

Frank glowered into his tea. Then he tasted it, grimaced, added a spoon of sugar, stirred it, tasted again, and leaned back into the sofa. "So what are you suggesting?" Deep-voiced and sour.

"First we have to listen to what she says, and then see if we can talk some sense into her. Leave the discussion to Michael and me. In fact, Frank, I think it would be best if you stayed out of it altogether since you're only likely to antagonize her further."

The door opened and Michael came in, followed by a hesitant Eilis.

"Your daughter has something to say." The ex-priest resumed his seat. Eilis remained in the doorway.

"I only came back out of respect for Michael. And I'll go again if I hear a single word of criticism from either of you."

"Who do you—"

"Shut up, Frank. Come and sit down Eilis, and let's talk like civilized people."

She came in slowly and sat on the edge of her chair. "Since you got my letter you know why I'm doing this."

"Abortion is wrong, Eilis." Bridget's tone was matter-of-fact. "That's not a criticism of you. Just a statement of fact. Amn't I right, Michael?"

"According to feminist theory," Eilis said, "a woman has

a right to reproductive freedom. She has control of her own body and no one has a right to tell her what to do with it. Especially not a male hierarchy of dried-up celibates." She glanced at Michael Heaney. "No offense meant to present company, of course."

"What about the rights of your child?" Bridget's tone was gentle, reasonable. "Doesn't *it* have a right to be born and to grow up and have rights like you? Where would you be yourself if I had had an abortion instead of giving birth to you?"

"At least *you* were allowed to decide who would rear your child, weren't you?" Eilis matched her mother's tone. "So why are you denying me my right to do the same?"

"Is that why you decided on..." Michael Heaney nodded as if he had just answered his own question.

"Of course it is! I said so in my letter. Do you think it's fair, Michael, for my parents to demand I give up my baby to them when I want to give her to Aisling and Eugene? Is that reasonable or lawful or legal or moral? I'd say what *they're* doing is what's sinful."

"So you're saying that if they agreed to let you make your own decision in this matter you wouldn't...?"

"Of course not. I want my baby. But there's no way on God's earth they're going to snatch her from me like they'd take a calf from a cow."

Michael Heaney glanced from Bridget to Frank. Both were staring at the floor. Street sounds invaded the room—the imperious honk of a car horn, the high-pitched shout of a prepubescent boy. Frank opened his mouth as if to say something, then slumped again. Eilis sat sideways, an elbow on the backrest of her chair, nibbling the nail of her index finger. Michael Heaney removed his hat and absently stroked his head. Bridget got to her feet abruptly. "You and I need to take a walk, Frank."

"Whatever you say." Frank stood.

"We'll be back in a while," Bridget said. They headed out the door, closing it gently behind them.

When their footsteps had died away, Eilis said, "Thank you for being so understanding." She removed her jacket and tossed it on the sofa.

"Ah sure, I didn't do anything." Michael Heaney put his hat back on.

"Will I light the gas fire for you? You seem to be cold. I'm so used to the place I hardly feel it any more."

"I'm a bit chilly, all right. Old age, I suppose, and not having much of a thatch on top." His smile had boyish embarrassment all over it.

"You're not old." Eilis squatted, lit a match and lurched back, startled, as the flame took hold around the imitation log. "That thing always frightens me the way it starts. Pull your chair up now and you'll thaw out in no time." She sat across from him as he leaned forward, warming his hands before the flames.

"I think it'll be all right now," he said.

"Do you really think so?"

"They'll talk it over and agree to your terms."

"Well, if they do it'll be thanks to you. If you hadn't come there would be skin and hair flying. Daddy shouting blue murder and Mammy screaming mortal sin and me crying my head off."

"'Tis useful to have a third party in these kinds of rows. It could have been anybody, of course."

"Indeed it could not. Give yourself credit. I think you're brilliant."

Michael Heaney took off his hat and dropped it on the floor. "Hardly, in the light of my recent behavior." He removed his raincoat and draped it over the arm of the sofa. "I'm getting warm now."

"I think you're great for doing what you did. I mean, what's wrong with priests getting married? They'd understand women a lot better. Be able to give some real advice instead of the clap-trap nonsense that most of them go on with. Sorry." She smiled at him. "My friend Mairead is a bad influence on me."

"Not at all. One of the reasons I left the priesthood was to do something about that very situation in my own life." Michael Heaney's cheeks reddened and his eyes focused on the gas fire.

"You intend to get married?"

"I'd like to. Of course I have to meet the right woman first."

"Oh, you'll have no trouble at all on that score. The women will be jumping at you from all sides as soon as they find out you're available."

"No fear of that, I'm afraid. I'm not exactly a bargain, you know. Fifty-one years old and no financial prospects. And without any hair to speak of." He smiled and stroked his head.

"Ah now, the kind of woman worth having won't be worried about your money or your hair." Eilis's voice had the enthusiasm of a punter touting a sure thing. "She'll be more—" She stopped at the sound of footsteps on the stairs. "They're back. Oh God, I hope…"

Bridget came in briskly and sat. She was already loosening the buttons of her coat when Frank came in sight. He paused in the doorway, glanced briefly at Michael Heaney, made as if to lean against the doorjamb, then went over and sat next to his wife.

"We've come to a decision." Bridget looked directly at her daughter. Eilis stared back. "We're dropping the court action to get custody of our grandchild."

"Thank you," Eilis said.

"We're doing it very reluctantly, mind you. It doesn't mean we approve of what you're doing."

"It's just that we don't want to have murder on our consciences," Frank said.

"But it's a terrible thing you're doing all the same, depriving us of our grandchild." There was real anger in Bridget's voice.

"You will not be deprived," Eilis said.

You scared the bejabbers out of me, Gran told Eilis that night as she was getting into bed. It was the first time her grandmother had spoken to her in weeks.

"Oh, Gran, I'd never have gone through with an abortion." Eilis smiled as she put out the light. "I just used the threat of it to bring Mammy and Daddy to heel."

Well, aren't you the terrible woman. But I trained you well, didn't I? Gran's distinctive chuckle—the one that used to announce victory over the forces of die-hard convention— sent shivers of delight through her granddaughter.

II. REVOCATION

Jamesie O'Malley, sitting in his Eyre Square office on the morning of Thursday, the thirteenth of February, was in terrific fettle. Six years. Six bloody years since he had qualified to put up his brass plate as a solicitor. And that was how long he had had to suffer Aunt Rose as his clerk. *Keep the money in the family,* his mother had insisted when he was setting up his practice. *Your Auntie Rose is your godmother and she has always been good to you and now she needs the bit of help since Uncle James died, the Lord have mercy on him.* And so it was. For though Jamesie was setting out to conquer the contentious world of law, there wasn't a snowball's chance in hell that he would ever defy his mother. Besides, he allowed himself to be convinced at the time, Aunt Rose wasn't really such a bad sort. A bit cantankerous, maybe, but an intelligent woman and a hard worker. Unfortunately, the cranky overshadowed the industrious. She would do things her way or not at all, with the result that Jamesie spent many an evening after her departure retyping documents or rearranging files.

After moving to Galway from Ballinamore, Jamesie bought the computer, more in hope that it would improve Aunt Rose's work than out of expectation that it would intimidate her into retirement. Though, optimist that he was, he had briefly indulged himself with the latter thought as well. Nevertheless, he *was* surprised when two weeks ago she marched into his office and said she was quitting. "That damn thing is the devil's own work," she shouted. "I refuse to sit here any longer and be told what to do by a dumb machine." Whereupon she gave formal notice that she was quitting.

So on this early spring morning Jamesie O'Malley surveyed his office and reminded himself with fine satisfaction that he would pass this day without having even once to argue with Aunt Rose, or to listen to her complaints about his writing, the office, the equipment, the clients, the city, the country, or the world. He would need a new clerk, of course: no upward-bound solicitor could manage without one. He rang the *Connaught Tribune* and placed an advertisement, emphasizing the need for computer skills. He facetiously suggested adding *no cranks need apply*, but the humorless *Tribune* person said that would not be appropriate.

Two weeks later when a young lady in the family way walked into his office, after he had already interviewed seven people for the job, his first reaction was that it would be ridiculous to hire *her*. By the look of her she had only a few months to go and then he'd be without a clerk again. But, being an expert in the law and careful in its observance, he decided to interview her anyway. Nobody would ever be able to accuse Jamesie O'Malley of discriminatory behavior in the workplace. Besides, she *was* pretty, if at present a bit ungainly, and the solicitor was ever willing to chat with a good-looking woman. "Tell me about yourself," he said.

"My name is Eilis O'Connor and I'm from Kildawree." He admired her quietly confident air, loved the way she spoke, and regretted he wouldn't be able to hire her, for none of the previous applicants had impressed him particularly. "It's near Ballinamore in Mayo. Now let me tell you what I've come about."

The synapses in Mr. O'Malley's brain were flaring in all directions, trying to connect that name and address with some information already present in his memory. "My parents came to see you recently about an adoption," she said. Instantly, as if resolving a harmonic dissonance, Jamesie connected this young woman's family condition with the anguished O'Connor couple who consulted him a couple of weeks ago.

"Yes," he let slip under the spell of her green eyes, realizing as he did that even that much information ought not be divulged, out of reverence for lawyer-client confidentiality.

"They told me they have dropped the case." Even her glasses couldn't dilute the effect of those luminous eyes. "But I don't quite believe them, and I wanted to hear from you that they really have."

He donned the mask of regretful sincerity he had assiduously cultivated these past six years. "As you may well understand, Miss O'Connor, I'm not at liberty to divulge information about clients, past or present." When her pretty face registered dismay, he added, "You'd probably find out for yourself, of course, if you were working for me."

She looked puzzled. "But I'm not working for you."

"I've been advertizing for a clerk, you see. So when you came in just now I thought you were applying for the job."

She gripped the arms of the chair and tried to settle herself a little more comfortably. "I already have a job."

And that should have been that. But Jamesie O'Malley,

who was quite successful in matters legal, was somewhat less fortunate in affairs romantic, and consequently always on the lookout. This young woman with her sympathetic air might be a possibility, despite her condition. Good family and that sort of thing, and from what the parents had said there didn't appear to be a steady man in her life. "How are you with the computer?" he asked.

"Not bad. Quite good, as a matter of fact. Will that help me get an answer from you?"

"I need a person with really good computer skills. And an interest in the law, of course. Actually, I'd prefer someone who wants to go on to an apprenticeship."

"I'm a librarian. At the county library. Where you go to get your books. I've seen your card many times. I recognized you the minute I walked in here."

"Did you now?" How could he possibly have missed seeing her at the library? "Have you ever thought of becoming a lawyer?"

She laughed. "You're very persistent, I must say. Actually, I did think about it. My father says I should be one because I always like a good argument."

"Well, it's never too late. I can pay you at least as much as the library."

"You're really serious, aren't you?"

"Absolutely."

The wrinkling of her nose suggested she was actually giving the matter thought. *You fool*, solicitor O'Malley yelped at Jamesie the romantic. *What are you going to do if she accepts?*

"Well, I'm not exactly thrilled with my library job. As a matter of fact I *have* considered doing something else. Can I think about your job offer? That is, if it's really an offer."

"It most certainly is an offer."

"Of course I'd need some time off in a few months."

"Certainly. No problem at all."

"So do you think you can assure me now that my parents have given up on their adoption claim?"

What was he to say? "I think you have nothing to worry about from that quarter," he said after a nanosecond of debate on the ethics of such an admission. And though his solicitor training reminded him to shut up at that point, he continued anyway. "If you *should* run into any further legal problems, you can count on my professional assistance." Even though Bridget O'Connor had informed him that she and her husband were no longer pursuing legal means to gain custody of their grandchild, his intuition told him the case wasn't over yet.

Monday, the fourth of March, began as a normal day for Joe Mahony, office manager of *Tribes' City Travel*. Anne Duddy rang to say she would be in a bit late: Anne was often tardy on Mondays. Sinead O'Gara was dealing with the first customers of the day, a couple who wanted to travel to Lourdes via Knock Airport. Maura McHugh was trying to look busy, shuffling papers. Joe himself was doing some bookkeeping. He was tapping his fingers on the desk, awaiting a response from the computer system, when the street door opened. It was then that an ordinary day became extraordinary. In strode his uncle and boss, accompanied by a gust of cold March wind.

Denis Brennan had been in the United States for the past month, attending travel industry conferences in Florida,

Chicago, and San Diego. Making the kinds of connections, he said, that would give the agency an edge in the fiercely competitive transatlantic tourist trade. A very nice man, Mr. Brennan, his staff agreed. Kind to his employees and always with the cheerful word and encouraging smile. Though he could be a bit more liberal with the wages, they murmured discreetly among themselves. A devout Catholic if ever there was one: at mass and communion before work every morning. And a staunch defender of the clergy and bishops against the depredations of a sensation-hungry media. His fiery remarks on this subject in the readers' column of the *Connaught Tribune* had brought him a certain local notoriety. A letter of his had even been published in the *Irish Times*. Last year he had founded, and become the president of, *The Society for the Promotion of Christian Marriage*, an organization, he told his staff at the annual Christmas party, that was badly needed in these days of rampant sex and pornography. Mr. Brennan's membership in the Knights of Saint Columbanus was not so generally known, for though that bulwark of Irish Catholicism was a national organization, it tended to hide the light of its membership and good works under a bushel, so to speak. It was a conversation with a fellow Knight after mass on Sunday that had kept Mr. Brennan from enjoying his usual good night's sleep.

At eleven o'clock he summoned Joe into his office. Long, lean, thin-faced, sharp-nosed, with just a hint of gray in his short dark hair, elegantly got out in a tailor-made dark blue suit, Uncle Denis looked the epitome of the successful businessman. Straight-backed now in his executive chair behind his cherry-wood desk, his visage looked unusually grim. Which was how he intended it to look at that moment. "Close the door, Joe, and have a seat." The voice, though kindly, had the sort of subtle edge that Torquemada's might have had on opening a conversation with a suspected heretic.

"Everything went well in your absence," Joe said brightly as he plopped into one of the cushioned armchairs. However, rabbits were starting to frolic in his stomach: ominous was the word for his uncle's mien.

"I'm sure it did. But I have something more important to discuss with you right now."

"Is there something wrong?" Had the uncle discovered his dreadful secret?

"A friend of mine was in the library the other day. He was looking for a particular book."

"A good place to go for a book, I'd say."

"Your girlfriend—Eilis isn't it?—helped him get it. He said she's a very efficient librarian; knows at her fingertips where everything is."

"She's the best."

"What my friend noticed most particularly about her was that she seemed to be pregnant."

"She is, as a matter of fact."

Uncle Denis joined his fingertips in an attitude of prayer, a pose he maintained for some time, while his nephew also sought guidance from heaven. "*You're* not, by any chance...?" The uncle lowered his hands and searched the young man's face for guilt. "Did you...? Was it...?" He shook his head in an effort to find the *mot juste*, but could not bring himself to complete the query.

"No, not at all, Uncle Denis." Joe waved innocent arms in utter repudiation. "Certainly not."

"You're absolutely sure?" The uncle's eyes bored into him, as if to read his innermost thoughts.

"Oh absolutely. I am, after all, a member of SPCM."

Relief flushed through Mr. Brennan like a dose of salts: he had absolute faith in the veracity of his nephew. "But what about...?" Although he believed now that Joe was innocent, his trust in the lad's reliability was shaken. "Shouldn't you have told me?" What *was* happening to the youth of today? Even the good ones could no longer be counted on. "You know the rule of our organization? All cases of unmarried pregnancy must be brought to the Board's immediate attention."

"Oh indeed, yes, I'm well aware of it. However, I had a special reason for not telling you before this."

"What reason was that?"

"I wanted to do something about her situation myself. I thought it would be better if *I* did it, since she's my girlfriend and all that." Through having to conceal his gay status he had become quite a resourceful liar.

"I see. What did you plan to do?"

"Actually, I've already persuaded her to give up the baby for adoption."

"You have? Well, that's very good, I must say. Is she going to do the retreat as well?"

"I'm working on her about that. I need just a little more time."

"Good lad yourself. But even so, remember for the future..."

Joe headed for the bathroom immediately on leaving his uncle's lair.

Between overload at the office, the time demands of Ger, and the pull of the great Irish novel he was struggling to write, Joe hadn't contacted Eilis for weeks. So he felt guilty when, on the evening after Saint Patrick's Day, she rang. "Guess what?" she said.

"What?"

"I started a new job today."

"Brilliant. Congratulations. I've been meaning to ring you."

"Sure you have. You don't care about me anymore."

"Uncle Denis has found out about you."

"Feck Uncle Denis. Oh my God, he didn't think…Oh Joe, I'm sorry."

"Actually he did for a minute, but I straightened him out. I had to lie a bit: I told him I was trying to get you to do the retreat."

"And what sort of retreat would that be now?"

"The SPCM retreat: the one fallen women are expected to make after they promise to give up their babies for adoption."

"I see. Well, you can tell Uncle Denis that I declined his kind offer. Speaking of adoption, would you do me a favor?"

"Uh-huh." Committing to favors for Eilis could be tricky, even dangerous.

"Would you drive me down to Kildawree on Saturday? I want to visit Gran's grave."

That seemed harmless enough. "I'll have to check with Ger first."

He rang back later to say he would. Which pleased Eilis no end. For weeks she had been having uneasy feelings that Gran wanted to tell her something. But no message ensued, not a word since the episode with her parents and Michael Heaney. Until this afternoon, her first day working for Jamesie O'Malley. She was playing with the computer, trying to get the hang of a legal-brief formatting program, when she felt her grandmother's presence. The phrase she was reading on the screen at the time was *a matter of grave concern*, and her eyes couldn't move from it. "You mean the baby's a matter of grave concern?" She whispered. But all she felt was Gran's impatience. "You want me to do something about it?" Then her nose itched. "You want me to fight someone?" Now her eyes could focus only on the word *grave*. "You want me to visit your grave?" At which Gran's presence dissipated.

"Thanks for coming with me." She sat in the back seat of Joe's car. "I don't want to be seen in Kildawree." She needn't have worried: the village was shrouded in heavy mist, there wasn't a person on the street, the graveyard was deserted. They stood in silence by the two mounds of earth that covered the last resting places of Mary McGreevy and Kitty Malone. Eilis suppressed a sob. Death was so unfair.

How do you know? Gran suddenly teased. *You haven't been here yet.*

"Oh, Gran."

"You must miss her a lot, I'm sure," Joe said.

Do you know what I want you to do?

"I'm afraid to ask."

"Is she talking to you again?"

"Ssh!" Eilis reached over and put her finger to Joe's lips.

I'd prefer to be raised by you than the Banaghans.

"Gran! I don't want to raise a child right now. It's not

practical."

You can do it. Anyway, you owe it to me: you wouldn't have been born if it weren't for me.

"Sometimes I wonder if...Never mind. But what on God's earth would I tell Aisling and Eugene?"

Tell them you changed your mind.

"Ah now, that wouldn't be fair; they've waited for years. And you yourself were always so hot on fairness."

We're all fair till it comes to our own needs. Anyway, I know that pair a lot better than you do: they'd do the same thing to you if the situation was reversed.

"But I don't want to be a single mother. Oh yes, I know *you* did it, but I don't want to."

Listen. You could do worse than marry that Jamesie O'Malley lad. His grandfather, Kevin Kelly, almost became your grandfather.

"I seem to remember hearing about him." Although Gran never discussed the subject herself, parish stories about her would-be lovers were legion.

Kevin turned out to be a terrible rake altogether, of course. But Jamesie is all right, they say.

"Gran, do you really..." But Gran was gone, leaving Eilis feeling wet and cold and horribly depressed.

"So what did she have to tell you this time?" Joe asked on the way back to the car.

"She wants *me* to keep her—I mean my baby."

"After I told Uncle Denis you were giving her up. And that I was going to get you to do the retreat. Horrors." Joe waved his arms in all directions.

"Feck Uncle Denis."

"You can say that again."

"Feck Uncle Denis."

"How does she communicate with you anyway? I mean *I* couldn't hear her."

"It's really weird. I can't explain it. Do you ever wake up from a dream and you remember what it was about, and then when you try to articulate it you can't? It's a bit like that: I know when she's there and I know what she says, but there's no way I can explain how it's done."

"She was a remarkable woman, your grandmother. The few times I met her I felt she could see right through me, that she knew exactly what I was thinking. Do you know what I mean?"

"Do I ever?" Eilis laughed. "She had extraordinary insight into what was going on in people's heads. You could never hide anything from her. She told me once—in great confidence, she said—that the parish priest thought she was possessed by the devil at the time Mammy was born. Then that same priest fell in love with her. Gran said she'd have married him only the archbishop sent him away for being too friendly with her. The old people in Kildawree still talk about the time she got up in the church on Confirmation Day and read the riot act to His Grace for getting rid of her parish priest."

"Are you scared when she appears to you, or whatever it is she does?"

"Not a bit. It's just as if she were still alive and I was visiting with her. I do miss her, though." She felt the tears.

"Ger wants me to come out," he said as they were driving back towards the village.

"Will you?" She had often wondered why it had taken them so long.

"I know I should. It's legal now and all that. Everyone is doing it. I don't suppose it's fair to Ger not to."

They drove through Kildawree in silence. Eilis kept her head down just in case. A mile farther on she couldn't bear the suspense any longer. "Well?"

"I was afraid it wouldn't be fair to you."

"You mean with Aisling and Eugene? Oh, I don't think there'd be a problem. I could simply say that was why you didn't want to take responsibility."

"Anyway, I can't do it for the time being."

"It's not easy, I'm sure."

"There's the novel, you see. I'm at a crucial stage right now, and I'm afraid the whole thing might fall apart if there was serious turmoil in my life—like losing my job and having to deal with my parents."

For the remainder of the weekend Eilis agonized over her grandmother's infuriating demand. On Monday at the office she could scarcely focus on her work. The Banaghans would go crazy. Her own life would be turned upside down. But what choice did she have? Gran must always come first. Hadn't she practically reared Eilis? So if she wanted Eilis to rear her reincarnation, that was the way it would be. In the fierceness of that determination Eilis didn't hear Jamesie's call till he left his desk and stood beside her.

"Is everything all right?" He spoke with concern, like a father worrying about the health of his child.

"Yes, everything is fine."

"You look upset. Is this place getting to you already?"

"No, indeed. Everything is lovely." She had an urge to tell him the reason for her pregnancy, and about Gran's latest demand. There was a quality about Jamesie O'Malley that encouraged one to make him a confidant. But she held back and merely asked if he had more work for her.

"Do I seem to be walking funny?" Aisling Banaghan asked her husband. Ten o'clock at night and they heading briskly towards O'Connell Street after coming out of the Abbey Theater.

"That's a weird question." Eugene looked sideways at his wife without breaking stride. "What did you think of the play?"

"Eugene, I think there's something wrong with me. I have this strange impression that I've changed shape or something and that I'm walking lopsided. Will you drop back for a minute and watch me and see if you can spot anything different."

"What's got into you at all?" He slowed anyway and observed her. When he caught up again he said, "I didn't notice anything; you're not waddling any funnier than usual."

"Aren't you the great comedian? You'd be as good as any of them lads up on the stage tonight."

"Wasn't that the strangest play you ever saw?" They turned left, heading for the bridge. "Who was the fellow that wrote it, anyway? Pyrex, or whatever. He's not Irish, is he? I thought the Abbey only put on Irish plays?"

"Pirandello. Luigi Pirandello. He's Italian. Or was. He's dead. I liked it, mind you. It's an interesting idea having the characters from the play wandering around the stage, taking over from the actors. I'll be wondering the next time I read a book if its characters are real, too, walking around somewhere. Thinking maybe I'd run into them in Ballinamore or Galway."

"I prefer a play with a good story. Give me Sean O'Casey any day."

"This may sound strange, Eugene, but the play reminded me a bit of the way things are between Eilis and us. I saw myself as the actor, getting ready to play the mother, while Eilis is the real mother. Do you know what I mean?"

"Are you afraid she'll take over from you as the mother?"

"I'd say she'll be glad to get it over and done with." Then Aisling stopped dead as they were crossing over into D'Olier Street. "Eugene! I *am* walking differently. Can't you see it?"

"You won't be walking at all if you don't get out of here before the traffic gets you." He took her by the arm and escorted her onto the sidewalk. Several years ago, on the spur of the moment, they came to Dublin for a couple of days during the Easter holidays, and now it was an annual event with them. Two nights in Buswell's Hotel, tickets to the Abbey and Gate theaters, dinner at a couple of good restaurants, shopping in Grafton Street, a visit to a museum, antique browsing in Francis Street. "You'd think we were rich," Eugene would grumble every year the minute they were home.

The day after their return, Aisling still sensed she was walking strangely, but the feeling was less pronounced and she didn't mention it again to Eugene, who would only laugh at her anyway. Then, two mornings later when she woke, her breasts were very tender, though in a different way from the usual cyclic discomfort. It couldn't have been Eugene's fault because they hadn't made love since they were in Dublin. Later in the morning when she was going over the farm accounts, it hit her like a jolt from an electric fence: she could be pregnant. Well had she memorized the symptoms over the years: tender breasts, fatigue, nausea…She *had* felt a bit tired for the past couple of days but attributed it to the aftermath of the city trip. No, she wasn't nauseous, though she remembered reading somewhere that nausea didn't always occur. The funny walking? Was that a symptom, too? Was it possible, after all these years and tests and fertility drugs? She *was* several weeks late already, though since that happened occasionally—a side effect of certain drugs, a doctor had once told her—she had thought nothing of it. *Now don't go expecting anything*, she cautioned herself. But she did anyway. And when another week passed without a period, she drove into Ballinamore after school to her doctor and asked for a blood test.

She was bursting to tell Eugene but she didn't dare on such slender evidence. It would break his heart if she got his hopes up and then sent them crashing. So she waited, and listened for the phone to ring after she came from school. Twice on Tuesday and three times on Wednesday it had her running fruitlessly out to the hall. Thursday afternoon she was in the scullery potting dahlia tubers when she heard the harsh clang. She dropped her trowel and raced, wiping her hands on her apron as she went.

This is Doctor Harney's office. Is this Mrs. Banaghan?
"Yes."
Mrs. Aisling Banaghan?
"Yes."

The result of your blood test has come back.

"And what did it say?"

It was positive, Mrs. Banaghan.

"Positive. What does that mean?"

It means that you are pregnant, Mrs. Banaghan. Congratulations…

At which point Aisling dropped the receiver. It crashed on the tile and dragged the cradle down with it. Aisling, who would brood all day if she dropped a cup on the kitchen floor, didn't even notice. She gasped and staggered and stumbled back to the kitchen and sat in a chair by the fire. It couldn't be. But it was. Ah no, not to her: all that ever happened to her was failure—*not this time, I'm afraid, Mrs. Banaghan; we'll have to try again; sorry, Mrs. Banaghan; but there's another possibility we haven't tried yet…*Nevertheless, the woman on the phone just now said *you're pregnant, Mrs. Banaghan*, didn't she? So she must be. She absolutely must be. At which mind-boggling tidings Aisling Banaghan raced to the back door and let out a joyful screech of such maniacal force that it reached the ears of her husband tending a newborn lamb three fields away from the house. He dropped the lamb precipitously and ran.

"What is it? What's the matter?" He charged through the scullery and into the kitchen, knocking over one of her tuber pots on the way.

"You won't believe it." She wrapped herself around him. "I'm pregnant, Eugene. I'm pregnant." She shook him and hugged him and squeezed the breath out of him. "Would you believe it? I don't believe it. But it's true. It's true. They told me it's true. I'm going to have our very own baby."

"Hold it! Will you hold still for a minute." He managed

to unlock her arms ever so gently and free himself and step back till he could see her face. "Who told you what?"

"The test. It's positive. It came back positive. Which means I'm pregnant. Isn't it great? Oh God! I'm totally and completely gobsmacked." She grabbed him again and led him in a spinning dance around the kitchen floor. This time Eugene let her have her way as she whirled and hugged and kissed and several times repeated her besotted screech of joy. After a time, when she showed no signs of abated energy he took control again.

"Slow down a bit now, will you. Slow down. Slow. Easy does it, that's it." Reducing the pace to a medium fast swing. "Now tell me, you have reason to think you might be pregnant?"

"I am. I am. The test proved it. Isn't it great, great, great?" She spun away once more.

"Listen. You went to the doctor, right? And he gave you a test, right? And the test said you're pregnant, right? Is that the way it is?"

She nodded vigorously to each question, then slumped suddenly, without warning, her head on his shoulder, her body a dead weight, dependent on his arms to keep her from falling.

"Are you all right?" The suddenness of her collapse was as terrifying as her mania.

"I'm all right." She tried to straighten but continued to lean on him. "Can it be true, Eugene? You don't think they're telling us lies, do you? I couldn't take that. Not now. After being told. I'm tired, Eugene. I think I need to lie down for a bit."

He supported her down the hall to the bedroom, rolled

back sheet and duvet, pulled off her shoes, helped her in and covered her. "Rest now for a bit and we can talk afterwards." In the hall he noticed the telephone on the floor and replaced it on the little table. Before he reached the kitchen it rang. Doctor Harney's office.

Sorry to disturb you again. Is this Mr. Banaghan? Is Mrs. Banaghan there? Oh! We got cut off before I was able to tell her that the doctor would like to see her as soon as possible.

"With reference to, if I might ask?"

Her pregnancy. Didn't she tell you about it yet? Oh dear, so sorry to ruin her announcement.

The woman rang off, clucking a chuckle. Eugene went back to the kitchen and sat by the stove to think.

Bridget had stayed angry at her daughter for more than two months. Though Frank said what was the use at all of carrying on a grudge against your own child, and her confessor repeatedly urged reconciliation, she remained obdurate throughout the entire penitential season of Lent. It was not in her nature to forgive lightly, especially an offense so egregious. When Frank visited Eilis, which he did faithfully every week, and reported home on her condition and progress, Bridget refused to show the slightest concern or interest. However, when Holy Week arrived and she was faced with the imminent passion of her Savior and the prospect of His glorious resurrection, she could no longer remain unrelenting. On Good Friday at noon she forgave her daughter in her heart and on Easter Sunday morning, after coming home from first mass, she rang her.

If she expected effusions of paschal joy from the prodigal daughter, and she did, she was not granted them. "How is your cold?" was Eilis's immediate follow-up on her some-what surprised "Hello, Mammy." She continued with "Daddy said you were having trouble shaking it off."

"It's almost gone now. Are you all right?" Which was a cry from a mother's heart. For, despite her adamant public stance of rejection, Bridget had privately worried every day about the health of her pregnant daughter. She had gone through it herself six times and, though always successfully, it was well she knew the perils that faced every woman who carried a child in her womb.

"I'm fine, Mammy, thanks." But in that brave and firm response Bridget detected the frightened cry of her little girl.

"Are you sure now? You have no health problems? Is there anything you need?" And with those quintessential maternal queries, and before her daughter had even time to respond, Eilis was returned to the family fold. Within days Bridget had invaded her flat—laden with food, uncooked and cooked—and, while Eilis was at work, proceeded to scour her dwelling till it gleamed like a builder's model.

It was days before Aisling was able to talk calmly about her pregnancy and discuss what it meant for their future. "There are such a lot of things to consider," she said to Eugene on Sunday afternoon. They were sitting in the parlor after dinner.

"Right," Eugene said, without taking his eyes off the telly: a football game was in progress.

"The first thing is: when do we tell people about it?"

"Right."

"I'd rather not say anything for a while. You never know what can go wrong."

"Right."

"I think we should wait three months before we say anything. Are you listening to me, Eugene?"

"I'm listening." Eyes still glued to the TV. "You said not to say anything to anyone for three months."

"The minute you tell one person the whole countryside will know."

"Right."

"So we tell nobody. Including your mother."

That got his attention. He turned and looked at her. "Ah now, we can't very well keep it from Mammy. You know her: she's always asking if there's any news. She'll keep it to herself, you can be sure of that."

"No, she won't, Eugene, and 'tis well you know it. If you tell her I'll never speak to you again."

He said no more, concentrating on the game. But when it was over and they were having tea in the kitchen he brought up the subject again. "We haven't said a word yet about the biggest problem of all."

"Eilis?"

"What are we going to do?"

"Do you think she'd want to keep her babby herself? There are a lot of single mothers around these days."

"She might, I suppose. Then again she probably wouldn't. We certainly couldn't ask her to do it, could we? 'Twould have to come from herself."

"I think we should make the suggestion. That way she won't have to be feeling sorry for us anymore."

"Don't you think that might be a bit insensitive?" He resented not being able to tell her he was the child's father.

"It would be awfully difficult for us to manage two

babbies almost the one age."

"But not impossible. People with twins do it all the time. For myself I'd be in favor of us taking Eilis's babby as well."

"Of course you would. You're not the one who'll be getting up three or four times in the middle of the night when infants are bawling and need to be fed and have their nappies changed."

"I'm perfectly willing to do my bit with the nappies and the feeding."

"I'm sorry. I know you are. It's just that I don't know if I can handle two of them. Isn't it ridiculous when you think about it? God certainly has a funny sense of humor. Here we were trying to have a babby for the past ten years without any success, and all of a sudden we're going to have two of them on our hands."

"But only if you want the two. Of course Bridget O'Connor would be delighted to hear we were letting go of her grandchild."

"Let me think some more about it. In the meantime, not a word to Eilis."

A week later, when Aisling went to Galway to visit Eilis, she refrained from telling her about her pregnancy.

Neither did Eilis tell Aisling about her grandmother's request.

Bridget was listening with amusement to her youngest daughter's blather on the way back from the Saturday shopping in Ballinamore. Suddenly, just as they were approaching Kilduff boreen, the girl interrupted her flow. "Mammy, listen. I think the Gardai are after you." She rolled down her window.

Bridget heard the two-tone sing-song and immediately an ambulance appeared around the bend ahead, coming towards them at a terrible lick, in the middle of the road, lights flashing, horn honking, siren blaring. She swung left till she was scraping the bushes and slammed on her brakes. The ambulance screamed by with only inches to spare. "Glory be to God. Who could that be at all?"

"Bad cess to them anyway." Marie was straining in her seat belt, head out the window trying to look back. "There should be a law against driving like that, shouldn't there, Mammy?"

"Someone must have been taken ill suddenly." Bridget swung the car into the boreen. "I didn't hear of anyone being sick." After they carried the groceries into the house she said casually to Marie, "Why don't you take a ride back the road on your bicycle. You might find out who it is."

Twenty minutes later Marie returned, out of breath. "I know who it was."

"Good girl yourself." Bridget was sitting in the middle of the kitchen ironing.

"But you won't be too happy to hear it, I'd say."

"Well, I certainly won't be happy if you don't tell me. Out with it."

"It was Aisling Banaghan."

Bridget put down the iron. "Are you sure?"

"Positive, Mammy. Didn't I meet Tara Moran back the road and I asked her. She said Eugene Banaghan came running over for her mother this morning. She said Eugene said his wife was himmerjing or something. What's himmerjing anyway?"

"Bleeding." Bridget continued ironing. "Did she say where they took her?"

Marie didn't know. A little later when her daughter headed down the yard—no doubt to find her father and tell him the news—Bridget went to the phone. When Frank came in to supper he asked, "Did you hear anything more about Aisling?"

"I'll tell you again."

"You just don't want *us* to know," Marie pouted.

Later, when the children had dispersed and she and Frank were sitting in front of the parlor fire, she told him. "The woman was pregnant, would you believe it? And she appears to have had a miscarriage."

Frank lowered his newspaper. "Are we talking about Aisling Banaghan?"

"Maggie Moran said she was about seven weeks along."

"But sure she couldn't be." He put the newspaper down on the sofa. "You're positively certain?"

"I'm as surprised as you are. But there's no doubt about it, according to Maggie Moran."

"Who told *her*?"

"Eugene. He came running over to Maggie in the morning looking for help. Aisling was hemorrhaging, he said, and since she was pregnant he was afraid she might lose the baby. Maggie said he was in an awful state."

"Well doesn't that beat the band. I wonder if Eilis knew about this?"

On Monday evening Eilis came home from work exhausted, and got herself a bit to eat. She had just found a halfway comfortable sitting posture—no easy task, with the little creature inside her flailing in all directions—when the footsteps sounded on the stairs. The Banaghans, on their way home from the hospital.

"I'm so terribly sorry," she said when they told her the sad news. There was an added earnestness in her tone that only she herself could appreciate.

Aisling cried. Eugene put his arm around her. Then she dried her eyes, got up slowly, and knelt awkwardly in front of Eilis. "You have no idea," she said, taking hold of her cousin's hands, "how much what you are doing means to me. I wanted your baby even when I thought I was going to have my own. Now…" She sniffled and tried to smile and started to cry again. "I don't know what in the world I'd do if it weren't for you."

Bridget O'Connor paid frequent visits to her pregnant daughter. Recalling her own first pregnancy, she was concerned that Eilis might be unduly nervous at the prospect of giving birth. However, whenever Bridget raised the topic, her daughter brushed it off with a casual, "I'll be fine, Mammy." Then, a few weeks before the delivery date, on the way back to the flat after a visit to the obstetrician, Eilis confessed that she *was* worried about all the things that could go wrong.

"It's my baby I fret about, Mammy," she whispered. "Oh yes, I know the statistics: giving birth was never safer for mother and child."

"So what's to worry about then?"

"She's not a statistic. She's *my* little girl and it would be no consolation to me at all that nine hundred and ninety-nine thousand, nine hundred and ninety-nine babies out of a million were born healthy and safe if she wasn't."

"Why are you whispering?"

Eilis leaned over and whispered. "Because *she* can hear what I say and who knows how much of it she may understand? I'm even worried that she may *sense* my worry and that that may affect her."

"Well, it's a good thing to talk to your baby anyway. I talked to all of you. Your grandmother taught me that. But you have to talk to her positively. Tell her it's going to be an exciting adventure. That the world she's coming into is a place of fun, of people who will love her to pieces, of colors that will dazzle her eyes, of sounds that will make her laugh, of food she'll love to taste."

"What if she chokes on her mucus? Or strangles on the umbilical cord? Or maybe she'll have a weak heart? Or her lungs won't function? What happens if she's brain-damaged by improper handling at birth? I've read about all these aberrations, Mammy, and I'm terrified that one of them might happen to her."

"I think you should come home now and stay with us till after the baby is born." Which statement surprised even Bridget herself.

"You can't be serious, Mammy? What do you think your neighbors would say?"

"Never mind the neighbors. It'll be a lot safer for you at home where I can keep an eye on you."

"I can't, Mammy. I still have to work. But thanks all the same. I'll be all right here. Mairead comes over every evening and Michael is always in and out."

"Fat lot of good *he'd* be if you needed help. Men are no use at all in those kinds of situations." She'd have to talk to Michael Heaney one of these days about not getting *too* friendly with her daughter. "Anyway, I'll have a bag packed and you're to ring and let me know the minute you have the first sign of going into labor. I'll be with you within an hour and a quarter." Back at the flat she made lunch before leaving for home. On her way out the door she said, "Your daddy says he can't wait to be a grandfather."

In retrospect, leaving had been less traumatic than

staying gone. There were days—and especially nights—
when Michael half wished he were Father Heaney again,
safely ensconced in his parish house in Kildawree. Those
moments passed—every time his imagination returned him
to his former state, he knew he *didn't* want to go back—yet
the desolation that brought them on could not be so easily
escaped. The aloneness inherent in priestly celibacy was of a
different order from the solitude of middle-age bachelor-
hood. *Father* Heaney, though deprived of that deep personal
companionship he craved, had nevertheless been enveloped
by his parishioners, friends *de jure* and often *de facto* as well.
Michael Heaney, bachelor, minor cog in the machinery of a
mighty corporation, was a man of no importance, and of
only slight interest, to his fellow workers. His background,
when it became known, seemed to make the men wary and
the older women reserved. To the younger set he was not
even an object of curiosity.

He had sworn to lay off the drink when he left
Kildawree. And he had, in the first weeks of elation
following his freedom from clerical obligations, buoyed by
unformed expectations of lay bliss. However, the euphoria
did not perdure and neither did his abstention. Whiskey—
though only in moderate doses, he assured himself—was still
needed till he found his feet.

Perhaps the severest pain on leaving his parish was
caused by separation from Bridget O'Connor. He
acknowledged now that he had been daft about her from the
time they first met. His love had been unstated and
unrequited, of course, but was nevertheless deep and
unvarying. He'd watch her through the confessional veil on
Saturday nights as she arranged the flowers and linens for

Sunday's altar, let fantasy transport him with her to places
he dared not go, and repress the discomfort of his own
hypocrisy as he lectured penitents about sins he himself was
committing. He couldn't advance beyond gaze and fantasy,
of course. Not then, when he was bound by celibacy, not now
when he was free. Bridget was married and pious and,
though she gave some indications that she returned his
passion, she would never, he knew, step over the bounds of
fidelity. Anyway, he could never himself engage in
adulterous behavior.

He became a little less sure of this latter principle after
Bridget sought his help in dealing with her wayward
offspring. She wasn't entirely happy with the outcome of
their meeting to prevent Eilis's threatened abortion, but she
thanked him for his help and said his intervention had saved
her daughter from becoming a murderess.

She invited him down to Kilduff for dinner the following
Sunday, an offer he gladly accepted: Sundays were difficult
days in his new lay state. She cooked a scrumptious meal and
looked ravishing herself. To ensure his enjoyment of both he
allowed himself only one whiskey—that after pressure from
Frank—and a single glass of wine with the dinner.
Immediately after the dishes were washed the children
disappeared. Unworthily, he wished that Frank, too, might
depart, but the man had obviously no such intention. The
three of them sat in the parlor and the O'Connors brought
him up to date on parish affairs. Then, when he was
thinking that perhaps it was time to leave, the phone rang.
Frank came in from the hall after answering it and said he
had to take a quick run up to Galway. Cattle mart committee
stuff, he explained vaguely. Michael stood and said it was

time for him to go as well. Frank said nothing but Bridget robustly not-at-alled—she was just about to make a cup of tea, she said. So after a polite demur he agreed to stay a little longer. Frank seemed about to say something but then changed his mind and departed after a cursory handshake.

"Well I'm delighted you stayed," Bridget said when she brought in the tray. She put two cubes of sugar in the cup, poured milk and tea, stirred and handed to him. "There's something I wanted to talk to you about that I couldn't very well do while himself was here."

"I'm glad I stayed, too. Now I have you all to myself for a while." He smiled at her, feeling thoroughly bold. A bit thrilled as well when he thought he detected a faint blush in her cheeks.

She sipped her tea and proffered a plate with tiny slices of cake. "I think Frank is seeing another woman."

He stopped dead in the act of reaching for a piece. "Oh dear!" What did one say? What kind of facial expression to adopt? Could he condemn the very act he himself was committing in fantasy and desire?

"I'm almost certain of it. Something he said made me suspicious—I won't embarrass you with the details." She put down the cup and joined her hands in her lap. "So I began to watch him. Then I came across this book in Easons that gives a profile of a cheating husband, and he fits it to a tee. The more I've watched him since the surer I've got that he's philandering."

"I'm terribly sorry. I don't know what to say." He was feeling a sort of indecent elation—cheated wife amenable to lover's advance, sort of thing—that was embarrassing to his moral self.

"I haven't let on that I know anything, of course. So he has no suspicion that I'm on to him."

"You don't think you might possibly be mistaken? I mean, could there be another explanation for his behavior?"

"I don't think so. It's simply a matter of who? Some slut in Galway, it would appear. He goes up there a lot and he's always in great humor heading off. I'm quite sure that's where he's gone just now."

He was startled at her composure: no tears or histrionics or visible anger. "So what will you do?"

"Wait till I get proof. More tea? There's plenty in the pot."

"Yes, please."

"That'll be the day he'll rue for the rest of his miserable life, let me tell you. I'll put a bridle on his head and a bit in his mouth that'll rein him so tight he won't go to the bathroom without my permission." She poured for him. "That is, if I don't throw him out entirely."

"It's a most unfortunate situation indeed," was all he could manage. It would be hypocritical to outrightly condemn what he might well do himself if he had the chance.

"But don't you think I'm right? Or do all men think this sort of thing is acceptable? You hear about it happening everywhere these days."

"No. It's not right. Of course not. Unfortunately, it's been going on for so long throughout history that one might suppose it's somehow part of human nature."

Bridget put her head between her hands. "I don't know what's happened to my life at all, Michael. First Eilis, and now Frank. Did I do something terribly wrong, do you think? Is God punishing me for my sins?" When she looked up at him there were tears in her eyes.

"Not at all. If there's one thing I've learned from life, Bridget, it's that virtue isn't even a distant cousin to either reward or punishment. So stop blaming yourself, my dear."

She wiped her eyes. "You're a good friend, Michael."

He desperately wanted to get up then and put his arms around her, but of course he didn't.

There were days when Eilis thought she was literally going to explode. So fat and stretched and pulled every which way. "I can't wait for the little joker to come out of hiding," she told Mairead. She was sitting at her kitchen table watching her friend wash the dishes.

"Won't be long now." Mairead had come over after work and cooked dinner, a performance of dedicated sisterhood on her part since she rarely cooked for herself. "Think of this, my dear, you're doing what no man, no matter how big or strong or powerful or rich, can ever do. No wonder they keep trying to put us down."

"You certainly don't like men too much, do you?" Being with Mairead was never a restful experience. Michael Heaney, after spending an evening in her company, called her the John the Baptist of feminism. "I can hear her preaching in the desert: *Prepare ye the way of the woman, make straight her paths. Every female shall be exalted and every male chauvinist pig brought low.*"

"I've nothing against them." Mairead finished the dishes, helped Eilis out of her chair, and they moved into the living room. "Except for the way they have historically treated us." She assisted Eilis to sit, then perched lotus pose on the sofa.

"Jamesie has been treating me very nicely," Eilis told her.

"For weeks he's been saying, 'Whenever you feel you can't come in any longer, just stay home.' He even said he'd pay me for the time I'm out. Of course I've only got ten more days to go if this young rapscallion comes out on schedule."

"Do I detect a touch of romance here?"

"I don't know; it's possible. I do like him an awful lot. And he certainly gives the impression that he likes me. Though he's so taken up with money and status and power that it's hard to tell."

"We're all a bit like that these days, I'd say. It's modern Ireland for you. The question is, does he have any compassion in him? That's how you'll know if he's worth having."

"He wants to be the richest and most famous lawyer in the whole of Ireland. The Tony O'Reilly of the legal system, according to himself."

"Women could do with a bit of that spirit, too." Mairead looked at her watch. "I better go home. I have to be at work at eight o'clock in the morning."

"There's something I want to tell you. Something I've been putting off for too long. If you can spare a minute."

"Fire ahead."

"I've changed my mind about giving the baby up for adoption to Aisling and Eugene." There! After arguing with herself for the past two months, she had finally said it out loud.

"You've what?"

"At least, Gran has changed it for me: she wants *me* to rear the baby." She told her friend about the episode in the Kildawree graveyard. "So I feel I have to, though I'm not very keen on it. Am I doing the right thing, do you think?"

Mairead got to her feet. "I have to be honest with you: I don't believe or disbelieve what you have told me about your granny. The whole business of voices from the other side is beyond me. I mean they *might* be coming from your granny. But, on the other hand, maybe they're coming from *you*. Maybe what prompted you to have a baby in the first place was some sort of mystical understanding—in a way that's not given to most of us—of what it means to give life. So that now you feel your baby is such a part of you, and always will be, that you must take care of it yourself." Mairead smiled. "That's the best I can offer you for now."

Eilis said nothing, but after Mairead left she dismissed her friend's speculation. It was *not* her imagination: she *had* heard Gran's voice and felt Gran's presence, so now she must carry out Gran's wishes. But how was she to resolve those wishes with her commitment to give her baby to Aisling and Eugene? Despite all the mental gymnastics and verbal contortions she had gone on with ever since her visit to Gran's grave, she had not been able to break through that wall of obligation. Then, later that night in bed, she remembered Aisling's miscarriage. Hadn't she promised them her baby because Aisling couldn't conceive? Now she had. Although she had lost her baby through very premature delivery, yet she *had* conceived. And if once, why not again? Aisling could even have several babies of her own yet.

However, Eilis didn't feel up to telling her cousin just now: best to put it off till after the baby was born. She thought, but couldn't be sure, that she heard Gran's murmur of approval in the darkness.

DELIVERY

Eugene Banaghan usually woke at six, his wife rarely opened an eye before seven. Since she lost her baby, however, she was awake before him every morning. "I don't sleep well anymore," she'd say.

"With a bit of luck," Eugene mused in bed one Monday morning about six weeks after the tragedy, "we'll get everything just right the next time." He gently plucked his wife's left nipple through her nightgown,

"What didn't we get right the last time?" Aisling was feeling more sensitive to the nuance of reproach than to the pleasure of his hand.

"Oh, I didn't mean to imply we did anything wrong." Trying to pull the nighty over her head but, without her cooperation, getting nowhere. "Just that it didn't work out in the end."

"Which was my fault, I suppose." Dragging the night-gown down from her face. She knew it was unfair to snap at him like that, but she couldn't help herself. The pain of her loss still repelled all consolation, and though she was aware that Eugene was only trying to be optimistic, she was not yet ready to be comforted.

"It was nobody's fault."

"So what didn't we get right and how are we going to fix it next time?"

He leaned over and nibbled her chin. His hand beneath the duvet lightly rubbed her smooth flat belly. "We'll fill this up one of these days, love." His tongue slid into her ear. It was his first attempt at making love to her since the miscarriage. But, though he tried both gentleness and passion, he failed to arouse her, so deep was her depression still.

Afterwards, as they lay side by side in their high brass bed, she returned to what had become almost her only topic of conversation. "Just a week to go."

"Aye."

"I'm going up to see her today."

"What about school?"

"I told them I wouldn't be in. She needs the company, the creature. Anyway, she has to see the doctor today and I promised I'd go with her." When there was no reply from her husband she added, "I'll bring her up a check." She swung her legs out of the bed.

"Didn't you already give her one last week?"

"We can't be stingy with the woman who is growing our baby." Over breakfast she stifled his attempts to discuss what bullocks he should take to the mart in Ballinamore on Thursday. "Do you realize we may have a crying baby in this house by the end of next week? How are you going to handle *him*, mister big cattle farmer?"

"We'll take care of it when it comes."

"Him! It's going to be a boy."

"Isn't it strange that she didn't want to find out ahead of time if it's a boy or a girl?"

"She's convinced it's a girl. But I'm cocksure it's a boy."

"I think maybe I'll wait another month before I sell any."

"I should probably get some more diapers as long as I'm in Galway."

"Still, there's a couple of them that aren't going to improve anymore, I'd say."

"Eugene! We're talking about our baby. Isn't he more important to you than your fat bullocks?"

"Of course he is, love. But we have to be able to feed him, and to do that I have to make decisions about selling those cattle. You do understand that, don't you?"

He could be so bloody patronizing at times. "Right now, I think the baby's needs should come before anything else."

"They do, my love. I'm as anxious about him as you are. But there's nothing we can do at the moment, is there? We just have to wait and let nature take its course."

"I better get ready."

"I don't know why you have to go. She's being well looked after, isn't she? In the hands of the most capable doctor in Galway. And her mother is in and out of there every second day, like a fly around a jampot. I think it might be best for us to keep our distance for the time being, just in case certain people get contrary again."

He was right, of course, but she couldn't sit around doing nothing. It was almost as if she was going to give birth herself, wasn't it? After all, the baby would be hers the moment he was born. "Maybe I'll go to Dunne's while I'm there and get a few more things for him."

He leaned back and laughed. "Musha God bless you, woman, you'll soon have enough baby stuff to start your own shop." He pushed back from the table and got to his feet. "I'll go have another look at them bullocks; I'm thinking maybe I'll sell the two biggest lads. That way we might have enough money to pay for all them baby clothes." He winked at her as he went. She stuck out her tongue at him.

Running her hands through the stacks of infant clothes made her feel like a mother. She imagined how his little wriggling body would look inside them. Then the jolt hit her, as it had been doing regularly and often since the miscarriage. From her womb that pain came, from the very spot where her child should still be nestling, growing, feeding, preparing for life. How unfair that same life was at times. Or—she might as well say it—how unfair God was. No, she mustn't blame Him. He undoubtably had His reasons. Though He might have made them clearer. Well, why not blame Him then? It hurt something fierce. She squeezed into a ball a pair of infant overalls in her effort not to cry. Then straightened them out and left the shop in a hurry. In the street she thought of returning to buy at least one item, but changed her mind and found a café where she ordered a cup of tea to soothe her nerves before going to visit her cousin.

Eilis had on a bright blue knee-length maternity dress with a white lace collar and gold buttons. Her hair was pulled tightly up and pinned at the top of her head. The bulging front looked almost comically incongruous on her slender frame. "I'll be with you in a minute," she said after letting Aisling in and waddling slowly through the kitchen into her bedroom. "I've started putting on makeup. I don't know why," she added when she reappeared. "When you're this ugly, what difference does it make."

"You have the bloom of motherhood on you," Aisling

said. 'Tis I should look half as good."

They took a taxi to Doctor Geoghegan's office on the Crescent. The doctor was short, stout, bald and, to Aisling who saw him only briefly as he ushered Eilis into his office, aloof as a monument. She observed this to her cousin later when they were leaving.

"He is, isn't he? There's more life in the statue of Padraig O'Conaire. But, you know, I prefer him that way. I hate having my most intimate parts poked and prodded by a stranger. So the less human he appears, the less the indignity."

"Do you have any idea how many times I've been poked and prodded? For all the good it has done me."

"He said everything is going, or rather coming, according to plan. My pelvis is big enough to accommodate the little creature. And her head is in the normal position."

"His!" Aisling smiled.

Eilis failed to reciprocate. "Anyway, he doesn't think there should be any problems."

"And the schedule? You're due in less than a week."

"He says it's hard to tell with a first baby." A hint of impatience in Eilis's tone, as if the question were somehow inappropriate. "I certainly hope she's on time. I'm tired, tired, tired." Tears appeared in her eyes.

"I'm going to take you straight home," Aisling said. As the car crawled through the narrow crowded streets she added, "I'll cook a nice dinner and maybe you'll feel better."

"I'm never going to feel better again." When they got to the flat she said she didn't feel like eating and would prefer to lie down. Maybe Aisling ought to just go on home since she, Eilis, was terrible company right now. And though

Aisling demurred, the mother-to-be uncharacteristically insisted.

"I'll come again then in a couple of days." Aisling was disappointed, having planned to spend the evening with her usually ebullient, but now morose, cousin.

"I'm not sure that would be wise." Eilis, still on her feet, leaning against the bedroom doorjamb, looked awfully tired and withdrawn. And, strangely, her expression was almost hostile, as if she resented Aisling for being still there.

"Why do you say that?"

"Mammy is going to be here a lot. She plans to come up every day from now on. I'm surprised she didn't come today. Maybe she was here while we were out."

"Which probably means she plans to go to the hospital with you, too." So stupid to think she herself could be present at the birth of her child. Though she had been imagining just that for the longest time. Ignoring the fact of Bridget and all her resentment and anger, she saw herself over and over again helping her boy into the world, till she had come to take her participation in the great event for granted.

"Oh indeed. She says with her own experience of childbirth no one is better qualified to help me out."

"Which means of course I can't be there. Dammit to hell!"

"I'm sorry, Aisling. Of course you'd like to be there. But you know the way Mammy is...Actually, what I'd prefer is for nobody to be around, except myself. Get it all over with quietly and peacefully and privately."

"I'll go home then." Aisling felt crushed. She was to be kept out of the entire drama of her son's birth. However, she'd make up for that by having him to herself for the rest of her life. "Who should I keep in touch with to find out what's going on?"

"Mairead Conneely. You have her number."

"I don't suppose there would be any point in my trying to…I mean, do you think your mother would resent…?"

"I think it would be the worst thing in the world you could do." Eilis's eyes were glazing.

Aisling cried several times on the way home.

She'd always remember where she was when she got the word. Tuesday, the eleventh, the due date, she raced home from school and rang Mairead, but got no reply. Thereafter she rang every fifteen minutes, feeling sure the baby had been born and that Mairead would be returning from the hospital any minute. But it was not until ten past eleven that Eilis's friend answered her frantic ring. No, nothing had happened so far, and there was no sign that labor was imminent. Had Mrs. O'Connor been to visit Eilis today? Oh, yes indeed. As a matter of fact she was planning on staying in the flat with her until the delivery. After that Aisling rang only at night and the answer was always the same. Until the following Tuesday, when Mairead said Bridget was of the opinion that Eilis might be showing signs of going into labor.

On Wednesday afternoon, after school, Aisling made herself go to Ballinamore to do the grocery shopping she had been neglecting. She shopped in a great hurry and drove home a bit too fast for safety. As she approached Kilduff boreen, Frank O'Connor pulled out in his lorry. He slowed and stopped and rolled down his window. She had to brake hard not to pass him. "We just got word," he shouted down at her. "The babby was born two hours ago."

"Oh, thank God," she said, though vaguely aware of her inability to absorb the news. It would come to her in time; for now it was enough that her swimming brain was in possession of the fact. "Are they both all right?"

"They're fine now. Though the poor girl was in labor for more than twelve hours."

"The creature. Is it a boy or a girl?" Not that it mattered a single iota this minute.

"A girl. Seven pounds, one ounce, they said." The complacent look on Frank O'Connor's face bespoke a proud grandfather. "She was born at ten past three this afternoon." Then, after raising his index finger from the wheel in minimal salute, he drove off.

Aisling floated home in a euphoric haze and raced screaming down the yard to tell Eugene. Mairead rang after supper. "How are they doing?" Aisling asked.

"The baby is great. The doctor says she's as healthy as a horse."

"And Eilis?" The woman's focus on the baby provoked in Aisling a sudden terrible fear.

"She's awfully tired, the poor woman, but otherwise she's fine."

"Well, thank God for that. Do you think it would be all right for us to visit her tomorrow?"

"I'd say probably not." Mairead was silent for a moment. "As a matter of fact she told me to ask if you'd wait until Friday at least. She says she's too exhausted to see anyone yet."

So Friday morning, after a day and a half of stomach-cramping, nail-biting, waiting, Aisling rang the hospital and talked directly with Eilis. "We're so thrilled, we're so thrilled," was all she could say for the first couple of minutes. After she calmed down a bit and asked how both were doing, she inquired if she and Eugene might pay a visit today.

After a brief hesitation Eilis said, "All right, but come after two."

At one minute to two she and Eugene entered the Regional Hospital and were heading for the reception desk when Frank and Bridget bore down on them, glistening like newly ordained grandparents. "We can show you where she is." They radiated goodwill as they led the way through a maze of hallways and corridors. "You have visitors," Frank announced, sticking his head in the door of his daughter's ward.

"We'll leave you, then, to talk," Bridget said.

"Come in." Eilis sounded subdued. Half-sitting, half-lying, propped up against a wall of pillows. Next to her bed a cot draped in white. Aisling wanted to cry. *She* should be in that bed, was her fleeting thought as she hugged her cousin. She did shed tears when she leaned over the cot and saw for the first time the infant that was to be hers.

"So beautiful. So beautiful. Like a sleeping angel." Touching the tiny fingers and marveling at their softness. "Her hair is black. Look, Eugene." She made way for her husband.

Aisling had been prepared for her own emotion and had let herself cry. But she had not anticipated Eugene's reaction. That phlegmatic man, to whom a woman's tears were an embarrassment, and whom she had never seen shed one of his own, was blubbering into his hand at the sight of his new daughter. So Aisling had to cry again to keep him company. She looked helplessly at Eilis and saw tears streaming down her cousin's face, too. The idea of all three of them crying made her smile through her tears. And, such being the affinity of weeping and laughter, she started to giggle and then burst into a full-throated guffaw. Eugene stared at her, as though she had gone daft. "What's so funny?"

"Sorry. It just seemed funny to see the three of us crying because we're happy."

"You produced a very fine babby there," Eugene said, then blew his nose loudly into his handkerchief.

"Was it very painful?" Aisling asked.

"I'll say this much, once is enough."

"How did your mother ever manage to do it six times?"

Eilis didn't answer. She who always loved to chat with her cousins and would stay up till late at night with them talking by the fireside now seemed curiously detached. Not in the least enthusiastic about discussing anything, even her baby. She's tired, the creature, Aisling excused in her own mind. When it became clear that the visit was going to be brief, Eugene brought up the business side of the agreement that would need to be concluded before they could take the baby home.

"Can we wait a couple of days before going into that?" Eilis asked. "I need a little more time to recover."

"Of course," Aisling said. "Since we've waited this long…" Though she was impatient to take possession of her child.

"Right then," Eugene said. "I'll go to the solicitor on Monday and have the papers drawn up, and when you're feeling better we'll all get together and sign them and then we'll have a nice celebration for the girleen." He was beaming at the prospect when Eilis waved a dissenting hand.

"Why don't you leave the paperwork to me, Eugene. Remember, I work for a solicitor."

"Fine so. Let us know as soon as you have them ready."

"How soon do you think that will be?" Aisling wasn't willing to accept such an indefinite schedule. "How about Monday?"

Eilis was looking at the cot. "Why don't I ring you." And that was how they left the matter.

On the way home Aisling said, "I'm worried, Eugene."

"What about?" His foot heavy on the pedal as they hurtled along the straight stretch of the Headford road.

"There's something bothering me. I'm not sure what it is, but between Eilis so down in the mouth and her parents so pleased I smell some kind of trouble."

"Arrah, what's there to worry about? It's just that you're anxious. Which is perfectly natural, of course. If you'll be patient a little longer we'll have everything settled within the week."

She said no more, but her foreboding persisted all through the day and into the night.

Postpartum

Jamesie O'Malley was badly smitten. In idle moments he liked to recall that first day when Eilis O'Connor walked into his office, with her radiant eyes and rounded belly. She had captured him in minutes. While at the time he tried to convince himself he hired her because she was the best qualified and because of his legal interest in her potential adoption troubles, he knew that he was giving her the job because of his attraction to her. He marveled now at this impetuosity. He still didn't understand why her condition failed to deter him. Mammy would have kittens if she knew that he was in love with what she'd call a streel without morals. Mammy was a pillar of Catholic virtue who had reared him so well that he had never until now consciously espoused a moral position that he felt she would condemn. As well as that, he himself had always looked on pregnant women, married or not, as being rather distasteful. So what was different about this young woman with the protruding tummy? Damned if he could say, but his viscera knew and they said *we want her*, regardless of present state.

So he hired her and admired her, while keeping his infatuation discreet. His behavior, he was proud to say, was ever courteously professional. Never once did desire overcome his duty to maintain a decent reserve. Nor would it, till she'd had her baby. Then, when the adoption was complete, with *his* legal help of course, she'd be free and ripe for his passionate overtures.

However, as a man of his generation and education and training, imbued with logic and realism and a dash of cynicism, he forced himself to stare squarely in the face, and respond with total honesty to, the question that skulked out of sight of his romantic persona: did this angel who so smote him with her sword of love reciprocate his passion? He was brutally frank in this inquiry. *Face it, Jamesie, you're not the stuff that women adore.* Advice begotten of bitter experience. It was not that he was terribly bad-looking or anything like that: persistent scrutiny in his bathroom mirror had failed to establish that he possessed any features which a normal woman would find abhorrent. True, his face was a bit on the round side and his nose somewhat wide. Overall, however, he was as presentable as many of his friends who seemed to have no difficulty in attracting good-looking females. The difference, he concluded after much analysis, had to do with his psychological inability to maintain his cool in the company of ladies with romantic potential. Whereas with the lads he was wit personified and urbanity incarnate, no sooner did a pretty young woman arrive on the scene than he felt himself reduced to the status of blithering idiot. Why this should be so was the subject of much agonizing analysis, from which he concluded that his lack of savoir-faire in the presence of fair femininity was due to subliminal fear of his mother's frown. For Eileen O'Malley (née Kelly), owner and proprietor of Kelly's Drapery shop on Castle Street, Ballinamore, was a disillusioned woman who trusted women even less than men. The latter, of course, she discredited with very good reason: her father was a philanderer who brought endless grief to her mother; and her husband was known as Don Sean of Castle Street before he took up permanent residence in England when Jamesie was only seven. But it was women who were the ruin of both men, and while Eileen in no way condoned either father's or husband's behavior she anathematized the sluts and streels who brought about their downfall. In so doing she consciously and subconsciously instilled in her son—her only child—a fear of attractive women. A fear that, at the onset of puberty and rebellion, transformed into paralysis Jamesie's natural fascination with those luscious creatures.

He still hadn't answered the question: would Eilis like him? Would she return his love? Would she accept a proposal of marriage? If she did, there was still the problem of Mammy. Eileen O'Malley, president of the Ladies' Altar Society like her mother before her, would never tolerate his marrying a woman who had a child out of wedlock. It had taken her years to live down the shame of her runaway husband. She had devoted those years to rearing a model son, so she wasn't about to permit that son to throw himself away on a wanton harlot—as she would undoubtably describe his beautiful Eilis. She must, therefore, never know about Eilis's unfortunate error. That was, of course, impossible: he was much too well acquainted with the practice of small-town gossip to have any illusions about secrecy. Which left him with two alternatives: concoct a story about the betrayal of innocence and the need for redemption and trust to his mother's piety to go along, or simply defy her. He was still arguing the merits of each the evening he rang his beloved to ask if he could pay her a visit.

"I can't believe it's the same flat." Mairead stood in Eilis's doorway, surveying the transformation. "Your mother, I suppose?"

"Who but?" Eilis rocked gently in her new upholstered chair, the very picture of mother-love as she cuddled her baby. "Mammy loves the paint pot. And buying new furniture."

"She did it all by herself? Well, she's a great woman." Mairead closed the door and came in.

"She shanghaied Terry and Ultan to give her a hand with the painting. They weren't too happy about it from what I hear."

"I suppose it all has to do with you changing your mind?"

"Of course. Daddy, the old skinflint, even shelled out for the furniture."

Mairead sat cross-legged on the new beige carpet. "Have you told your cousin yet?"

"I'm afraid to even think about Aisling. I have to break the news on Saturday when they come up." How she was going to accomplish that heartrending disclosure she had as yet no firm idea, though she had spent weeks trying to come up with reasons that would justify her action to Aisling and Eugene. Several times she had even tried to invoke help from Gran—thinking hard about her, speaking aloud to her in the dark of night—but Gran, wherever she was, was silent; not so much as a squawk out of her since she gave her orders that day at the graveyard.

"How does it feel to be a mother?"

"It's incredible, Mairead. Though to tell you the truth the first time I saw my baby I was a bit shocked. She looked like a tiny red-faced old man. My first thought was I couldn't possibly have brought this critter into the world and I certainly didn't want to have anything to do with her. But of course *she* changed, and *I* began to feel differently about her. It was the touching that did it, I think. Something happens when your fingers come in contact with the tiny body. You're hypnotized so that you have no choice except to want to take care of her."

"You look happy."

"I am now. Though the first couple of days after I came home from the hospital were hard. Mammy stayed with me until Sunday evening, and when she left I started crying and I couldn't stop. I felt as if I was alone in the entire world with this little morsel and I hadn't the faintest idea how to take care of her."

"So sorry I couldn't come over and keep you company. The Bank auditors are still with us, so we're working late every day. It was a big deal to sneak out early tonight."

"It's all right. I got over my panic. Now I just look at her and I can't tell you how good I feel. I know you won't believe this, but I sense the presence of Gran in her. Anyway, my baby is so beautiful and I gave her life and she's part of me. Never mind that my breasts are sore, my nipples hurt, my whole body is uncomfortable. I just want to hold her and feed her and feel life pulsing through her. I've even talked myself into believing her dirty diapers are a part of her. And I love washing her. There's something soothing about—"

The phone rang. She lifted herself carefully out of the rocker, placed the baby in the lovely old wicker bassinet that had been in the O'Connor family for generations, and moved slowly into the kitchen. Jamesie O'Malley. Congratulations and all that sort of thing and how was she doing and how was the baby and could he come to visit her? He could. That would be grand. How about tomorrow evening? Fine. Actually, it would suit her, too, though she didn't tell him that: she was worried about how she was going to survive as a single mother.

"When are you going back to work?" Mairead so often seemed to know what she was thinking.

That question was answered the following evening. "I dropped over to find out when you're coming back," Jamesie said. He stood inside her door, right hand behind his back.

"I still have a job?"

"*Do* you have a job? I have these for you, too." Pulling out the concealed hand and flourishing a bunch of roses, pink and white and yellow.

She wanted to laugh: it was so like a gesture from one of those old fifties films. But then she wanted to cry as well. She and Mairead had more than once discussed the sad fact that while women had not yet gained the equality with men that they sought, in searching for it they had forfeited many of the privileges associated with subservience that their mothers had enjoyed. Like getting a bouquet of flowers. "You're such a gentleman, Jamesie. There should be more men like you in the world."

"Isn't she lovely?" He stared for a long time at the sleeping infant.

"You'll have a cup of tea," Eilis said after she found a vase for the flowers. It was the first time she had met him outside of the office and she could feel the strain of his shyness.

"If it's not too much trouble."

"Why would it?" When she returned he was standing by the fireplace, staring at an abstract watercolor that hung over the mantelpiece.

"That's a very fine work," he said. "Where did you get it?"

"My friend Mairead brought it to celebrate the baby's arrival."

"And all I brought was a bunch of flowers."

"Don't be silly. You didn't have to bring anything. Mary Kate is all the present I need."

"Mary Kate?"

"The baby. That's what I decided to call her. After my granny and my Aunt Kitty."

He was looking around the room. "Are you going to live here?"

"Of course." She poured the tea and handed him a cup. "Don't you like it?"

"It's very nice. But a bit small, isn't it?"

"It's all I can afford. We're not all big-shot solicitors out to conquer the world, you know."

He reddened. "I suppose it's all right for one person."

"Two. I'm keeping Mary Kate."

He stared, as if not comprehending. "I thought you were giving her up for adoption."

"I've decided to keep her."

"That's a very big decision." He made himself comfortable on the sofa, crossed his legs and sipped his tea. "What about the parties who are expecting to adopt?"

"I'm awfully sorry for Aisling and Eugene. I really am. But I love my baby too much to give her up." No way she could tell *him* about Gran's request.

"They could take you to court, you know. Have you thought about that?"

It *had* crossed her mind. "Would you help me if they did?"

"Of course I'd help you." He made a display of examining his watch. "Let the record show that the defendant retained my services as and from June the twenty-sixth at seven forty-five p.m."

"I couldn't afford your fees, of course. I'd have to work for you for nothing for the rest of my life."

"An indentured clerk. And a computer whiz to boot. I suppose I could live with that."

He left soon after, saying he had some things to do. Then at about ten o'clock when she was feeding the baby he rang. "I hope I'm not disturbing you."

"Not at all." She was standing by the kitchen door holding the phone in her right hand, cradling the baby in her left arm and trying to remain composed as Mary Kate sucked on her tender right nipple.

"I've been doing a bit of thinking."

"Dangerous habit, that."

"About where you're living. It's really awfully small for you and the baby. And the thought came to me—this is just an idea, mind you, but you might want to think about it—that, you know, maybe…Well…" He paused and coughed into the phone at exactly the moment Mary Kate let her know with a squawk that she'd had enough of the right and was ready for the left.

"Can you hold on a minute?" Eilis placed the receiver on the stove, transferred the baby to her right arm, introduced her to the left nipple, picked up the phone with her left hand

and, by raising her elbow, managed to connect it with her right ear. "Hello."

"It was just an idea."

"Sorry. I'm trying to feed the baby and I missed what you said. What was the idea?"

"Not a very good one. I shouldn't have brought it up in the first place."

"Well, out with it anyway, now that you have excited my curiosity."

"I had this thought on the way home from your flat tonight. You know I bought a house a couple of months ago. It's kind of big and I'm rattling around in it. So I thought maybe I could share it with you. On a strictly business basis, of course. You could pay me rent. Not more than you're paying where you are now, mind you, but you'd have a lot more space. And...So that was the idea. I don't know what you might think of it?"

It was extraordinary how much pain a tiny infant could inflict with toothless gums. Eilis wanted to scream at that moment. "I'm not sure it would be a good idea." Her life was already too complicated.

"You're not? Well, maybe you'd like to think about it some more before you give a definite answer?"

"All right." Anything to get him off the phone so she could attend to this painful feeding.

"I'll ring you again soon."

"Oh, by the way," she had almost forgotten to ask, "when do you expect me back to work?"

"I suppose we'll have to give you a month anyway."

Jamesie O'Malley was far from accepting her refusal to

live in his house as final. What he needed was a wife. An attractive wife. An intelligent wife. And Eilis O'Connor was both. The baby was a drawback, of course. Goddamnit anyway! Why did she have to do such a stupid thing? Nevertheless, in the Ireland of today, as distinct from the Ireland of even five years ago, her foolishness need not be an obstacle to the career of an upward-bound solicitor. Once they were married and settled, the people who mattered would forget the whole embarrassing episode. Especially in a city like Galway, which was becoming more and more cosmopolitan every day. Ballinamore would have been a different kettle of fish, but he was no longer languishing in that backwater. So the important question now was, how to accomplish the deed? Should he immediately pursue her, woo her aggressively, let her know his intentions, and rely on those powers of persuasion that worked so well for him in courts of law to prove equally effective in courting his love? Or would it be superior strategy to first lead her safely through the legal minefield she must surely traverse when the wrathful adoptive parents discovered she had broken her contract, and then count on her gratitude to secure his prize? He went to bed happily debating the merits of both approaches.

Eugene Banaghan, too, climbed into bed a happy man that night. Secretly, ever since hearing the good news, he had reveled in his accomplishment of fatherhood. Yes, he admitted, it did matter that Aisling was not the mother. Nevertheless, he himself had achieved the immortal glory sought by every man worthy of the name. Now, in just four days' time, his baby—*his* baby—would be here in this house, in this very room, sleeping in the new bassinet that was already waiting for her over in the corner.

"Good night," Aisling murmured from the other side of the bed. "Only four more peaceful nights."

"Just what I was thinking myself. For you, anyway."

She kicked him in the leg. "If you think, Eugene Banaghan, that you're not going to be getting up to her in the middle of the night, you've got another think coming, let me tell you."

He was down the yard late Friday afternoon when she drove in from school. A few minutes later he heard her agonized scream. "Eugene! Quick! Come here!" He raced to the house, imagining blood or broken limbs. She was standing at the back door, her face covered by her forearm, a letter in her hand.

"What's the matter? Jesus! You scared the daylights out of me. I thought you were hurt."

"Read this." She thrust the letter at him, then leaned against the doorjamb and cried.

Dear Aisling and Eugene,
It is with very great sorrow and regret that I write to tell you this. I have decided that I must keep Mary Kate, my baby.
I know you will be very upset, and that you will be very angry with me. I am most awfully sorry. I would not want to hurt you for all the world. I am doing this only because I absolutely have to. It's terribly hard to explain but when I saw her I knew that I could not give her up. She is mine, a part of me, and I could never live with myself if I gave her away, even to someone as kind and as good as you both are.
Once again, I am most awfully sorry to disappoint you like this.

*I can only hope that you will be able to have your very own baby
in the near future.*

   Your loving cousin,
   Eilis

"God damn her to hell!" Eugene kicked fiercely at a
pebble lying on the concrete and sent it scudding down the
yard.

"I want to die." Aisling beat her fist against the door. "I
just want to lie down and die."

"Come inside, love, and sit down and we'll talk about it."
He put his arm around her and half-carried her into the
kitchen. When he got her into a chair by the table she
wouldn't let go of him, holding tight to his shirt collar and
gazing piteously up at him. "I don't want to live if I can't
have my baby. Do you hear me, Eugene? I don't want to live
without her." She banged her head off the table till he had to
restrain her. She stamped her feet on the floor, pushed
brutally away his attempt to place his arms around her, and
beat a furious tattoo on the table with her fists. There was
nothing he could do except wait and watch and make sure
she did herself no harm, his own grief and anger for the
moment subsumed under the terrifying despair of his
desolate wife. When her wailing resolved to syncopated sobs
he knelt and pulled her to him. This time she let him, and
her head rested on his shoulder till her shuddering subsided.

He stayed with her for the rest of the day, ignoring his
farming chores. They hardly spoke. She somehow managed
to make dinner, shuffling around the kitchen like a zombie
from a horror film, but then ate none of it. They stared at the
telly till it was time for bed, neither speaking. On the way

down the hall he said, "I need to get some air for a few minutes," and made his way out the front door. She didn't follow. He went around to the back of the house, got into the car, pulled the door shut without slamming, and rang Eilis from the mobile phone. She picked up after half a dozen rings.

"Who's this?"

"Eugene. We got your letter. You can't mean it, surely?"

A long silence. Then she said, "I'm so sorry, Eugene. The saddest thing I ever had to do in my entire life was write that letter."

"Well, just tell me now that you didn't mean it and we'll forget all about it."

"I can't, Eugene. I wish to God I could, but I can't."

"For God's sake, Eilis, the child is mine as much as yours. Remember that."

"I'm afraid she belongs to neither of us anymore, Eugene. That's the problem."

"What kind of nonsense is that? Are you drunk?"

"I can't explain it, but that's the way it is. And she has to stay with me. Again, I'm so sorry."

"Damn you to hell, Eilis. I'll get you for this. You wait and see. You're not going to get away with it."

Throughout the night he slept and woke, slept and woke, and each time he regained consciousness he heard Aisling crying. After finishing his porridge in the morning, while she sat silently in her dressing gown, her head resting on the table, he said, "By Jesus, we're going to do something about this."

She raised her head, stared at him, and said in a voice of total despair, "What can we do?"

"We can take her to court, that's what we can do. And by hell we will. She made us a promise, and by God if she doesn't want to keep it we'll find a way to make her."

"She's the mother. You can't take the baby from her if she doesn't want to give it up."

"We'll see about that. I'm going into town first thing Monday morning to talk to your man—what's his name—Branagh, and we'll find out what can be done."

She looked sadly at him, as if searching for hope in his face but not finding it. "I think we should go up to Galway first and talk to her. Maybe she wrote the letter in a sudden fit of something. She's a very impulsive girl at times. We might get her to change her mind."

"All right, if that's what you want."

"Let's go now. I can't stand moping around here doing nothing."

On the way up they debated how best to approach the traitorous cousin. "Threaten her with the courts," Eugene said. "That'll bring her to her senses. A promise is a promise and it can't be broken."

"But she's so fiercely stubborn. That sort of line will get you nowhere with her."

In the end he agreed that his wife should try persuasion first. "But we'll throw the bloody book at her if that doesn't work." Anger, cold and pervasive, was submerging his disappointment and frustration. *She has no right! She has no right!* hammered in his brain like the beat of a rock drum. To which *We'll get our child! We'll get our child!* responded as counterpoint. How dare she? The slut who seduced him into adultery. And what was that nonsense about the child not belonging to either of them?

"I hope she's home," Aisling said.

She was indeed home, but she had a visitor. "Hello," said Michael Heaney from the sofa. His presence dampened Eugene's anger for the time being and forced neutral and civilized, though awkward, conversation. The baby was sleeping in the bedroom, Eilis responded in a strained voice to her cousin's eventual inquiry.

"I'd love to see her."

"I'll be going." Heaney rose like a man who suddenly remembered he had urgent business elsewhere and headed for the door.

"Would you stay for a while, please, Michael? I think I know what you've come about." She was looking at Aisling. "Michael knows all about it."

Eugene could feel his temper rising again. He was not going to be put off by the presence of this fecking ex-priest. "Don't think for a minute…" he began before he caught his wife's eye.

Heaney looked back, hand on the doorknob. "Well, if nobody has any objection?"

"Of course we'd like you to stay," Aisling said. Heaney returned to his place on the sofa. "As you know well, Michael, Eugene and I have been trying to have a family for years, without any success. Then last August Eilis out of the blue and out of the goodness of her heart suggested that she'd have a baby for us. It was an extraordinary offer, wasn't it? Naturally we couldn't tell you about it in your capacity as parish priest, since we didn't think you could approve of it. Truth to tell, it took ourselves a bit of time to get used to the idea. But when we did we were thrilled out of our minds. So you can imagine the joy it was for us when our baby was born. We had prepared our house, decorated her room, bought her clothes, bought her furniture." She pushed the flat of her hand against her nose to restrain the tears. "We had everything ready to receive our child. Then we got this letter." She turned to Eilis. "You wrote it in a fit of depression, didn't you? I know you didn't mean it. I said that straightaway to Eugene. I'm right, amn't I?"

Eilis bent over, head in hands, elbows on knees. "I'm most awfully sorry, Aisling. Eugene. I would to God this had never happened. Everything you say is true indeed. I'm not denying it. Only something has arisen that I didn't expect. She's a part of me and I can't give her up."

"What about us?" Eugene shouted. "Isn't she part of us as well? How do you think we feel after almost a year of waiting?" He'd have said more but Aisling signaled him to shut up.

"Listen, Eilis." She knelt in front of her cousin, like a suppliant before the Sacred Heart altar. "Give yourself a little time. We'll be patient, don't mind us. Then this feeling will pass. You have your life to live, remember. You don't want to be saddled with a baby as a single mother. You couldn't properly take care of her that way. Amn't I right, Father?" She looked pleadingly at Michael Heaney.

The ex-priest sank back into the sofa cushions. "I don't think it would be appropriate for me to say anything at this stage."

"Please, Eilis. She'll be well looked after by Eugene and me. You know that. You can visit her as often as you want, I promise you that. You'll get to see her grow up. And in a certain sense she'll always be your baby. Won't you think about it? Ah, do, please. Before I lose my mind." She broke down and dropped her head onto Eilis's lap.

Eugene couldn't move a muscle to save his life. *It's now or never, never or now, now or never,* kept beating in his brain to the rhythm of Aisling's sobs. Eilis remained rigid as the Sphinx, head down, eyes closed. But when Aisling eventually stirred, lifted her head and stared up pleadingly at her cousin, Eilis turned away, covered her face with her hands and cried. Eugene, after an eternity of waiting, could restrain himself no longer. "Well, what is it to be, Eilis?" Then her miserable tear-filled expression provoked an anger within him that seared his flesh. Out of which *don't forget, you bleddy little bitch, that I'm her father,* almost erupted. So close did those words come to the surface that for weeks after he sweated at the thought of them. Instead, he jumped up and yelled, "You'll be hearing from our solicitor. Come on, Aisling, let's go home."

After another wretched sleepless night and perfunctory attendance at Sunday mass, Aisling said over dinner, "Let's talk to the solicitor."

Though he said "Yes, to be sure," he was less certain of that course now. What if his fatherhood should be divulged in court proceedings?

Bridget came to visit at eleven o'clock on Sunday morning. After she goo-goo'd and tidley-didley'd Mary Kate a few times, she asked Eilis, "Have you been to mass?"

"How could I?" She wasn't about to tell her mother she had gotten out of that habit, other than when she was home in Kildawree on weekends.

"Well, you can go now; I'll take care of her ladyship." What could Eilis do except get herself together and head off for the twelve o'clock at the Sacred Heart. She knelt at the back and tried to focus on what was happening at the altar. But she was a stranger now in this house of God; she no longer took part in the sacrifice she had been reared to believe was the central act of human existence; nor did she feel a flicker of the emotional surge she was wont to receive at consecration and communion. Of course, she didn't partake of the sacrament: it had no meaning for her now. Joe still went to mass, and to communion, too, a fact that surprised her when he had mentioned it. Though he didn't go to confession anymore, preferring, he said, to go straight to God Himself with his sins.

On the way out she spotted Michael Heaney and came up behind him. "Well, aren't we getting lazy in our old age, going to last mass."

"This is amazing, Eilis. I was going to ring you as soon

as I got home."

"And I wanted to talk to you." She linked her arm in his, the way she'd do with her father. "I'm having a terrible case of the guilts for what I did to Aisling and Eugene."

"That's only to be expected, I suppose." They were walking in the direction of her flat. "You've caused your friends pain, though you didn't want to. Which is exactly the mixture that brings on guilt."

"I'd give anything to undo it."

"Not quite anything, of course."

"Oh God! I wish I could. Unfortunately, I can't, Michael. Anything within my power, yes. I think I'd be willing to cut off my right arm if it would rid them of their suffering. But the one thing that would help them I can't do. Isn't it awful?"

"Mother-love is such a powerful force."

"It is." She dared not tell him the real reason. She had indeed become very fond of her baby: how could she not love the little bundle of soft skin and tiny limbs and adorable face, flesh of her own flesh. Though there were times in the past month when she'd have cheerfully handed her over to Aisling. Incessant crying that tattered her nerves, nocturnal awakenings that fragmented her sleep, unvarying demands on her time and patience with no one to share the burden, all had combined to sap her energy and even occasionally to weary her commitment to her beloved grandmother. Hardest to bear was Gran's total silence. If only she'd give an indication, some hint that she was present behind Mary Kate's big dark eyes.

"'Greater love no man hath, that a man lay down his life for his friends,' Saint John's Gospel tells us. I suppose this is the kind of thing the sacred writer had in mind."

"I suppose." Michael didn't know it was her love for Gran she had in mind.

"I was wondering," he said as they approached the flat, "if you'd like to go for a drive? It's a lovely day."

"I'd be delighted to." Would she ever! Anything to get out of the flat after being housebound for almost a month, her world circumscribed by the demands of her baby. "Mammy is up. She's minding Mary Kate at the moment."

The man's face lit up in a happy grin. "Brilliant! We'll take her with us. That is of course if she wants to come."

"Certainly," Bridget said. Her pleasure at seeing the former priest seemed not a whit less than was his at seeing her. "They're expecting me home for the dinner, of course. But Niamh is doing the cooking today, so they'll manage without me." She looked very smart in a flowered summer frock and white pumps.

They took Eilis's car because she'd had it fitted with an infant seat. Michael drove, with Bridget in the front and Eilis in the back where she could keep an eye on Mary Kate. They went northwest towards Moycullen and Oughterard, with the intention of going on to Cong and Headford, a trip that would take them all the way around Lough Corrib. A perfect day for a ride: glorious July with unclouded sky and scarcely a whisper of breeze. The first truly fine day in a month, Michael remarked as they left the city behind. At Oughterard they stopped for lunch, for which Bridget insisted on paying, over Michael's protest. On the road between Oughterard and Maam Cross Mary Kate whinged, bawled, and finally began to scream. "We need to stop," Eilis said. "It's her feeding time."

Michael pulled on to the margin by a ribbon of blue lake. "You and I can take a walk while the mother does what needs to be done," Bridget said, and off the pair went, down a steep path that led to the lake. They were soon out of sight.

"Aren't you the lovely girleen?" Eilis crooned to her suckling child. "Worthy of your great-grandam indeed. Only I do wish, Gran, that you'd let me know you're here." Was Mairead's surmise correct? That Gran's command was just a figment of Eilis's bereaved imagination? What utter chaos it had brought to her life. But then Gran always had a way of creating turmoil around her. Not that she had ever set out to make life troublesome for others; it was just that she saw the world from her own peculiar standpoint and made her demands accordingly. Like having her child without being married. And falling in love with a priest in the days before priests could get free. Apparently this Father Mulroe had packed up and gone off to a diocese in Kansas, USA, lest he fall from grace through his infatuation. "I'd have married him, too," Gran once admitted, her eyes moist as she said it. Then when Eugene's Uncle Jack, whom she *did* marry, died six years ago, she invited her longtime friend Kitty Tarragh, widow of the National Teacher, to come and live with her. A lot of tongues wagged about that, but did Gran care a fig? She was retired from politics by then.

"I'm sorry, Aisling; I'm sorry, Eugene." The refrain kept going through Eilis's head. The most awful thing that anyone could ever do, she had done to that unfortunate couple. And they her very best friends. "You've a lot to answer for, Gran," she shouted out the window into the still Connemara air. Mary Kate squawked and stopped feeding.

In Cong they visited the ruins of the Augustinian Abbey. "Isn't it about time you had her christened?" Bridget asked as they admired one of the well-preserved ancient doorways of the monastery Saint Feichin had founded in the seventh century. Eilis was carrying her sleeping child in a sling around her neck.

"I suppose." She hadn't given the matter any thought.

"I have your own christening dress still."

"Grand."

"And maybe *you* could do the ceremony, Michael?"

"It would certainly be a pleasure for me. Unfortunately, I'm no longer permitted to be an official minister of the sacraments. However, maybe I can smooth the way for you."

"You think there may be a problem?" Bridget asked.

"Well, some priests are insisting that what they call marginal Catholics, into which category they tend to lump unmarried mothers, take a course of instruction before they'll baptize their babies. However, you and I, Bridget, will vouch for this mother's good moral character, so there shouldn't be any problem."

Immediately on their return to Galway, Bridget and the ex-priest went to the parish church and scheduled the baptism for a week from the coming Saturday. Two days later Bridget was back in town with Eilis's christening dress. "Frank and I would very much like to be godparents," she said, to which Eilis had no objection. Furthermore, the entire O'Connor family would be present at the Sacred Heart Church for the ceremony. Then they'd all adjourn to Monaghan's restaurant for lunch to celebrate the occasion. Eilis's friends were of course welcome to join the festivities. Even Mary Kate's father, if he so chose.

Friday evening Joe Mahony came by after work. He had a habit of dropping in when Ger was occupied elsewhere. This particular evening Ger was off playing golf, a game in which Joe had no interest. "Anyway, I needed to get away from him for a bit." He seemed morose, in contrast to his usual cheerful self.

"Why so?" Eilis was glad to see him.

"Things are a bit strained between us at the moment."

"I'm sorry to hear that." She was taking advantage of Mary Kate napping to clean the flat. "Nothing too serious, I hope?"

"Ger wants to set a date for us to come out."

"That's a major step indeed. I take it you're not quite ready yet?"

"I want to finish my novel first. Ger had always agreed to that."

Mary Kate caterwauled from the bedroom. "Damn. I thought I'd get the cleaning done before she woke."

"Would you like me to pick her up?"

"If you wouldn't mind. Mammy has this habit of running her fingers over things, testing for dust."

He strolled into the bedroom. The crying stopped. He came back swaying and cooing, with Mary Kate nestling into his shoulder. "Someone came to our door last week while *I* was at my SPCM meeting. You know, the weird group that Uncle Denis bullied me into. By the way, did I ever tell you that they originally named the organization *Families United in Christian Marriage*? Until someone pointed out the acronym to Uncle Denis. Anyway, this fellow told Ger he was doing a survey of families in Galway for a marketing organization. He didn't need any names, he said, only numbers from which to compile statistics. Which sounded all right to Ger until he started asking questions like what were Ger's family arrangements: married, single, or in a homosexual partnership?"

"Very interesting indeed."

"Ger passed that one off by saying he was single. It was only afterwards he recalled that the guy was wearing a medal of the Immaculate Heart of Mary around his neck—the very same one I had shown him that SPCM members are supposed to wear. Now he's convinced the fellow was one of Uncle Denis's crowd checking up on *me*. I think he's afraid the Uncle might try to pry me away from him, so he wants us to come out first."

Eilis was giving a final rub to the stove when a gentle rat-tat-tat sounded. She went through the parlor and opened the front door.

"Are you Miss Eilis O'Connor?" The woman was wearing a dark blue polka-dot dress with collar, and elbow-length sleeves. She had a kind face and a pleasant smile.

"Yes." She didn't look like the type who'd be trying to sell you something.

"I'm Mrs. Nora Cloherty. From the church, you know. I came to talk to you about the baptism of your baby. Mary Kate, isn't it?"

"It is, yes."

"May I come in, please?"

"Certainly." She stood aside to let the woman enter. When she turned around Joe and the baby were nowhere to be seen. "Have a seat. I need to wash the grease off my hands; I was doing a bit of cleaning." She hurried into the kitchen. They weren't there either. After washing and drying her hands she stuck her head in the bedroom door. Joe was sitting on the bed rocking Mary Kate. He put a finger to his lips and waved an imaginary something hanging from his neck. Eilis smiled and returned to her visitor.

"Nice little place you have here," the woman said.

"Not bad. It's quite suitable for myself and the baby."

"But no husband and father? You're not married, I understand?"

"No. I'm not."

Mrs. Cloherty joined her hands and lowered her head and seemed to pray. Then she looked up. "That's what I was sent to talk to you about." The soft eyes were wet with sincerity. "As I'm sure you know, the church does not deem it appropriate for an unmarried woman to raise a child on her own. The feeling is that it would be better if she gave the infant up for adoption to a suitable married couple. That way, you see, the baby is placed in a good Christian family environment, and the mother is enabled to put her life back together again."

"In what way put it back together?" Eilis's hackles were rising. "I don't think I understand you."

"Well, let me put it this way: having a baby out of wedlock involves conduct that, shall we say, the church does not condone. So in order to return to the fold, as it were, one needs to set one's house in order."

"I'm doing that; I just this minute finished cleaning." The colossal nerve of the woman!

Mrs. Cloherty smiled with her mouth, but her eyes were cold. "We'll have our little joke. However, we're dealing here with a very serious matter—nothing less than the salvation of one's soul, and that of our baby as well. We can help you find adoptive parents; there are so many worthy couples out there who would just love to have the opportunity to bring up your child in a good Catholic home. As well as that we can offer you a course of instruction and a weekend retreat, all expenses paid, to enable you to reflect on your past and see where you went wrong, and to start you on the path towards a good Christian life in the future." She looked earnestly at Eilis. "So what do you say to that?"

Eilis stood. "Thank you for your time, Mrs. Cloherty. I know you mean well, but I feel perfectly capable of making my own decisions about my child and my life and the needs of my soul."

At the door Mrs. Cloherty offered her a card. "I do urge you to think about what I said. You can ring me any time."

When the door closed, Joe came dashing out with Mary Kate. "Ger was right."

"How did they find out about the christening?"

"They hold their meetings at Sacred Heart. Uncle Denis is thick as thieves with the priests there. One of his tricks is to check the baptismal lists for unmarried mothers. Of course it's my fault for introducing you to him; he knows your name."

"Feeding time," Eilis said when Mary Kate began to cry in earnest.

"I'll go get us some pizza," Joe said. On his way out the door he added, "Anyway, that's the last you'll hear from that crowd, I'd say."

It wasn't, of course. The following Friday evening, the day before the christening, while Mary Kate was sleeping

Eilis napped on the sofa. The corncrake sound of the phone startled her into confused consciousness. "Hello."

"This is Father Gibbons from Sacred Heart. I'm looking for Eilis O'Connor."

"Oh yes, Father. I'm Eilis."

"I have to inform you that there is a problem regarding the baptism of your daughter." The formal civility of his tone was chilling.

"Oh dear! What's the matter?"

"It has come to our attention that you are an unwed mother. This parish requires, as a matter of policy, that a person in your condition take a special course of instruction before we can baptize your child."

"But my mother made the arrangements last Sunday week and she was told then that everything was in order."

"Apparently we were not given all the information at that time. You'll need to come in to the presbytery and register for the course as soon as possible."

"What's this course all about?" Mammy would be furious at the postponement. She had cajoled every member of the family, regardless of previous plans, to commit to tomorrow's ceremony and lunch.

"You'll get the details when you come in. It involves a one-hour class each week for eight weeks, followed by a weekend retreat, confession and communion, and a pledge regarding the upbringing of your child. The important thing is—"

Her annoyance at this pompous clerical voice erupted into sudden anger. "Keep your damn christening. Who needs it anyway?" She slammed down the receiver with enough force to wake her child in the bedroom. When she hurried in, still fuming, she was greeted by a smile from the infant. Her anger evaporated. "Well, aren't you my happy little baby."

At that moment Gran broke her long silence. *I can't tell you how glad I am that I don't have to go through that mumbo-jumbo. Especially the part about having my own daughter as my godmother.* All the while she was speaking, Mary Kate continued to smile.

Eilis laughed so hard that even an hour later she could scarcely summon a doleful tone with which to inform her mother about the postponement. She didn't mention that the event was unlikely to take place at all now.

Michael Heaney was madly, sadly, distractedly, pathetically, deeply, devoutly, despairingly in love with Bridget O'Connor. But what was he to do, except subtly impress her and see what happened? Which he had been doing quite well, he thought. He had changed his image and his behavior. No longer the parish priest turned layman, lost and lonely in a sudden secular world. Didn't Saint Paul talk about putting on the new man? Well, that was what he had done. You'd hardly know him from a few months ago. Spiffed to the nines in the latest mod duds. A well-trimmed mustache that came out fox-red with just the teeniest tint of gray. Contact lenses in place of the old horn-rims. In his morning mirror he thought he looked ten years younger. He had gone off the booze, too, and into Alcoholics Anonymous.

There remained but to woo. That was the crux, of course, the sticking point, the barrier he could not surmount. He went down to Kilduff almost every week now. Ever since that Sunday when he had taken Bridget and Eilis and the baby for a drive. Just to chat with herself and Frank, he'd say. Though each time he promised himself that if the opportunity presented—if Frank were away—he'd burst through his wall of reserve, mention the love word, hold her and kiss her and pour out his soul.

But he couldn't do it. Her husband was gone to Galway

to see his harlot, Bridget said one Sunday, with tears in her eyes. Which only raised anew the conundrum that had stumped Michael Heaney before: how to suggest infidelity to a woman who was berating her spouse for being unfaithful? Besides, he, Michael Heaney, had been her parish priest, for God's sake. How could he propose himself as her lover? She might actually be horrified. Or maybe she'd just laugh at him. Worse still, what if she said yes? Was *he* ready? For adultery? Or for that matter for physical love? Fifty years of abstinence was a poor preparation for a man. Though he *was* exercising at a gym these days—the older you got, the more you had to work at keeping fit and healthy. He also engaged in sexual fantasies about her, fighting guilt from a lifetime of sin-fear, till arousal told him he had nothing to worry about. But still he held back from declaring his love, despite the warmth of her greetings and the look in her eye that said she might be willing. There were times when he'd be sitting on her sofa calmly talking philosophy or bemoaning the state of the country and Frank would be gone out the land somewhere and all he wanted to do was reach out and touch her and...He couldn't bring himself to do it. The books he read on love—he had bought several modern studies at Kenny's bookshop—said it was perfectly acceptable to exhibit a bit of energetic lust. One said that the best love-making was hot and sweaty and calorie-burning. But he had no practice at the grand passion: Maynooth at eighteen, and nothing before, and nothing while he was there, and nothing since—he had faithfully observed his vow of celibacy throughout his priestly career. So, while his virtue was untarnished, his experience was nil.

One time he almost plucked up the courage. Frank was

at a meeting of the cattle mart committee. Out of the blue Bridget said, "I wonder if I should confront him?"

"What was that?" Admiring her profile while she poured him tea. He noticed she was wearing makeup, though it was Friday evening and she wasn't going anywhere.

"I was wondering if I should tell Frank to his face that I know what he's up to?"

"That's a difficult question." It would hardly be to his benefit if she challenged her husband: she couldn't very well do herself what she was lashing out at Frank for doing, even if she *were* so inclined.

Then she said, with malice he had never before heard from her, "Maybe I should tell him that two can play that game."

This was, for sure, the moment of truth, the perfect opportunity to declare his love. But before he could swallow and clear his throat and formulate the words she added, "unfortunately, he knows me too well to believe I'd ever do such a thing." That sapped the energy out of Michael Heaney for a moment; until from somewhere within him came the riposte, *though you might, with the help of the right man.* Sadly, before the words could get past his lips she concluded, "Of course he's right."

Eilis was beginning to feel secure in her mother role, and was even coming to terms with her guilt for what she had done to her cousin. She had found, a few doors away, a wonderful care-giver for her baby—Mrs. McDonough, a kind woman who had two small children of her own. Then, just a month after she returned to work, and had gotten a few more intimations that Gran was present in Mary Kate, the letter came.

Looking back, it was hard to believe she hadn't taken Eugene's threat more seriously. Of course, at the time she thought he was just blustering, and that after he calmed down he wouldn't *do* anything. True, she did remember half-jokingly asking Jamesie if he'd defend her if she were brought to court, but deep down she hadn't really believed it would ever happen. So the letter was a fierce jolt altogether: a plenary summons to appear before the High Court in Dublin on a breach of promise to deliver her baby for adoption. She screamed, feeling as if she were falling through space. Mary Kate began to whimper. Eilis let the letter drop as if it were an IRA bomb, and cried.

"Jamesie," she wailed into the phone. He was still at the office. She had left an hour earlier, collected Mary Kate from Mrs. McDonough, and come home.

"What's the matter?"

"They want to take away my baby." Then she was bawling again. Mary Kate was crying, too.

"Just take your time and tell me what happened, whenever you're ready." After she quieted Mary Kate and read him the contents of the letter, he said, "We were afraid that might happen, weren't we?"

"I know. But I didn't really believe it would."

"Actually, I've been doing some reading up on the law that pertains to this particular situation. Just in case."

That was Jamesie for you. You never quite knew what was going on under that curly black thatch. His mind was as crooked as a ram's horn, as Gran used to say. Never letting on what he was really thinking, then springing it on you with that grin of his. Like the night he rang and suggested she move into his house. Which offer she had managed to fend off by saying she'd think about it. She did give it some thought, too, for all of two seconds, but didn't say a word to him until he asked again a week later. "It wouldn't work," she told him then. He clearly wasn't happy but he didn't get mad, just continued to play his patient game of wooing her. Flowers at the office for her birthday, followed by dinner at Paddy Burke's Oyster House after work. A casual visit to her flat of an evening when he knew Bridget and Frank were up to see Mary Kate. Presents for the baby three times already, including an expensive pram when she invited him to the christening that didn't take place.

"I can't afford to go to court."

"Of course you can. You have me for your solicitor, remember?"

"We were joking then, but it's for real now. I know your fees, Jamesie, and I won't let you do it for nothing." She had grown very fond of him, and a debt like that could destroy the equality between them that she felt was necessary to preserve their relationship.

"We'll cross that bridge when we come to it."

For Jamesie O'Malley, Eilis O'Connor's legal predicament gave his strategy for marriage a significant boost. So his expressions of condolence were simply masking his urge to cheer. She was going to be in his debt. He was going to be her hero. His reputation as a solicitor would soar when he won her case in the High Court.

For the rest of that evening he reflected and planned, decided and scrapped decisions, concluded and refined conclusions. By bedtime he knew that he knew what to do.

Next day he asked her to go to Ballinamore with him on business. They got there about noon. He drove up the Glebe, into Castle Street, stopped in front of *Kelly's Drapery* and hustled her into the shop before she realized what he was up to.

There was nobody behind the counter. "Mammy," he called. A woman appeared through a door leading into the back. "I was hoping I'd catch you in."

"What are you doing here?" His mother was a big-shouldered woman with hair an unnatural shade of red.

"A spot of business. So I thought I'd drop around for a cup of tea." He sensed the tension in his companion: he had occasionally told her awful things about his mother in the course of conversations, yet here he was saying, "Mammy, I want you to meet my colleague, Eilis O'Connor."

Eilis was a brick. "Hello," she said, friendly but cool. He had once brought home a girl who was patently afraid of Mammy, and the Ma, sensing blood, had needled her till the girl broke off the relationship. Since then he had brought no one home, waiting for the woman who could stand up to his mother.

After the briefest of nods to Eilis Mammy said, "I suppose you better come in then." Grudgingly. Obviously not thrilled to see a potential rival.

"Eilis is studying to be a barrister," he said when his mother brought them tea in the parlor. "She already has her BA."

"Is that so?" He could almost see some of the gloom rising up from her, like a misty day giving way to mere gray clouds. For the first time she looked at Eilis, and then back to him. "So you work together?"

"Eilis is my clerk right now. But that's only until she finishes her law degree and does the King's Inns and gets called to the bar. After that we're going to be partners. Right, Eilis?"

"It's all a long way off yet."

"You won't feel it catching up on you." He smiled affectionately at her in full view of the mother. "And who knows what else might happen in the meantime. We're very good friends, Mammy, Eilis and myself."

"Is that so?" He could see the gloom descend on Mammy again.

An hour later as they were driving out of town Eilis said, "What was that all about, if I may ask?"

"Well, as I've been saying for some time, I think you'd make a very fine lawyer. And we'd make a great firm, you and I. Can't you see the shingle: *O'MALLEY and O'MALLEY*. We'll show Galway a thing or two."

"You're daft, Jamesie. Anyway it would be *O'MALLEY and O'CONNOR*."

"Not if you were to marry me."

"Watch out!" He had taken his eyes off the road to gaze on her and a lorry was coming straight at them on a very narrow stretch.

"It was a bit disappointing," Mairead said. They were strolling along the bank of the Corrib in the twilight.

"A waste of my evening out," Eilis agreed. "Except for the company, of course." Bridget had come up in the afternoon and offered to baby-sit if she wanted to go somewhere. So she and Mairead went to a play at the Nuns Island Arts Center.

"Feminism is not served by bad art," Mairead pontificated.

"That play made women look like a bunch of humorless fanatics. It's not enough to believe in the cause: you have to translate it into ideas people can understand and sympathize with. This sort of production would turn anyone away from acknowledging women's rights."

"I wish you humorless feminists would come up with some ideas that'd help *me*. The primordial rights of biological mothers, or something of the sort."

"Maybe we can. I've discussed your case with the Women's Rights Association—without giving your name, of course. Not everyone agreed straight off with what you did, but they'd like to hear more about surrogate motherhood, and why you feel justified in keeping Mary Kate."

So Eilis O'Connor and her solicitor were invited to a gathering of Galway feminists, held late one Friday evening in a meeting room of a Salthill hotel. "Am I safe here, do you think?" Jamesie whispered out of the corner of his mouth. Only half-facetiously, judging by his nervous expression. They sat in a circle, without benefit of table: fifteen women in all kinds of dress, and one lone male in a dark business suit.

"They won't bite you," Mairead said. "Though they may pinch you, so watch out." The women ignored him as they chatted and smoked and joked and laughed for a good twenty minutes after the official starting time, while the late-arriving sisters straggled in. Eventually Mairead formally addressed the group from her seat.

"I'd like to begin our meeting this evening by drawing your attention to a lawsuit that will be coming before the High Court early next year, and which may have important consequences for the rights of women in this country." She went on to describe the case in some detail, without of course mentioning the preposterous role played in it by that great deceased feminist, Mary McGreevy. In conclusion she said, "We have the defendant in this litigation, Eilis O'Connor, here with us tonight. With her is her solicitor, Mr. Jamesie O'Malley, who would like to address a few words to us about the case."

Jamesie coughed, straightened his tie, and uncrossed his legs. "I'm honored indeed to address such a group of distinguished women." He tried to make eye contact with them but only a few were actually looking at him, the rest were staring elsewhere or searching their purses or lighting cigarettes. "I must say I'm impressed at the way Ms. Conneely has just outlined the problem. As you may know, there is no statute in Irish law dealing with surrogate motherhood. However, we—"

"I object to the term *surrogate*." A pretty woman in shorts and tank top and gold pendant earrings and black fingernails almost shouted the words at him. "If a woman gives birth to a real baby she's a *real* mother, isn't she? Not a surrogate."

"Well, I don't think we need—"

"She hardly gave birth to a plastic baby, did she?" Somebody snickered.

"Or to someone else's baby, either," said a woman in a print frock and with black hair drawn severely back.

"The terminology 'surrogate motherhood'," Jamesie said, "is the accepted way of describing the condition in America, which is about the only country where the practice is prevalent at this time."

"Well, they're bloody wrong," the woman in the print

frock retorted. "There's a principle at stake here, you know. By calling her a surrogate you're downgrading her to the status of a brood mare or a milch cow. If she carries a baby and gives birth to it, she's entitled to be called a mother, with no denigrating adjective added."

"I think I'd disagree with that," a woman in jeans and glasses said. "It seems to me that if a woman has reproductive rights over her own body—and all we women here acknowledge that she has, I'm sure—then surely she has a right to carry a baby for another woman if she wants to, especially for one who can't have a baby of her own. So *surrogate* would appear to be a reasonable term for describing what she's doing."

"The whole wretched business seems to me to be just one more example of degradation for the less fortunate," a beautifully coifed woman in a black dress stated in the deliberate tone of one accustomed to being listened to. "Will we soon have the rich commissioning babies from the poor? Handing them their own eggs and sperm no doubt, just so they won't have to go through the messy business of pregnancy and birth themselves."

"Could we focus on the present case, please?" Mairead said. "It's a *fait accompli,* so there's no point in saying it shouldn't have happened. It will likely happen many more times in the future, as well. The question at issue is, must the mother who carries the baby and gives birth to it, under contract to another, give it up to that other, even if she has changed her mind in the meantime? That's the position Eilis O'Connor is in and that's the case that the High Court will decide on."

"Thank you," Jamesie said. "Any ideas that you may

have will be most welcome. We are raising a legal question here that has never before been posed in this country, much less answered. It's a question, furthermore, that has been resolved every which way you could think of in America, in the few instances in which it has been raised."

The discussion lasted more than an hour. During which Jamesie O'Malley had his perspective on the lawsuit considerably broadened by the views of women grown accustomed to defending their rights against the depredations of a male-dominated society. At the end he acknowledged his debt of gratitude to all present for their candor and their wisdom.

Eilis had fallen asleep fairly quickly after putting her head on the pillow just after eleven, but when Mary Kate made a rumpus at about one and she got up to feed her, the mind started churning with the flow of milk. How could she part with this happy energetic cherub? Unthinkable now, even if she didn't have a duty to Gran. The question was: how were they to convince a cold unfeeling court of her right? Yes, Jamesie was sure the law was on their side, and he had begun to lay out his logic of law and fact. "We have a strong case," he concluded, but her instincts refused to trust these purely rational arguments. The fact was she had made a commitment, and commitments must be kept. Didn't the well-being of society depend on such fundamental principles? What kind of justice system would allow her to renege?

"So what have you got to say to that?" she whispered to her suckling child. At which Mary Kate bit her nipple hard enough to elicit an ouch. Eilis pulled her quickly away from her breast. The baby screwed her face into an expression of martyrdom and began to cry. Eilis let her have the nipple again.

It was then she heard Gran's voice: *When I was in the convent I took perpetual vows. A lifetime contract, they said. Yet, when I found I could no longer live there, even that hidebound old institution called mother church gave me a dispensation.*

"That was different," Eilis retorted. "We're dealing with the law here, not with the church's rules."

Any and all commitments can be rescinded with the blessing of the powers that be. You just have to find the right arguments. So you tell Jamesie he'll find one for you if he studies my *case.*

"How can he study your case? You left the convent fifty years ago." But Gran had stopped talking. So when Mary Kate, fed and diapered, returned to slumber Eilis was left wide awake to grapple with her grandmother's enigmatic solution. At three she was still no closer to resolving the puzzle. She remembered the clock registering four and half past four, and then had difficulty waking when the alarm went off at seven. While she bathed herself and took care of the baby, she decided to ask Michael Heaney about vows as contracts, and when and why dispensations from them could be granted.

III. CONSEQUENCES

Jamesie O'Malley rose and shaved and brushed his teeth, contemplated a shower and rejected the notion, having had one yesterday, then changed his mind on recollecting the day that was in it, his very first formal appearance at the High Court in Dublin. "You're on your way, Jamesie, my lad," he told his mirror image. "As long as Mullen doesn't muck it up on you."

He had breakfast in a place down at the Temple Bar with Dermot Mullen, Barrister-at-Law, whom he had briefed for the case. He had been tempted to be his own counsel: it would be quite a feather in his legal cap to present before this court. But he refrained when he learned that a mere solicitor who had the temerity to argue a case before the High Court seriously risked incurring the snobbish ire of the judge, himself of course a former barrister. Anyway, though Jamesie regularly argued cases in the District Courts of Mayo and Galway, he had only twice seen at first hand, and never actually engaged in, the fearsome formality of this highest tribunal of first instance.

"Are you ready for battle?" He checked out Mullen over the rashers and eggs. The barrister, tall, blond, athletic, younger-looking than himself, had the tailor-made pinstripe and sheen and confident air of the big-city man.

"It will be a rather difficult case." In the toney accent of a Jesuit old boy. "No laws touching directly on it and no real precedents. It won't be easy."

"But somebody has to win it, and it's going to be us."

"This client of yours, is she really quite *compos mentis,* do you think?"

The curl of his lip transformed the lawyer into that vicious schoolboy, Roddy Monks, who had made boarding school miserable for Jamesie O'Malley eighteen years before. Until he had learned to fight back and discovered that Roddy Monks, bully, was in reality Roddy Monks, coward. "She's perfectly sane. A fiercely intelligent young woman who has made a very wise though terribly difficult decision and needs the law to support her in it."

"She's a good friend of yours, then, I take it?" Again the sardonic grin that Jamesie felt a sudden urge to obliterate with his fist.

"She's my client."

"Molyneaux will crucify her on the witness stand."

"She'll give as good as she gets."

"You country lads are all the same. So fucking naïve. You have no idea of the kind of game these fellows play up here. They tackle from behind, they gouge, they kick, they bite, they rip your balls out. I've worked with Molyneaux. He's a sadistic bastard. A girl with a bastard is grist to his mill. He'll make serious fun of her, he'll grind her to dust, he'll prove she's a liar and a slut. By the time he's finished she'll be sorry she ever went to court."

"Listen, Mullen. I'm paying you to make sure he does no such thing. So you better fucking well take good care of her or I'll kick your fucking arse into the Liffey." He was proud of the fact that he spoke without raising his voice or showing a semblance of annoyance, even though the *country lads* jibe rankled. There was, of course, no earthly reason why Mullen should fail him. Jamesie's affidavit left nothing to chance, if he said so himself. It included every minute particle of information that could possibly be relevant. And he had his witnesses thoroughly coached, ready to cope with the most withering cross-examination Con Branagh's counsel could devise.

"Don't worry about Molyneaux. I'll take care of him. The fellow I'm most concerned about is Beirne. He's supposed to be a very brilliant judge—they say he'll go to the Supreme Court eventually. But he has delivered a few rather strange judgments. At least in my opinion."

That conversation would have seriously disturbed Aisling and Eugene Banaghan, had they heard it. The euphoria of fighting for their baby had worn off, both through the many months of waiting—all through autumn and winter and into early spring—and by the immediate prospect of presenting in a public courtroom their most intimate feelings of love and frustration.

"I wish to God we never got involved in this whole stupid affair," Aisling burst out, sitting on the bed stretching her nylons over her ankles and up to her knees.

Eugene, combing his hair in front of the mirror on the wardrobe door, was taken by surprise. It was the first time she had said anything like this. But, though no less unnerved himself by the prospect ahead, he faked courage and confidence. "Don't be foolish, now. We've come this far, and by hell we're going to see it through. It'll be well worth the trouble; you'll see."

"I'm not feeling in the least bit hopeful." She stood, wriggled the hose up over thighs and midriff, and ensured its smoothness with a quick run of her hands before stepping into her green skirt.

"Listen! We made our decision, we paid our money, and now we have to take our chances. Anyway, I have a lot of faith in Con Branagh."

"That man gives me the willies." She buttoned her lacy white blouse. "If it was left to me I'd have hired somebody else."

She had been saying this for the past six months, much to Eugene's annoyance. "Listen, he's the best man for the job. And don't forget, he knows how to deal with that other bugger. O'Malley, they say, would make a liar out of Saint Patrick himself, the way he has of twisting your words to make you say what you didn't mean at all." He straightened his tie and put on his jacket. "Let's go down and see if they have some grub for us."

They were staying at a bed and breakfast in Glasnevin, having come up the night before. February not being tourist season, they had the dining room to themselves. While they waited for the fry Aisling said, "Do you know what I've been thinking, Eugene? Our child has a natural father as well as a natural mother. Now if we could get a hold of this lad, maybe we'd get *him* to agree to the adoption. Don't you think he might have as much legal say in the matter as Eilis?"

"But didn't Eilis say Joe has no interest at all in the baby?" He barely managed to get the words out without choking.

"Well, between you and me now, I've been wondering for some time if maybe Joe isn't the father at all."

Once when Eugene was young and foolish, he had two double whiskeys in rapid succession. He would never in his entire life do that again because, although he had remained conscious, he felt as if his brain and his entire body were paralyzed for the next hour. Which was exactly the way he felt this minute. For a long time he had lived in a state of terror that his wife might find him out. Then, as the months went by and she never questioned the father's identity—taking for granted it was Joe Mahony, as Eilis had told her—his fears had dissipated. "What are you talking about? Didn't Eilis herself tell us it was him?"

"Listen to this. It's something that happened one time I was up visiting her before the baby was born. Her friend, Mairead, came by in the evening and somewhere in the conversation Joe's name came up, and Mairead referred to him and a friend of his called Ger as being a very nice couple. The thought crossed my mind at the time that Joe must be gay, and that if he *was* gay wouldn't it be unlikely...? But then I forgot about it until a few nights ago when I was trying to get to sleep and I remembered that scene and the thought came to me: what if he isn't the father? I do think it's something we should look into."

Fortunately for Eugene, the proprietress chose that precise moment to appear with the breakfast tray. After she served them and left, he had calmed enough to be able to say, "I wouldn't put much store in that idea. Joe's our lad, you can bet your bottom dollar on it. Anyway, who else could it be?"

"She's had lots of dates over the years. Let me tell you something else: when I enquired who the father was the first time—you remember that day Eilis came back to tell us she was pregnant?—I asked her was it Joe. Now, she admitted it was him when I asked her, but she never said outright on her own that it was him. I remember thinking from the way she talked around it that she might almost be telling me a lie. I don't know why I thought that but I did. And she never seemed to want to discuss the matter afterwards. Which until lately I took to be just shyness on her part. But I bet I was right." Aisling poked her finger deep into Eugene's shoulder to emphasize her point.

"You're dreaming, woman. Goddamnit, it has to be Joe."

"Let me remind you that everybody thought Bridget's father was your Uncle Jack. Don't forget that. Until it came out in the end that it was my grandfather. A man no one in the world would have suspected. You know something else? I remember Eilis saying when she was pregnant that she was glad the baby's father was who he was. She didn't use Joe's name; she just said she was glad it was who it was. Now isn't that suspicious in itself?"

There was more animation in his wife's face than he had seen for months. Which in other circumstances would have pleased Eugene mightily. He finished the last piece of rasher, put a final crust in his mouth, and looked at his watch. "We better get a move on."

"But don't you think," she continued as they returned to their room, "that maybe we should go and see Joe and ask him right out if he's the father?"

"Too late for that now, I'd say. We have to be in court in an hour."

Mr. Denis Brennan's involvement in *Banaghan vs. O'Connor* came about by accident. However, he immediately saw it as a divinely ordained opportunity to help him resolve the religious and social crisis that was most dear to his crusading heart. The accidental element was his membership in the same Council of the Knights of Saint Columbanus as Mr. Cornelius Branagh. Because the two men were close friends resulting from their common Knightly brotherhood, Mr. Branagh, normally a model of professional propriety in preserving the confidentiality of clients' business, happened to discuss casually with Mr. Brennan the extraordinary case for which he had just finished preparing an affidavit. They had adjourned after a Council meeting to one of Galway City's more discreet drinking establishments.

"Appalling," Mr. Brennan lamented on learning the facts. "As if she were a brood mare. You wouldn't think there could be so much evil in the world."

"Oh, it's a common enough occurrence in the States nowadays. They call it 'surrogate motherhood.' Though we've never before had a case of it in the courts here in Ireland."

"And it's a local girl, you say?" Mr. Brennan would never be so indiscreet as to ask for details, much as he wanted the identity of this wretched sinner—with a view to pursuing her conversion and salvation, of course.

"A respectable farmer's daughter, if you don't mind. Today's *cailíns* are not what they used to be when you and I were growing up."

"The country is in such a sad moral state." Mr. Brennan stared piteously at his Hennessy as if it might hold a clue to current degeneracy. "Will you win your case, do you think?"

"Well, I'll put it to you this way: I think Mr. Jamesie O'Malley and Miss Eilis O'Connor have a hell of a surprise in store for them; that's what I think." Mr. Branagh winked confidently at Mr. Brennan, and noticed the sudden expression of pain passing over his fellow Knight's countenance. He put it down to the man's well-known susceptibility to heartburn.

"Are we talking about Eilis O'Connor from Kildawree?"

"You know her? In that case I shouldn't be naming names, of course."

"My nephew, Joe Mahony, used to date that girl. But of course he was in no way involved in her fall from grace—Joe is a fine young man, a great lad indeed. When we found out about her illegitimate child I had someone visit her from the SPCM apostolate. But obviously we didn't know the half of what she was up to."

"Well, isn't it a small world indeed." Mr. Branagh sniffed his brandy before taking another sip. And there was silence between the Knights as they contemplated the sometimes minuscule scale of God's infinite universe.

It was Mr. Brennan who shattered their pious reverie. "Do you need any help with the matter, do you think?" Spoken in the confidential tone of a travel agent who has only his client's best interests at heart.

"I don't think so, Denis." Mr. Branagh's abrupt response implied that his drinking companion was now meddling in a sphere where he did not belong. "I have written my affidavit and I have retained Counsel to present my case."

"What I had in mind was the moral aspect of the litigation. I do know a little bit about adoption laws, you see, particularly the part that says the welfare of the child is paramount, and that defines welfare as including religious and moral well-being. My organization has a lot of experience in that aspect of the matter. That's where I'm coming from, Con: we'd be most willing to assist you in any way we can." Mr. Brennan rested his case with a generous slug of brandy.

Mr. Branagh's quick intake of air suggested the onset of another peremptory dismissal. But then he relaxed, laid down his drink, folded his arms, sat back in his chair, and surveyed Mr. Brennan with a speculative eye. "They say women can't be too thin or lawyers too well prepared. Well, for myself, I like a little roundness in the fair sex, but when it comes to a trial I'm in agreement that the more angles you have going for you, the better. What exactly do you have in mind that might be useful in *Banaghan versus O'Connor*?"

"Character, Con. The unwed mother is *de facto* an unfit mother, at least by the moral standards of this once great Catholic country. And we believe that given the chance we can prove this to a court of law. As for the moral character of Miss O'Connor, I have no doubt that we'll be able to dredge up some very interesting facts."

They discussed the possibilities at length over a second round of Hennessy.

"Thanks very much, Mrs. O'Connor." Michael Heaney folded his serviette. "It was a lovely dinner."

"Bridget had a fair hand in it, too," said Aunt Nora from the other end of the long dining room table.

"It was delicious, indeed," Jamesie O'Malley added. "And it was very good of you to ask me."

"Why wouldn't we ask you?" Frank belched discreetly. "Aren't you the man of the hour?"

"Anyway, you all needed a good meal after the day that was in it," Uncle Tom said.

"Let ye adjourn to the parlor now while I do the wash-up." Aunt Nora began to collect the dishes.

"I'll help you," Eilis said.

"Indeed you will not. You must be exhausted. Go and sit inside now like a good girl. My own pair will help me." Her two daughters had come home from the university for the evening to have dinner with their relations.

Eilis didn't protest. She was very tired. She and Bridget and Frank had arrived in Dublin yesterday evening and were staying for the duration of the court hearing with Frank's brother Tom, and Aunt Nora. Away out of the city, near Howth Head, in a secluded neighborhood.

Michael Heaney smiled at her before heading out the door after Frank; he had insisted on coming up for the trial, though she didn't know why. Jamesie O'Malley dawdled until she came around the table. "Are you holding up?" His entire person dripped solicitude.

Eilis grimaced. "I feel as if I've been mauled by a gorilla. Why do people have to say such mean things? Especially when they're not true and they know it."

"Justice, my dear, is unfortunately too often not about truth, but about winning. Them lads today, both ours and theirs, wouldn't recognize the truth if it walked up and smacked them in the gob."

"I'd like to smack that fellow Molyneaux in the gob. He had no right to call me..." Her eyes teared.

"What's the matter?" Bridget asked, coming in from the hallway.

"Lies," Jamesie said. "Rotten stinking lies were told in that courtroom today."

"I was afraid of that," Bridget said. "Which was why I didn't go. I'd have had to get up and say something."

"That would hardly have helped our case." Eilis smiled at Jamesie.

"Would you like to go upstairs, pet?" Mammy was at her best when her children needed comforting. And when she called you *pet* you knew you'd get her undivided care.

"I'll stay for a bit." They had agreed not to discuss the case during dinner and she wanted to hear what Jamesie had to say about it now.

"Are you sure?"

"Just for a short while. Then I'll go check on Mary Kate."

The oversized parlor had a roaring fire, an elegant arrangement of stuffed chairs and sofas and lamp tables. The sideboard was booze-laden and there was a grand piano at the far end from the fireplace. The walls held a mélange of Impressionist prints and original oils by Aunt Nora herself, who everyone said was a very fine painter. "First you'll have drinks in your hands," said Uncle Tom, presiding at the sideboard. "Then we'll have a blow-by-blow account of the day's proceedings."

"'Twas an experience," Frank said, in the tone of a man ready to elaborate. Eilis wondered if maybe she should have gone to bed after all.

"Not yet." Uncle Tom, as bald as his brother was hirsute, had a voice like a trumpet. "Not another word now till everyone has a drink. I don't want to miss a syllable." He held them to silence about the case till all were served. "*Slainte*," he said then, raising his glass. "Who wants to go first?"

"As I said," Frank began, "it was quite an experience."

"Maybe we should hear from our solicitor first," Bridget said. Frank glared at her.

"Well, I'd agree with you, Frank." Jamesie nodded to the silenced husband. "It was an experience. Even for me, and I'm fairly used to courtrooms and the paraphernalia of justice."

"I liked the wigs, mind you," Frank said.

"I thought myself they were a bit scruffy," Michael commented. "The color of dirty sheep's wool."

"The judge had a good one. A nice steel gray with neat tails hanging down—"

"I'm all for fashion in its place." A sharp edge to Bridget's tone. "But for now I'd prefer to know what actually transpired in the courtroom."

"Sorry." Michael Heaney smiled at Bridget. "Very sorry.

Take the floor again, please, Jamesie."

"I suppose I should start with the opening arguments." Jamesie put down his drink and hooked his thumbs in the vest of his three-piece.

"Was it like "Rumpole of the Bailey"?" Uncle Tom asked. "With the judge sitting away up there and lots of wood paneling and the jury box and the witness stand and the prisoner in the dock?"

"And wigs," Eilis said.

"I give up." Bridget slumped back in her chair and sipped her sherry.

"Sorry, Bridget," Uncle Tom said. "I won't open my gob again. Go right ahead, Mr. O'Malley. No more interruptions."

"I'm going on memory now, since I don't have my notes with me, but I'll try to give you the gist of the plaintiffs' affidavit."

"Is that what they call that long speech he read at the beginning?" Michael asked.

"Right. In it he said that—"

"He read it so fast you'd think he was being chased by a fierce dog or something. Sorry. Carry on."

"He said first that the ultimate issue society must face in this matter is whether it wants to prohibit surrogacy contracts or to enforce them."

"What he reminded me of," Frank said, "and he standing there with his left hand on his hip and his right hand holding his papers and he looking up at the judge's bench as if it were a goalpost, was a Mayo footballer waiting to take a free kick."

"Molyneaux contended that, although there is no Irish case law dealing with this subject as yet, acknowledging the legality of surrogacy and upholding its contracts is not only consistent with existing law but necessary to maintain our status as an enlightened member of the European Union."

"Do you think he's right?" Uncle Tom asked.

"It's all humbug. Both the French and the Germans are already treating surrogacy contracts as baby-selling. As I had my counsel point out to the court later in the day."

"Is that what you were passing all the notes about?" Eilis looked across at her mother. "He was hopping up and down and going back and forth to what's-his-name—Mullen—with little bits of paper. You'd think he was playing postman."

"Go on, Jamesie," Bridget said.

"He argued that the case was about a contract that had been broken. The defendant contracted to conceive and bear a child, he said, which she would regard as the child of the plaintiffs, and would at birth deliver to the plaintiffs."

Eilis glanced up to see how her mother was taking this. She found Bridget staring at her. "Surely you didn't do it deliberately, Eilis?"

What could she say—*Gran told me to*?

"Oh my God!" Bridget turned on Frank. "Did you know this?"

"Faith I did not."

"This is what surrogacy is all about, Mrs. O'Connor. I thought you understood that." Jamesie gliding to Eilis's defense. "It's a contract made to have a baby and then—"

"Bad enough for her to get in the family way accidentally. But to do it deliberately!" Bridget was almost screaming. "Were you out of your mind, Eilis?"

"Listen a minute, Bridget." Michael got on his knees

beside her and took her hand. "What your daughter did was a wonderful, generous, courageous act. She felt the pain of her cousin who wanted a baby so badly for more than ten years, and she undertook to do what Aisling couldn't do for herself. Is it really so terrible to do something that kind?"

"It's a common practice now in many parts of the world, Mrs. O'Connor," Jamesie said. "The Americans have been doing it for years."

"In Europe, too," Uncle Tom added. "I've read about it. Though they say *in vitro* fertilization is the way of the future."

"You made a *contract* with them?" Incredulity dripped from Bridget's every word. She made no attempt to withdraw her hand from Michael's grasp.

"We're arguing that there was no contract, Mrs. O'Connor," Jamesie said. "Only a simple promise between relations. That's the basis of our legal response."

"Will you tell me, what's the difference between a promise and a contract?" Uncle Tom asked.

"What they call consideration, mainly. The other side of the bargain, if you like. The plaintiffs argue that they provided financial support to the defendant in the form of payment towards her medical and hospital bills."

"So because they paid part of the bills they think they're entitled to the child?" Aunt Nora was standing in the doorway, a scowl on her face that would have scattered Molyneaux to the four winds.

"Exactly. And they claim that serious damage ensued to the plaintiffs because the defendant reneged on her contract. The Banaghans invested emotionally in their child, they looked forward with the keenest anticipation to its arrival, and they let their friends and relations know they were expecting a baby. They also prepared their home and bought furniture and a wardrobe for their child." Jamesie picked up his glass and sniffed. "All this is a great pile of you-know-what calculated to appeal to the judge's soft side. Just emotional fluff. I wouldn't worry about it. The fellow up on the bench didn't look the type who would be unduly swayed by sentiment. Now if it had been a jury...I'm very happy the Banaghans didn't opt for a jury."

"Is he proposing to you, dear?" Aunt Nora came forward and sat on the sofa next to her sister-in-law.

Michael Heaney got quickly off his knees and let go of Bridget's hand. "So how are you going to answer them?" Picking lint off his trouser legs as he returned to his seat.

"We'll argue, first of all, that there was no contract."

"I still can't believe you did it on purpose," Bridget said.

"Secondly, that even if there was a contract it is not enforceable." Jamesie reached for his glass again. "However, I think it's time to let the rest of you talk for a while."

"No, no," his audience objected.

"I for one would like to hear *your* arguments," Uncle Tom said.

"Indeed! Certainly! Of course!" sang the Greek chorus.

"It's fairly technical stuff, but I'll keep it as simple as I can." Jamesie cleared his throat. "First, we're arguing that there was just a promise between cousins. Eilis did it out of the goodness of her heart with no expectation of anything in return. A promise like that has no legal standing at all. Besides, it was rescinded after the baby was born. So it's really like a promise to give a baby up for adoption, which of course—"

"Which *we* told her not to do." Frank wagged a finger at his daughter.

"—which a mother has a right in law to rescind anytime up to the moment the Adoption Board makes the order."

"It seems like an open-and-shut case, then," Aunt Nora said.

"Unfortunately, we can't be certain the court will accept this argument. So we follow it up with another one: namely, even if the court agrees there *was* a contract, it shouldn't be enforced. The reasons we give for that make up the bulk of our case." Jamesie sat back in his chair and sipped his drink.

"Well, go on, man. Don't keep us in suspenders." Uncle Tom said.

"The argument here is…" Jamesie stopped and pointed at Eilis. "Maybe you should tell it to them. It was you who came up with the suggestion in the first place."

"*I* got the idea from Michael. He can tell you about it a lot better than I can."

Michael Heaney glanced at Bridget. "I'll be glad to try." He put his lemonade on the lamp table and rubbed his hands together as if building up energy. "From a number of things Eilis said, it struck me that the type of promise she made mightn't be much different from the one I made myself at ordination—I'm talking about the commitment to celibacy, of course. As you might imagine, I had done a bit of soul-searching in recent times about that particular promise, and come to a certain conclusion. The result of which is that I'm here tonight instead of in the parish house in Kildawree."

"That took a lot of courage, I'd say," Uncle Tom voiced.

"The question I put to myself was this: if you make a promise, can you ever be justified in going back on it? I made my promise freely, you see. I knew what I was doing. Ah! But did I? I asked myself. Of course I did. Then the thought came to me: I knew what I was doing as a twenty-three-year-old lad, bursting with religious fervor but ignorant of the long-term consequences. I made a promise for life not knowing what my life would be like in twenty-seven years. Or what I would become in twenty-seven years. A different man, you see: different in knowledge, different in understanding, different in feelings, different in needs. So the question was, had the twenty-three-year-old the right to make a promise for the fifty-year-old? The big decision I came to was that he hadn't. I met a Brazilian missionary a few years ago who told me that parents there often make promises for their children to keep, like that they must get married at the national shrine a thousand miles away. Which I thought was sort of like what *I* did to myself: a young lad making a vow for an old man to keep. So when Eilis told me about her problem, I realized that the same reasoning might apply. When she promised her baby to the Banaghans she had no idea of the extraordinarily intimate relationship that was going to develop between herself and her child: a relationship that would change her sense of herself so profoundly that she couldn't even be said to be the same person who made the promise in the first place. I believe we're defined in part as human beings by our most intimate relationships. Like the one between a religious person and God. Or between mother and child. Or between lovers. When you become a mother or a lover you're a different person from what you were before, and the difference *is* that relationship. To make a contract, then, that would break up such a relationship is like making a contract to cut off a piece of yourself." He stopped. "Am I making any kind of sense at all?"

"By God you do make sense," Uncle Tom said. "I always felt priests and nuns shouldn't make promises for life."

"Maybe we should put Michael on the stand on Monday," Jamesie said to Eilis.

"Oh yes." She grabbed Michael by the shoulder. "You'd say it a thousand times better than I could."

The phone rang out in the hall. Aunt Nora got up, but before she got to the door one of her daughters could be heard saying hello. "Well, I don't know," Michael said. To Eilis that sounded like assent.

"I don't want to belittle your argument, Michael," Frank said, "but—"

Maeve, the older of the O'Connor daughters, put her head in the door. "There's a man on the phone wants to speak to Mr. O'Malley."

Jamesie shot up like a greyhound coming out of the box. "I left your number at the hotel in case anyone wanted to find me." He hurried out the door.

"As I was saying," Frank continued, "if what you say is true, Michael, wouldn't anyone be entitled to get out of any promise using the same argument?"

"Ah no. Definitely not. Let me put it to you this way, Frank. The argument is only valid when there's such a profound change brought about in the person who made the—"

Jamesie O'Malley returned. "That was Con Branagh on the phone. The other side has issued a subpoena for Joe Mahony. They're going to have him in court first thing on Monday morning."

Eilis's stomach knotted. She was going to be sick.

"Who's Joe Mahony?" Uncle Tom asked.

"Mary Kate's father," Jamesie said.

"So what does it mean for your case?"

"More than likely they'll argue that as father he has an equal say in determining the baby's future. There have been some recent laws that give unmarried fathers certain rights regarding their children. But I don't think we have anything to worry about in this case. Those fellows are just grasping at straws now."

"What would happen," Bridget asked, "if Joe were to deny he was the father?"

Eilis felt certain now that she was going to be sick.

That Joe Mahony should stand up in the witness box and refute the defendant's avowal that he was the father of her baby was Denis Brennan's idea. He talked Con Branagh into it when the two of them were walking into the Four Courts on Friday morning. He returned to the subject that evening when they met for dinner in Jury's Hotel. "It's going to be a fierce surprise to the lot of them when my nephew gets up and issues a ringing denial."

"It will, Denis. It will indeed." Mr. Branagh flaked off a piece of poached salmon with his fish knife and hoisted it onto the back of his fork. "Of course, I'll have to tell O'Malley in advance that we've got a subpoena for your nephew."

Denis Brennan stopped cutting his filet mignon. "Why would you want to do that?"

"Ah now, you have to do the decent thing, even with your adversary of the day." *Bloody hypocrite* was what went through Branagh's mind. Nothing worse than those sanctimonious fellows on a crusade. But no one was ever going to be able to say Con Branagh was mean, least of all Jamesie O'Malley.

Mr. Brennan meditated while he chewed. "We have to make sure Joe gets here on Monday morning."

"I've got the subpoena in my pocket. We'll bring the lad back with us Sunday evening."

On Saturday morning, as they were driving through Kilbeggan on their way west, Con spotted a place to park and pulled in. "I've been doing some more thinking about this business. It would be better still if we let them know in advance what Joe is going to say."

"But if you let them know now, won't they be ready with an answer for you on Monday?"

"What answer can they have? Listen, Denis, this is what I'm thinking." Con took his mobile phone from his pocket. "If we let them know that Joe is going to deny paternity after their affidavit has affirmed him as the father, there's a fair chance they might back down altogether. Their credibility will be gone, you see, and the character of the mother will be further tarnished."

Mr. Brennan admitted that it might be worth a try. Con rang the Banaghans' B&B. He had to wait a couple of minutes while the woman who answered went to fetch Eugene. It was Aisling who came to the phone. Her husband had gone for a walk, she said.

"I want you to ring the O'Connors and tell them that on Monday in court Joe Mahony will issue a categorical denial that he is the father."

"Hah! I knew it." The phone seemed to explode in his ear with her triumphant shout. "I knew it all along. I told Eugene that we—"

"Listen to me now. I'd like you not to make any comment whatever when you tell them. You understand? Just give them the bare-bones information. And ring them right away now, that's a good girl." He rang off before she could say any more. Women! He hoped she wouldn't make a hames of it, getting their backs up with her crowing.

Aisling was sitting alone in the B&B dining room when the phone call came. They'd had a row at the end of breakfast and Eugene got up without waiting for her and said he was going for a walk to clear his head. Rows between them were getting more frequent these past six months. The loss of their two babies had put a terrible damper on their lives and, seemingly as a consequence, on relations between the two of them. This morning's scrap was really about nothing at all. *She* said maybe it would be nice to visit the Botanical Gardens, which were within walking distance of where they were staying. *He* snapped back how about consulting him first for once in her life to see what *he*'d like to do. To which she had quietly responded that it was just a suggestion on her part and if he had any other ideas she was perfectly willing to accommodate. But by then he was on his high horse, muttering that she always got her say in first and he was forced to go along because if he so much as hesitated she made him feel like he was just being disagreeable. She had been about to retort that she never said any such thing when another couple entered and sat at the table by the window. Eugene got up and left. She was exchanging pleasantries with the new arrivals when the proprietress came into the dining room and said, "There's someone ringing for Mr. Banaghan."

"I'll take it," Aisling said.

It was a good job Eugene wasn't there to hear her I-told-you-so squeal of delight at the news. She felt suddenly lighter. There was a chance after all. The longer the whole business dragged on, the less confident she had become that they'd ever recover their lost child—which was how she thought of Mary Kate. But this news sparked hope. Maybe, just maybe. Oh dear Blessed Mother, let it be so.

Then the import of what she had to do next dawned on her. Ring the O'Connors, the solicitor said, and tell them. Oh God, she didn't want to talk to those people now. Anyway, she had no idea where they were. Branagh said letting them know was very important to their case. So maybe leave it till Eugene came back? No, she wouldn't. Not after their recent spat. Be independent, Aisling Banaghan. Have a bit of courage. Find out for yourself where they are. But how? Ring their home of course: the children must know. Wouldn't that be awfully cheeky in the circumstances? Well, be cheeky then. She rang. A young man answered. "Is this Ultan?"

"No, it's Ciaran. Who's this?"

"This is Aisling, Ciaran. My, but your voice has deepened; you're really a man now." She babbled on to get him in a mood to help her: there was no knowing what Bridget might have told her children about awful cousin Aisling. If she *had* said anything, Ciaran gave no hint of it. Yes, he knew where his parents were staying in Dublin: with Uncle Tom and Aunt Nora out in Howth. He went away and came back with their phone number. She rang Howth.

"The O'Connor residence." Eilis, of all the clan the person she least wanted to talk to, except maybe for Bridget. Aisling almost hung up. Instead she managed a strangled "Is that you, Eilis?"

"Oh." A brief pause. "It's you."

"I have a message for you. I've been asked by our solicitor, Mr. Branagh, to give some information to your solicitor."

"More insults, I suppose."

"I had nothing to do with what was said yesterday, Eilis. Neither had Eugene. We were both terribly—"

"What was the information?"

"He said to tell your solicitor that they're putting Joe Mahony on the witness stand on Monday, and that he's going to deny he's the father."

"Is that it?" Eilis's tone was mild.

"Yes, that's it." The consequences hadn't yet registered with her, was what went through Aisling's mind.

"Well, thank you for the information. I'll be sure to pass it along to my solicitor." A click signaled the end of the conversation.

Aisling couldn't wait to tell Eugene: it would be a good way to patch up the row. It wasn't. "What?" He had just returned rather sheepishly to their room and the first thing she said was, listen to this. He seemed stunned by the news, as if she had informed him his mother had just dropped dead, or something equally tragic.

"What's the matter? It seems like a very good idea to me. Isn't it what I've been saying to you for the past couple of days?" But he slumped onto the bed and covered his face with his hands. "I don't know what's got into you at all," she said. "I thought you'd be delighted. It'll improve our case."

He jumped up, walked to the window, stared out. "It's the very worst thing that could possibly happen to us. Do you know why?" When he turned, there was an expression of fear on his face. "Let me tell you why. Do you know what's going to happen? Let me tell you what's going to happen." A slight froth of spit at the edge of his mouth. "The minute that lad denies he's the father, they're going to put your cousin on the stand and they're going to ask her under solemn oath who the bloody father is and she's going to tell the truth and then we're going to have this bastard, whoever he is, coming into court and demanding *his* rights as the father of *our* child, and whatever chance we had up to now of getting our baby we won't have a bloody goddamn snowball's chance in hell after this. Jesus Christ Almighty!" He stamped his foot hard on the floor before swinging around again to face the window.

What in God's name had got into him? They didn't even know yet who the father was and here was Eugene already making dire predictions about what the fellow was going to do. "I think you're overreacting." She reached her hand out to touch his shoulder. "I mean, he must know already what's going on. God knows there's been enough about it in the media. So if he hasn't come forward by now, it's got to be because he doesn't want it known that he's the father."

He pushed her hand away. "Weren't you listening to what Branagh told us a long time ago about the rights of the unmarried father? That joker has equal rights with the mother when it comes to deciding what's going to happen to the child."

Nothing she could say would change his mind on the subject, so she gave up and went off to the Botanical Gardens by herself.

Saturday afternoon Con Branagh rang Joe Mahony from his home in Ballinamore. The lad expressed surprise that he should be called as a witness and immediately declined the honor. However, when Con explained the nature of a subpoena and the fact that he had no alternative but to respond to it—and testify truthfully, since perjury was a

criminal act punishable by jail—the young man reluctantly
agreed to cooperate. But how was he going to get to Dublin?
And what about his job? He had to be at work on Monday
morning. Not to worry, the solicitor assured him: his uncle
Denis was going to Dublin on Sunday evening and would
take him with him, and put him up at Jury's Hotel, and take
him to court on Monday morning, and then put him on the
train back to Galway in the afternoon.

In moments of malice, which were not few since she
received the plenary summons, Eilis fantasized betraying
Eugene to his wife. Just seeing him squirm in mind's mean
eye and mentally hearing his bellow of pain—ironically
similar to his cries of delight on that night of pleasure—gave
release to her anger and softened her fear. She would never
actually inform on him, of course: there were some things so
wicked that one simply could not do them and continue to
live with oneself. Besides, though the information might
wreak havoc on the Banaghans' marriage, it would
strengthen their chances of being awarded Mary Kate.

So what was going to happen on Monday when Joe stood
up in court and denied *he* was Mary Kate's father? Eilis
would certainly be called a liar and, God forbid, might even
lose her child. A tragedy not even to be thought about. It was
her own fault for lying in the first place. Joe had given her
permission to tell *Aisling* he was Mary Kate's father, with
the clear understanding that she wouldn't spread the lie any
further. But she *had* spread it when Jamesie asked her who
the child's father was—they were discussing their legal
defense after the Banaghans sued. Jamesie said she was
fortunate that Joe wasn't interested in custody because

nowadays fathers had almost equal rights with mothers in custody suits. "Now if Eugene Banaghan had been the father," he hypothesized with a smile, "we'd have no case at all."

So when Jamesie affirmed in the affidavit that Joe was Mary Kate's father, Eilis allowed the lie to stand. She agonized over it, realizing the harm it could do to Joe's relationship with Ger. However, she convinced herself that if she asked his permission to name him as father in the document he'd most certainly refuse. Whereas if he didn't find out till after the event, he wasn't likely to expose her. It was unfair, of course, but what was she to do? If Jamesie knew the truth he'd surely drop the case, and then she'd lose Mary Kate. In the end, she persuaded herself that Joe would be able to explain the truth of the matter to Ger without having to make a public denial of paternity.

Now Jamesie would have to be told the truth, whatever the consequences. She was playing with Mary Kate in Aunt Nora's parlor—Bridget and Frank and Tom had gone into Dublin for the day—and trying to pluck up the courage to ring him when the phone rang again. The last time she answered it she had found herself talking with Aisling, so this time she stayed put. After six rings Aunt Nora came out from the kitchen. A few seconds later she stuck her head in the parlor door. "It's for you, dear. A man. Here, let me take herself for a while."

Maybe Michael Heaney? He had gone back to Galway early this morning, after Jamesie decided not to call him as an expert witness. It was Eugene. "Eilis." His voice cracked, hoarse, frantic. "You heard what they're going to do on Monday?"

"Yes."

"We can't let it happen, you know."

"*You* can't. It doesn't matter to me."

"Listen to me now."

"I'm listening."

"When Joe gets up in the witness box on Monday and says he's not the father, do you know what the next step is going to be?"

"I have no idea."

"Well, I know. And damn well you know, too. They're going to put you in the same bleddy box and ask you who *is* the father."

"So you'd like me to perjure myself, I suppose, to save your bacon?"

"No, I don't want you to perjure yourself. But there must be some way around it that you don't have to say who the father is."

"I know one way to get around it."

"Well, good on yourself. Tell us."

"You can withdraw your case."

There was a long silence. Eventually he said, in a slow, painful tone, "There are times when I wish I could. Honest to God I do. But you and I know it's too late for that now. Eilis, please. We used to be friends, the best of friends. This whole business has done terrible things to Aisling and me, to our marriage. We're fighting all the time. If she finds out about you and me it'll be the end. So I'm asking you, please."

Her toes were curling in anguish, but she said, "Tell her to withdraw," and hung up.

Jamesie wouldn't be back till later in the evening, his

hotel said, so she left a message. He rang just as they were beginning supper. "What's up?" Ebullient as usual.

"I have a message from Mr. Branagh for you."

"Indeed! And what does the bold Con of a hundred battles have to say for himself?"

"I can't tell you over the phone." She kept her voice low, even though the conversation in the dining room would make it difficult for a listening Bridget to pick up her words. "We need to talk about it. Can you come out?"

"I'll be there in half an hour."

When he arrived she left a protesting Mary Kate in the care of her mother and went for a drive with him. "It'll be good for you to get out for a while," Aunt Nora said. They sat in his car down by the pier: it was too cold and blustery to go for a walk. She told him what Aisling had relayed on the phone. Then she informed him that Eugene was Mary Kate's father. Finally, she gave the gist of Eugene's frantic phone call. Through it all he sat in silence, looking out on the water. He might have been composing a legal brief for all the emotion he displayed.

"So that's it now, as Gran used to say." Still he said nothing. "It's not going to be a problem for us, is it?"

He turned in his seat and faced her. "We stated in our affidavit that Joseph Kieran Mahony is the father." There was a cold anger in his voice, the bite of a man whose pride has been hurt. "So when Joe denies it, our credibility will be gone. Maybe our defense as well."

"Don't say that, please, Jamesie."

"Do you realize," he looked at her with a hurt expression, "that they can use Eugene's paternity to their advantage? Under the law he could get custody, even if they throw out the argument for a surrogate contract. On the other hand, if you don't tell them who the father is, your good character will be gone completely and the judge is liable to declare you an unfit mother. Shit!" He started the car and backed out of the parking space. "I need to go back and talk to Mullen." He left her at Uncle Tom's front gate, confused and half-paralyzed with fear.

Sunday morning Frank O'Connor woke with a headache. Whenever he and his brother Tom got together they generally drank too much whiskey, with predictable consequences. So he was in no mood to be pleasant when Eugene Banaghan rang him. Bridget and he were getting into the car in the driveway, heading for nine o'clock mass, when Tom came running out the front door. "Phone for you, Frank."

"Who could that be?" Bridget asked.

"I don't think you and I have anything to say to each other at this stage," Frank responded after Eugene identified himself.

He was about to hang up when he heard Eugene say, "Julia." At that very same instant Bridget came through the front door and stood there, just two feet away from him.

"What was that you said?"

"I said it might be in your best interest to listen to what I have to say."

"All right." Frank did his best to keep a straight face with Bridget eyeing him, dying of curiosity to know who he was talking to.

"We need to talk, Frank, man to man. I can't say what I have to say on the telephone now, and neither can you, I imagine."

"That's true."

"I'll meet you in the lounge of the Westbury Hotel at eleven o'clock." Then Eugene Banaghan hung up.

"Who was that?" Bridget asked.

Frank had a flash of inspiration. "Ah, just a fellow from the Farmers' Association. Martin Brannigan," he added, pulling a name out of memory's hat. "He wants me to meet him in town this morning to discuss a bit of Association business."

"How did he know you'd be here?" He didn't detect suspicion in his wife's tone, just her usual curiosity.

"I left him word before we came up." The lies were coming thick and fast, but what else could he do?

Eugene was at the Westbury before him. "What are you drinking?" Sprawled on a couch in the elegant lounge, he looked like a farmer up to town for the day.

"Nothing now, thanks. I still have a bit of a head after last night."

"I ordered a pot of tea. You can have some of that."

"Best get down to business. I'm in a bit of a hurry." He had gotten away after mass on the understanding that he'd be back for the one o'clock Sunday dinner.

Eugene stretched his intertwined fingers till the knuckles cracked. "Jesus Christ. I can't believe we've got ourselves into this pickle."

"It wasn't my doing."

"Listen to me now, Frank, and listen good. I'm in a very vulnerable position at this moment. Have you heard what them jokers of lawyers are planning to do next?"

"I have no idea what they're planning to do." If

Banaghan thought he was going to divulge any of their plans he had another think coming.

Their waitress brought a tea tray. "They're going to put Joe Mahony into the witness box tomorrow morning." Eugene's hand was shaking as he poured the tea. "And he's going to deny that he's the father of your grandchild. What do you think of that?"

"Do you see what you've done? You and Aisling, the pair of you." Frank's anger bubbled like a boiling kettle. "It isn't enough that you're trying to take away Eilis's child from her but you have to destroy her character as well with your lies. Well, let me tell you, Eugene—"

"Frank, listen to me." Eugene put down his cup and waved his arms. "'Tis I'm as sorry as you are about the things that have been said. And so is Aisling. She cried all Friday night about it, if you want to know the truth. But that's not the point right now. The point is what's going to happen tomorrow when Joe Mahony says under oath that he's not the father."

"I don't give a damn what happens. You can't make things any worse than you've made them already." What began as a shout ended in an almost whisper as Frank realized he was making a spectacle of himself in this quiet lounge.

"Well, maybe you *will* give a damn when I'm finished telling you what's going to happen next. They're going to put your daughter in the box and make her say who *is* the father. And do you know who that's going to be?"

A prickly cold sweat erupted over major parts of Frank's body. "I can guess."

"If she says it, I'm ruined." Eugene grabbed his cup and

with trembling hand slurped the hot tea.

"I'd be sorry indeed if that happened. We all make our mistakes." Appeasement was his only hope.

"I want you to do something for me." Eugene leaned so far forward that he was barely sitting on the couch. "I want you to talk to Eilis and get her not to say anything."

"Maybe you should talk to her yourself." Fat chance either of them had of getting Eilis to change her mind.

"I did. I rang her yesterday and I didn't get anywhere. But I've been thinking about it since, and she doesn't have to perjure herself. All she has to do is say nothing. It's as simple as that, Frank. They can't make her tell if she doesn't want to. That way is best for everyone concerned."

Except that Eilis might see things differently. However, Frank's sweat was abating: his initial fears were not being realized. "Well, of course, I'll try. But there's no guarantee she'll listen to me, either. You know how she is."

The cunning expression on Eugene's face brought back the terror. "I know full well how stubborn she can be. So I thought up a little incentive for you to give her. You can tell her I said that if she rats on me I'm going to tell her mother about Julia."

"Julia?" Stupid to feign ignorance of course, but the shock of actually hearing the threat prevented him from responding sensibly.

"You don't have to play the innocent, Frank. Didn't I meet her with you that day in the restaurant? And I've made some enquiries of my own since. Enough said. You'll persuade Eilis to do the right thing now, won't you?"

"Jesus Christ, Eugene. No one would ever do a thing like that to a friend."

"I'm not particularly proud of it, if that's any help to you. I never thought in all my born days that I'd stoop so low. But you don't know what you're capable of until you're put on the spot. I have a marriage I desperately want to save, and if this is the only way I can do it, then so be it."

"You're a dirty stinking rotten bastard and may you rot in hell for it." Frank stood abruptly. "You'll get no help from me." However, on the train ride back to Howth sanity returned. Surely, after all he had done for her over a lifetime, Eilis owed him that much. After dinner he got her to take a walk with him and put the proposition to her in terms of the total destruction of the O'Connor family.

"Part of me sympathizes with you, Daddy," she said, "and part of me says you deserve it. On the other hand, Jamesie says I'll certainly lose Mary Kate if I don't tell who the father is."

"But Eilis! You don't want to see your parents' marriage broken up, do you?"

She stopped and faced him on the road, with the sun glistening on the sea below them. "I've thought many times about what might happen if Mammy found out about your affair. And I've come to the conclusion that she'd make your life hell for quite a while, and you'd never be let outside the door again on your own. In the end, though, she'd forgive you because she's the good Catholic woman that she is. So, Daddy, you're going to have to take your chances with her."

Early Sunday afternoon Con Branagh drove up to Oranmore and picked up Mr. Brennan, who had already collected his nephew. The young man acknowledged him with a frigid hello, and for the entire trip to Dublin hardly spoke another word. After they finished dinner in Jury's Restaurant, Con said, "I'd like to brief you now on what to expect tomorrow."

"It's terribly important that you know exactly what's going on." Mr. Brennan placed his elbows on the table and leaned forward to get closer to the scene of the action.

"If you wouldn't mind, Denis, this is going to be a solicitor-client conference, which by its very nature of course has to be private." Con gave Mr. Brennan the sign of the raised eyebrow, and received no small satisfaction from the less than gruntled glare he got back.

"I'll go for a stroll." Mr. Brennan got up and left.

"You know what's going on, don't you?" Branagh asked Joe.

"All I know is the Banaghans are suing Eilis for custody of her baby."

"Miss O'Connor claimed in her affidavit that Joseph Kieran Mahony is the child's father. And my question to you is, are you?"

Joe looked at him in surprise. "I don't believe it."

Con Branagh stared at him. "Are you?"

Joe looked down. His lengthy silence eventually taxed Con's patience. "Yes or no?"

Joe looked up at him. "No."

"So we have them by the bollocks, then."

"What does that mean?"

"It means that young lady will be caught with her britches down in the middle of a big fat lie—she may even go to jail for it. It means, too, that the child will now go to its rightful parents. So what you have to say in court tomorrow is terribly important. Now listen. There's no need to be nervous in the box. You're not the nervous type, are you?"

"I don't want to do this."

"I'm sure you don't, and I can't say I blame you. But the law is the law, as I'm sure you well understand, and we all have to abide by it. Now here's the procedure. You'll step into the witness box when you're called. You'll answer the questions that counsel will put to you. You'll say nothing more and nothing less. That's the most crucial thing you have to remember—say nothing more and nothing less. A lawyer, you see, must never ask a question unless he first knows the answer he's going to get. So you and I must now rehearse our questions and answers for tomorrow."

They were still at it twenty minutes later when Denis Brennan returned.

The O'Connors were watching the telly after supper on Sunday evening when Jamesie O'Malley arrived unexpectedly. "I hope I'm not intruding." He sat next to Eilis on the sofa near the fire. She was laughing at Mary Kate's gyrations on the carpet: the child's attempts to crawl backwards were giving the family more entertainment than the television program. Uncle Tom, after muting the sound with his remote receiver, offered the visitor a drink that he refused. Aunt Nora suggested a cup of tea, which he said he might have later.

"I came out to tell you all something important," he said. "I thought you should know about it before we go into court tomorrow. We got further word over the weekend about what the plaintiffs are going to do when they put Mr. Mahony in the witness box: he's going to deny his alleged paternity. We'll have to respond by asking Eilis to expose the name of the real father."

"Do you think that's a wise thing to do?" Frank asked.

"Naturally, we'd be happier if we didn't have to do it, but in the circumstances Mr. Mullen and I have decided that it's better for our case if we do it than if we don't."

"I think it's a great idea," Bridget said. "It's about time the father of our grandchild came forward and identified himself. Can you tell us who he is, now?" Bridget put the question in her sly offhand way: with eyes cast down, hands joined in the lap, an innocent look on her face that said butter wouldn't melt in her mouth. Eilis's butterflies took off in all directions.

"Unfortunately," Jamesie said, "we can't divulge that information yet. We expect it to cause no small amount of consternation to the plaintiffs, and we feel that its effect will be greater if they have no inkling of it beforehand. So to protect you all from any accusation of having blabbed out of turn, we're not going to tell you. I hope you won't mind."

After a general chorus of *not at all*s and *why would we mind*s, Jamesie turned to Eilis. "Now Miss, you and I need to talk about tomorrow in some detail." He followed her upstairs, made faces at Mary Kate while Eilis changed the child's diaper, and watched with amusement while Eilis tried to settle her into her crib. Mary Kate was in no hurry to give up for the night: several times she stood, holding on to the rails, and protested loudly each time her mother placed her back down. Jamesie showed no impatience during the half hour or more it took for the baby to go to sleep. Afterwards, he and Eilis sat on the latter's bed.

"Our biggest problem, as you know," he took her hand in his as he spoke, "is that we affirmed in our affidavit that Joe was the father. Now we must try to minimize the loss of credibility that will accrue from that statement. So here's what Mullen and I came up with. You'll begin by identifying Eugene Banaghan as the father, in answer to the question Mullen will put to you. Then, when he asks you why you led everyone to believe that Joe Mahony was the father, your answer will be that you did it to protect Eugene Banaghan from the scandal that would befall him and the hurt that would be done to his wife if you let it be known that he fathered your child. That's all true, isn't it?"

"It is." But that was small consolation for the awful deed she must do.

"Now let's go over again your explanation for why you decided to keep your child." They worked at it for half an hour, but though at the end of it she was exhausted, physically and emotionally, Eilis hardly slept a wink all night.

She had tried to prepare herself, but it still came as a shock to Eilis when she saw Joe Mahony walk into the courtroom on Monday morning in the company of his uncle, knowing that he was about to make a public liar out of her. She forgave him in advance: he couldn't commit perjury. Besides, it was her fault that he was here at all. Of course she hadn't expected the situation to come to this pass.

She was sitting with her father on the right side of the visitors' gallery, saying nothing, feeling wretched, watching Jamesie O'Malley down below chatting with Mullen, when sudden silence broke the low drone of conversation. All rose. The judge entered from a door to the left of the bench, like a priest coming out from the sacristy to say mass, with brisk step and flapping gown. He was a good-looking man to the point of being handsome, youthful for the post, several years younger than her father she'd say, and quite natty in his iron-gray wig.

When he sat, all sat, except Molyneaux, to whom the man on the bench nodded with quietly understated arrogance. "My first witness this morning is Mr. Joseph Kieran Mahony," the barrister intoned.

Denis Brennan put an arm around Joe, as if his nephew needed to be lifted bodily from his seat. But Joe rose lithely and marched like a soldier to the witness box. Or perhaps like a martyr to the gallows, for on turning he revealed a look of sad defiance to the court. When he swore to tell the truth, the whole truth and nothing but the truth, his closed eyes and rigid posture suggested he might well be in direct communion with the great Judge of all. His name was Joseph Kieran Mahony, he responded in a clear though somewhat strained voice to Molyneaux's perfunctory question. Eilis had an urge to dash up and stroke his hair and tell him everything was going to be all right, that she didn't really mind what he said. "What is your occupation?" Molyneaux asked, standing there, with obnoxious confidence, one hand on hip, the other holding the paper from which he read.

"I am office manager of the Tribes' City Travel Agency in Galway." There was a marked increase in Joe's agitation, as if he were preparing to panic.

"You are acquainted with Miss Eilis O'Connor, the defendant in this litigation?"

"Yes." Joe almost choked on that simple word and had to clear his throat.

"How long have you known Miss O'Connor?"

"About four and a half years."

"Would you say you are very good friends?"

"Yes."

"Would you say your relationship is that of boyfriend and girlfriend?"

"No. We're just good friends."

"The defendant's affidavit states that you are the father of her child. Mr. Mahony, *are* you the father of Miss O'Connor's child?"

"Yes."

"You are quite…" It was here that Molyneaux's confident

posture slipped. The hip hand left its post, the other lowered the paper. He glanced up at the judge, then glanced down at Con Branagh; finding no comfort in the latter's puzzled stare, he looked again at the paper in his hand. "Let me repeat the last question, Mr. Mahony: Are you the father of Miss O'Connor's child?"

"I am," said Joe, serenely now, as if he had been waiting for this admission to soothe his agitation.

Eilis had to hand it to Molyneaux: he recovered his composure almost immediately. "You are quite sure of this?"

"I am."

Eilis found herself clutching her father's arm. "Is he telling the truth?" Frank whispered out of the side of his mouth.

"No." It had to be a trick, a scheme to pry her baby from her. But Molyneaux himself had seemed shocked. Anyway, how could *he*, or anyone else for that matter, get Joe Mahony to perjure himself? So he must be doing it to protect herself and Mary Kate.

"No more questions," the barrister said.

Mr. Mullen declined the opportunity to cross-examine. As Eilis watched Joe leave the box and walk back to his seat beside his uncle, she thought the expression on his face was that of a devout communicant returning from the altar after receiving his Lord.

Before Aisling Banaghan had time to reconcile this unpleasant departure from the evidentiary script with her own theory, she was called to the witness box. Afterwards, Eugene told her she had responded in a barely audible voice when asked if she would swear to tell the truth, the whole truth, and nothing but the truth. She herself couldn't remember that part of the interrogation. Neither did she recall answering Molyneaux that she was indeed Aisling Margaret Banaghan. She did, oddly, recall the change in her body temperature, from the cold of nervousness to the heat of embarrassment, as counsel picked his way through her extremely personal history of failure to achieve motherhood. From that ordeal of inquiry she had attained the calm of uncaring by the time Mr. Molyneaux placed his first prepared question about Eilis O'Connor's commitment.

"How did you react, Mrs. Banaghan, when the defendant, Miss O'Connor, solemnly promised to have a baby for you?"

"Objection." Aisling didn't look to see who uttered the statement she had heard so often in film and television dramas.

"Rephrase," the judge commanded.

Molyneaux removed his wig, wiped his long sloping forehead with a handkerchief, and replaced the headpiece. "Did Miss O'Connor, the defendant, commit to have a child which she would then give to you?"

"Yes."

"Did she commit to surrender all her maternal rights to that child in your favor?"

"Yes." Eilis had never really said so explicitly, but Aisling had acceded beforehand to counsel's vehement assertion that such a promise was definitely to be understood from her cousin's behavior.

"Did you consider this commitment to be quite an extraordinary one at that time?"

"Yes."

"How did you respond to it?"

"I told her she was daft."

"You told her she was daft." Molyneaux leaned down, retrieved a bottle of water, drank briefly and replaced the bottle. "What was her response to that?"

"She explained that what she was proposing was called surrogate motherhood, and that it was quite a common thing in the United States of America."

"How did she—" Molyneaux stopped abruptly. "Rephrase. Did Miss O'Connor explain to you what she understood by the term surrogate motherhood?"

"Yes."

"Would you please tell us how she described it."

"She said it involved her having the baby and then handing it over to us as if it were our own natural child. She would give up all her rights as mother." There! She had said it exactly as rehearsed, though she did feel she was skirting the borders of perjury: Eilis had simply asked if she and Eugene would adopt her baby. But Molyneaux and Branagh were fierce in their insistence that she never use the word *adopt* in evidence. It could destroy their entire case, they said.

"Did Miss O'Connor, in those terms, offer to be a surrogate mother for you?"

"She did."

"Did you accept her offer?"

"Eventually. I was reluctant at first."

"Why were you reluctant?"

"Because it involved a tremendous sacrifice on Miss O'Connor's part."

"Did you state that to Miss O'Connor?"

"Yes, I did."

"What was her response?"

"She said she was very fond of us and having our baby was something she really wanted to do for us."

"And that argument persuaded you to accept?"

"Yes."

"Did you make any reciprocal commitment to Miss O'Connor?"

"Yes. We—my husband and I—promised to pay all her out-of-pocket expenses associated with having the baby. National Health, of course, paid most of the medical costs."

"Did you actually pay the out-of-pocket expenses she incurred?"

"Yes."

"Did you view the commitment made to you by Miss O'Connor as irrevocable?"

"Yes."

"When did Miss O'Connor inform you that she was going to keep the baby herself?"

"Shortly after the baby was born. She wrote us a letter."

"What was your reaction?"

He ought not have asked that question. She had explicitly ruled it out when they rehearsed this examination. Molyneaux had pleaded that if she were to break down in the witness box it would help their case, but she had furiously rejected the suggestion: she was not about to make a spectacle of herself. Anyway, her case was about her right to her baby; soggy emotional appeals would cheapen instead of strengthen it. Even Branagh had agreed with her on that. Now, predictably, her answer was a reenactment of her original response to the letter. Her entire glandular system rose up like a tidal wave and engulfed her. Vision swam, throat constricted, nose ran, ears blocked, sweat erupted, diaphragm spasmed. A fearsome cry escaped her tight-clenched teeth.

"Court will recess for ten minutes," the judge said. Someone placed gentle arms around her and led her pain-racked body elsewhere.

Eugene, standing in the Four Courts Rotunda after lunch listening to Molyneaux and Branagh discuss the morning's events, was still alternately tingling and going weak-kneed with blessed relief. What possessed that young man he could not say, nor did he care. He had to suppress the cry of jubilation that periodically rose to his throat ever since Joe uttered his famous, or infamous, *yes*.

Eugene was less pleased with his lawyers, though he managed to remain silent as they tut-tutted their disbelief that such perfidy as Joe Mahony's perjury was possible. He didn't accept that Joe's lie was a setback to their cause. Neither did he share the barristers' view that his wife's breakdown was the best thing that could have happened to their case. In fact, he felt like thumping them both in the ribs for causing it, or flattening their noses with a couple of belts of his fist. He did neither, of course, and when he took to the box himself to corroborate his wife's evidence, he answered counsel's questions as dutifully as if he bore the lawyer no grudge.

Afterwards, he sat with Aisling in the visitors' bench—she insisted on staying—and watched Eilis O'Connor walk gracefully to the witness box with the baby in her arms. The gall of that girl! *Their* baby, gorgeously dressed in a pink frock with pink shoes and a pink bow in her red hair. He saw Molyneaux shoot to his feet at the sight, and then abruptly sit again. Having just endured the ordeal himself, feeling nervous as a horse in a new stable all the while, Eugene grudgingly admired Eilis's poise as she replied to counsel's questions. Yes, she had given birth to the child she was now holding. Mary Kate kicked her feet and waved her arms and gurgled happily, as if to confirm her statement. Yes, before she became pregnant she had promised to have a baby and to give that baby up for adoption to her cousins, Aisling and Eugene Banaghan. At the word "adoption" Eugene exchanged a significant glance with his wife: so this was going to be the tactic.

Yes, Eilis admitted demurely, she had changed her mind. Could she tell the court why, Mr. Mullen asked ever so gently.

"First of all, I would like to apologize to my cousins, Aisling and Eugene, for the hurt I have caused them." She was looking up at them. "I dearly wish I could undo that hurt," she said in a voice that broke with emotion. Eugene felt the tightness in his throat, and he put his arm around Aisling as his wife wept quietly into her hand. "But I gradually found, as my pregnancy progressed, that I was growing so close to my child that the thought of having to part with her—to give her away, even to friends as dear to me as my cousins—was completely unbearable."

"Were you aware before you made the offer of adoption to your cousins that this attachment would occur?" The barrister's tone oozed sympathy.

"No. Not at all. I had no idea whatever. I knew about mother-love, of course—who doesn't?—and I certainly experienced it from my own mother. But I never thought until it happened to me with my own child that it could be so overwhelming." Eilis O'Connor then wept in the witness box, and hugged her baby tightly when Mary Kate wound tiny arms around her neck.

Eugene Banaghan, chagrined, could swear he heard a sigh of sympathy arise from the courtroom. "It's not fair," Aisling whispered. "She's using our baby to get pity from the judge."

After a decent pause to let Eilis recover her composure, Mullen continued. "People frequently give up things, even relationships, that are very dear to them in order to keep promises made to their friends. What is so special about this relationship you have with your daughter that you could not bear under any circumstances to part with her?"

"Because—because she is a part of me. I gave her life. She grew out of me, out of my very own flesh." Eilis's response had the slow drawn-out quality of an attempt to express the ineffable. "In my womb she could not exist without me, and out of it she still belongs with me." Mary Kate was standing on her lap, wriggling happily, arms outstretched as she tried to touch the back of the witness chair. "The Scripture describes the marriage bond as two in one flesh, which no one should set asunder. But an even more real two-in-one-flesh bond exists between mother and child. No one ought to put that asunder either." Her baby grabbed the chair and held on to it.

"What do you think would be the effect if your child were to be forcibly taken from you?"

Eugene found his cousin's ability to weep on cue distressing. "I'd feel mutilated. As if a part of my very own body had been cut off." Eilis dabbed a handkerchief to her eyes with one hand while holding on to Mary Kate with the other. "A baby is not separable from its mother during gestation. Neither is she suddenly separable as soon as she's born. Separation in either case would injure both mother and child."

"Are you saying, then, that giving up a newborn baby for adoption is wrong?" Just the slightest edge on Mullen's tone suggested he himself might not be entirely sympathetic to this line of argument. Eugene felt a burgeoning hope that perhaps Eilis had gone too far.

"Adoption is not necessarily wrong, no. It's like divorce, isn't it? It's a separation that ideally should not occur." Eugene sensed a perkiness now in her voice that said she was beginning to feel at ease with this examination. "It may be the lesser of two evils—for instance, when the mother is unable to care for her child—but it's still an evil."

Mullen ceded his witness to opposing counsel. "Miss O'Connor," Molyneaux held a single sheet of paper in his hand, "Do you believe women and men should have equal rights before the law?"

"Yes."

"So you believe women should not be discriminated against on the basis of their sex?"

"I do."

"And you would also hold, then, that women should be held accountable for their acts equally with men?"

"Yes."

"You're quite sure of that?"

"We're all equal before the law, aren't we?"

"Then you would agree, Miss O'Connor, that when a

woman makes a contract she ought to be held to it in the same way as a man who makes a contract?"

"If it's a valid contract, yes." Mary Kate, turning and spotting Molyneaux for the first time, let out a squawk and grabbed her mother tightly around the neck.

"Perhaps you'd even agree that *not* to hold women to the same standard as men with respect to contractual commitments would imply that women were not competent, by reason of their biological sex, to act as rational moral agents?"

"Men aren't always held to contractual agreements either. For instance, priests are allowed to resign now, and divorce is—"

"Just answer the question, yes or no, Miss O'Connor."

"I agree that women should not be held to a lesser standard than men." Slowly, carefully, each word weighed.

"So you would accept, then, that *you* should be held to the contract you made with your cousins to have a baby for them?"

"Objection." Mullen barely raised his voice.

"Rephrase," said the judge laconically.

Molyneaux bent and picked up his water bottle, drank slowly, put the bottle away. "No further questions."

"It was a terrible mistake altogether," Mr. Brennan fumed, "not to put me in the witness box."

"I did my best for you, Denis, you know that." Con Branagh shoveled another forkful of champ into his gob and savored it with tender appreciation. "This is great stuff, man. I'll tell you something: you won't find it this good anywhere else. I'd say it's better even than the missus makes."

"The most solid reasons why the child should be taken from that wretched girl, and they were never even mentioned. It makes my blood boil, Con. The strongest arguments are always the moral ones. Remember that." Mr. Brennan stabbed the air with a minatory fork. "Truth and rightness can never be gainsaid. The sanctity of the family. The moral welfare of the child. The unfitness of the unwed mother. These are the rocks on which a winning case should have been built." There were tears in the SPCM founder's eyes as he cut open his sole *Alla DiaVolo*. "And the bloody fellow never once brought them up."

"It wasn't for want of my trying, Denis. I laid them all out for him." Con chewed on his lamb chop. "But he wouldn't hear of presenting them." They were dining at Lord Edward's, and by unspoken agreement had avoided mentioning Joe Mahony's perjury.

"It's a travesty," Mr. Brennan lamented.

"'Mr. Justice Beirne,' the great Molyneaux said to me, 'is not a practicing Catholic. He may even be a Freemason. So it's worse than useless trying to convince him with arguments that have meaning only for the strong in faith and pure of heart.' That's what the bugger said, honest to God, Denis. 'You have to appeal to reason with the man on the bench, not to faith or morals,' he said. That was his argument for proceeding the way he did."

"Maybe you should have gone for a jury then."

"'Twas a toss-up on that. Molyneaux's argument was that the finer points of his case would be lost on a jury. 'Tis hard to say. Time will tell."

"The only reason I put myself into this case, Con, was to

strike a blow for the faith. Somebody has to stand up and proclaim God's message to the world. This wretched unfortunate lawyer—God forgive me, he's probably a decent man according to his lights—can say nothing better than that the law must recognize the validity of a surrogacy contract and enforce it. Well, I'll tell you this, Con, *I'm* against recognizing surrogacy contracts. To that extent I'm with the other side. I fully agree with their position that having a baby is a sacred activity and that it should be kept out of the marketplace. As their counsel said, even the godless French—and the Germans, too, for that matter—are in agreement that surrogacy treats babies as merchandise."

"I think we'll win all the same, Denis. The way I look at it is this: the judge either accepts that the surrogacy contract is valid and enforceable—in which case we win hands down. Or he decrees that it's not, which forces him to decide which of the parties is best for the child. The law says, you see, that the court must always regard the welfare of the child as the first and paramount consideration."

"It all has to do with Paisley and his ilk in the North."

Con Branagh halted his last forkful of champ midway between plate and mouth. "How's that now?"

"There was a time in this country," Mr. Brennan declaimed, "when it would have been sufficient to state that the whole question of surrogacy was profoundly contrary to the teaching of the Church's magisterium for an end to be put to the whole discussion. But not anymore. We're more concerned these days with accommodating ourselves to the feelings of heretics in the North of Ireland than we are to defending the eternal truths of Christendom."

"Ah, sure no one listens to the bishops anymore." Then,

spotting the glint of battle in Mr. Brennan's eye, Con Branagh added quickly, "But your point is well taken."

No one was more flabbergasted at Joe Mahony's perjury than Jamesie O'Malley. However, he was a model of legal propriety that evening among the assembled O'Connors. "What that young fellow did in the witness box certainly didn't hurt us," he allowed. "Though it's not clear that it did us any particular good either."

It was Bridget who raised the question everyone wanted to ask. "Why did he perjure himself?" She looked accusingly at her daughter. "Unless of course somebody got at him. Someone with a lot of influence."

Eilis's flash of anger gave a jolt of pleasure to Jamesie: she'd be well able to stand up to Eileen O'Malley. "Don't look at me, Mammy, I wouldn't dream of asking Joe to tell a lie."

"Did you talk to him afterwards?"

"I did not. He went straight out of the courtroom after he finished. And I haven't seen or heard of him since."

"Well 'tis worth a drink or two, anyway," Uncle Tom said from the sideboard.

"What happens next?" Aunt Nora asked. She was sitting briefly with the rest of them in the parlor while dinner was cooking.

"It's in the judge's hands now." Jamesie gazed adoringly at Eilis, who was sitting on the floor making silly noises at the baby. "He'll deliver his judgment three weeks from tomorrow."

"And we're going to win, you think?" Frank accepted a glass of Tullamore from his brother.

"We're in a better state than we were this time yesterday, I'd say. Between what Mahony said and the superb job herself here did on the stand, I think we have more than a fair chance." He smiled at Eilis.

"You were brilliant, Eilis," Frank said.

"I was terrified. That's what I was. Your mammy was scared out of her wits, so she was," she told her daughter.

"Well, it didn't show one bit."

"Why would it? Isn't she her mother's daughter?" There was an expression of pure pride on Bridget O'Connor's face.

The convivial atmosphere and the sight of Eilis playing with Mary Kate brought marriage and family to the forefront of Jamesie's thoughts. He had kept the subject at bay while his mind was on court; now it was time to focus on it once more. So he stayed on, into the evening, and when Eilis came downstairs after putting the baby to bed he asked if she'd like to go for a walk.

"I'd love to," she said.

The street lamps were dim but the moon was bright. A good omen: what better setting for a man to propose. He bided his time, leaving the talking to her, till they reached the end of the street and the sea was below them, glistening a jagged white in the moonlight. They stopped in the middle of the road to enjoy it. "Marry me," he said abruptly. It wasn't the way he imagined or planned it, but that was how it came out.

"Don't be daft." Her reply as swift and blunt as his plea. Followed by her tinkling laugh that had so beguiled him at their first encounter.

"I am no such thing daft. I'm proposing marriage to you. What's so daft about that?"

"Oh Jamesie! You're brilliant. Everyone knows that. But right now you must admit you're being rather foolish." She turned and walked a few paces down the road, then stopped, folded her arms, and stared anew at the water.

He followed. "What's foolish about asking you to marry me?" His hands were cold, so he stuck them into his trouser pockets.

She was silent for a while. "I'd be a terrible burden to you, Jamesie, and I don't want to be that."

"You mean because of Mary Kate? Now you're the one who's being foolish. I love Mary Kate, as you well know, and I'll adopt her and treat her as if I were her biological father."

"It's not just Mary Kate. There's this whole court business and all the things that were said about me by the media. You wouldn't want a wife you'd be ashamed of every time you were seen in public with her." She shook her head as if to ward off a swarm of flies. "I couldn't do that to you. It wouldn't—"

"Yerra stop, will you!" The discipline snapped and his emotions took over. "I don't give a witch's curse what people say or think." His hands shot out from his pockets, grasped her by the shoulders, and turned her to him. "Do you think I haven't thought about all this? Well let me tell you I have, and thought about it a lot. And I still want you to marry me." He took in a great gulp of air: "I love you, Eilis O'Connor." Then, stunned by the enormity of what he had said, he let her go, folded his arms, and stared unseeing out to sea.

Waves crashed unheeded on the rocks below. Traffic

rumbled in the distance. But from Jamesie and Eilis no
sound came forth. Until she spoke eons later, half in
defiance, half in despair. "I love you, too, Jamesie O'Malley.
So if you want me you can have me."

Oh God! Had he heard right? The tone meant nothing,
only the assent. She had assented, hadn't she? He grabbed
her and hugged her and kissed her, with all the aplomb of a
neophyte lawyer grappling with an unfamiliar tort.

Mr Justice Niall Beirne delivered judgment in *Banaghan
vs. O'Connor* on Monday, March 23, 1998. His decision was
lengthy and learned and, he said at the outset, had been most
difficult to arrive at. This was due, his lordship noted, as
much to the lack of precedent in Irish law—or indeed, for
that matter, in English, European, or American law—as to
the harrowing consequences for those concerned.

The justice said he would begin by summarizing the
evidence presented. What he read then, in clear well-clipped
words and utterly dispassionate tone, was a rather long
meticulous narrative that Jamesie O'Malley, listening
intently in the visitors' gallery, had to admit was an
outstanding and succinctly put statement of the facts of the
case. When his lordship paused briefly at the end of his
narration of facts to sip water from his glass, Jamesie
whispered to Eilis, "Now he's going to discuss the law.
That's the important stuff."

In the matter of law, Mr. Justice Beirne said, there were
no specific statutes in Irish law that dealt with surrogate
contracts or indeed with anything relating to surrogate
motherhood. Neither were there any judicial precedents in
the matter. The only precedent in English law was a statute

that forbade agencies to arrange surrogacy contracts but did not forbid individuals to do so. In the absence of specific law or precedent, therefore, he must find a solution in more general principles of law that related to the subject matter.

The plaintiffs' case hinged on whether what they called a surrogacy contract, which they entered into with the defendant, could be construed to be a valid application of general contract law. If it were, then a valid contract might exist and the defendant could be obligated to deliver her child to the plaintiffs.

Jamesie heard Eilis's anguished intake of air as she grabbed his arm for support.

He, the justice, was of the opinion that the essential elements of a contract existed in this case. However, even where there was a presumption that a contract was *prima facie* in existence, events might occur either at the time of contracting or afterwards that would render it unenforceable or void. A void contract, even though it complied with the formative prerequisites, was one that never legally existed because of a particular aggravating factor. An example would be a contract whose purpose was to perform an illegal act. This situation had specific relevance to the case at issue. The legality of the act that was the subject of the contract had to be called into question in making a decision as to whether the contract was enforceable. He determined, however, that since neither the Constitution nor the statutes dealt with surrogate motherhood, the act which was the subject of the contract could not be illegal.

Eilis groaned. Jamesie took her hand and squeezed it.

However, Mr. Justice Beirne continued, a contract could be void at common law without being invalid. Such was the case with contracts that were against the public interest; for example, contracts that were in restraint of trade or which prejudiced marriage.

The tight squeeze of her hand so overcame him that he almost lost concentration on the *res judicanda*.

It was this latter ground which most concerned Mr. Justice Beirne in the present case. Article 41 of the Constitution stated that "The State pledges itself to guard with special care the institution of Marriage, on which the Family is founded, and to protect it against attack." So the question at issue was whether an act of surrogate motherhood prejudiced marriage. His lordship held that it did, for the following reasons: the family, founded on marriage, was the home of the child, both by nature and by law. The guardians of the child were the natural parents, who bore full responsibility for the upbringing of their offspring. Children had the right to be reared and nurtured by those who brought them into the world. Only by way of exception, when the parents failed in, or were unable to perform, their duty to their children did the law permit that responsibility to devolve upon others.

Eilis gave one final squeeze to Jamesie's hand before withdrawing hers.

The concept of surrogate motherhood ran completely counter to those principles, the justice continued. Its specific objective was the conception and birthing of a child with the explicit intention of handing over responsibility for its upbringing to a third party. This was not in the best interests of the child, who had an inalienable right to be nurtured and cared for by its natural parents. Therefore it was not in the public interest to condone or in any way to legitimize the practice of surrogate motherhood. For these reasons he held that the contract entered into between the plaintiffs and the defendant was void because its subject was contrary to the public interest.

Eilis clutched his arm and squeezed till Jamesie imagined the blood flowing from the sharp pressure of her nails through jacket and shirt sleeves.

There remained, the justice continued, the determination of which placement was in the child's best interest in this particular case. He quoted from the Guardianship of Infants Act of 1964: *Wherever in any proceedings before any court the custody, guardianship or upbringing of an infant is in question, the court, in deciding the question, shall regard the welfare of the infant as the first and paramount consideration.* He, Justice Beirne, had thought long and hard about this aspect of the case under adjudication. He had agonized over it. It was his decision to make, and a most difficult decision it was. The law could help him, but the law dealt only with general principles, not with the specifics of the case at hand.

It was his decision, then, after mature deliberation, that the best interests of this child would be served if it remained in the custody of the defendant, her natural mother.

Treachery

Michael Heaney was stopped at a traffic light Tuesday evening on his way home from work in Spiddal when the pair crossed the road in front of him. Frank O'Connor and a woman, and they holding hands. A fine-looking woman she was, too, he just had time to notice before they disappeared through the door of a restaurant.

So Bridget was right was the thought that drummed in his head the rest of the way home. He was barely inside the door of his flat when the phone rang. "How are you, Bridget. It's so nice to hear your voice. I was just about to ring you as a matter of fact. I saw the verdict in the paper this morning and I was thrilled for you all." Babbling at a terrible rate to cover the vast discombobulation of his mind at that moment.

"We're all very pleased, of course." Though her matter-of-fact tone hardly suggested elation. "It was a most distressing business altogether and we're grateful that it's finally over and done with."

"Indeed."

"The *really* good news is that Eilis has got herself engaged. At last. To Jamesie O'Malley, if you don't mind. And I always thinking she'd marry Joe."

"I'm delighted to hear it."

"Of course it's past time for her to settle down, Michael, as you and I have often said; especially with the baby. And

Jamesie's a fine man, with a good future."

"Well, isn't it wonderful."

"So we're having a little dinner here on Thursday evening to celebrate the two occasions, and we'd be most pleased if you'd join us."

For the next two days he was counting the hours, when he wasn't stewing over what to do about that vision of Frank and the woman. He owed it to Bridget to tell her, didn't he? Well she certainly had a right to know. What kind of man was Frank anyway to be unfaithful to a woman like Bridget? Good God Almighty, what he himself wouldn't give to have...If he told her, of course, who knew what she might do? She had mentioned the possibility of two playing that game. Even talked about throwing Frank out.

On the other hand, telling her might be playing with fire: slay the messenger sort of thing. She'd definitely be traumatized, and might possibly blame Michael Heaney, at least in part, for her pain. Thursday evening driving down the Headford road he made his decision: *keep your big mouth shut, Heaney; blabbing would do more harm than good.* The O'Connors were delighted to see him, they said. It was the first time he had seen all the children together. Marie stood with arms akimbo overseeing Mary Kate crawling. Eilis relaxed on the sofa next to a self-conscious-looking Jamesie O'Malley. The rest of the younger generation sat on the carpet.

Bridget welcomed him with a warmth that set his whole body tingling. But her smile quickly vanished when her husband said, "How about a drink, Michael?"

"Frank!" Her scowl was as dark as a rainy sky.

"I meant a mineral, of course." Frank grinned and

Michael smiled back, though he felt like thundering *adulterer* at the fellow.

When they were all seated at the dining room table, Bridget said, "Would you please say grace for us, Michael?"

He felt embarrassed: he hadn't led a public prayer since he left Kildawree. "Bless us, O Lord, and these Thy gifts, which of Thy bounty we are about to receive. Through Christ Our Lord."

"Amen," the family responded.

As soon as they blessed themselves Frank was on his feet. "I'd like to propose a toast to the happy couple." He had obviously been toasting himself for some time, though his speech was in no way affected. "I'd like especially to welcome our future son-in-law to the family. It's a great pleasure for us all, Jamesie, I can tell you, to have you among us. We know you'll take good care of our little girl, and our granddaughter, too."

"Some little girl," Ciaran jeered.

"Shut up, Ciaran," Marie said. She was holding Mary Kate on her lap. The baby grabbed a fork and banged a plate.

"Now, children," Bridget said. "Politeness, please."

Jamesie raised his glass. "I'd like to toast my new family. I feel honored to—"

That was when the phone rang in the hall. Niamh went dashing out.

"I feel honored," Jamesie repeated, "to be accepted into such a wonderful clan."

"Wait till you get to know us," Ultan chirped. "Trying to get out you'll be then."

Niamh came flying back in and scrunched her way the length of the table behind the chairs to reach her mother and whisper in her ear. Michael, sitting next to Bridget, caught only the name *Eugene*. But that was enough to cause him intestinal fibrillation as Bridget rose and left the room.

Bridget, too, was disturbed. Whatever it was that Eugene wanted to say was surely not going to be pleasant. On Monday after the verdict when she and Frank had come face to face with the Banaghans in the Rotunda of the Four Courts, hatred had twisted Eugene's face into an ugly sneer. "Ye'll live to regret it," he shouted at them before taking Aisling by the arm and stalking off.

She picked up the receiver. "Hello," as politely as she could manage. If there was to be unpleasantness she would not be the one to initiate it.

"Good evening to you, Bridget." His voice was slurred.

"Hello, Eugene." She couldn't keep the disdain from her tone: she hated drunks.

"I heard ye were shelebrating this evening, so I thought I'd give ye something else to shelebrate."

"Indeed." She barely refrained from hanging up on him.

"Listen to this now, Mrs. O'Connor. Do you know what your fecking husband is up to?"

"Eugene, you're drunk. Go away and sleep it off." She would have hung up then, but his question held her. *In vino veritas* sort of thing.

"I'll tell you what he's fecking up to: he's up in Galway cavorting with a tart, that's what he's doing. Her name is Julia. Are you listening to me, Bridget? I know it for a fact because I met them in a restaurant up there."

"Goodbye, Eugene."

But before she could go he shot back, "Your daughter saw

them, too. Fecking Eilis was with me the day we met them. And they holding hands like a pair of lovers. Ask Eilis if you don't believe me." Then drunken Eugene Banaghan, having delivered his bomb, hung up on her.

She remained in the hall, transfixed, clutching the phone, limbs shaking, nausea sweeping over her, unable to think, while she underwent the sharp piercing pain of the deceived. The cheerful chatter of the dinner table wafted out the half-open dining room door, heedless of the calamity that had just befallen this home she had built on peace and love. She shook herself, like a duck shaking off rain, and walked steadily down the hall into their bedroom. *Their* bedroom, hers and Frank's. Well, it wouldn't be his for long, you could be sure of that. This very minute she was going back into the dining room to break his neck and send him packing. She would, too. She would. She would. The nerve of him! After all she had done for him. No consolation to know she had suspected this for the longest time. Suspecting and knowing were worlds apart, weren't they? When you only suspected you could say maybe it wasn't so. Now she could no longer pretend. The only question was what to do. Go right in this minute and make a scene in front of everyone? Was that what she should do? No. Unfortunately, no. Her pride would not permit that. Anyway, he'd deny it; Frank was the great denier. Wait till she questioned Eilis. If it was the case that she knew all along…That little trollop—after all she had done for her. The least she owed her mother was to tell her. Drunken Eugene had mentioned a restaurant. She'd love to catch them there. Then he couldn't wriggle out of it, could he? That was it: surprise them in the act. Then there could be no denying. Calm down now, Bridget; you're your mother's daughter. You can handle this in a sane, cool, rational, manner. Walk straight back into that dining room as if nothing had happened. Smile and be a devil and bide your time.

Which she did. Sweet as pie to Frank all evening. Not a cross word to any of her children, not even when Niamh and Marie fought over who would put Mary Kate to bed, or when Ultan and Terry told a couple of off-color jokes. But when at nine o'clock the future son-in-law looked at his watch and said it was time they went home they had to go to work tomorrow, she took Eilis by the hand in motherly fashion, excused herself to Jamesie and Michael, walked her out of the parlor, down the hall into the bedroom, and shut the door. "Let's sit on the bed and keep our voices down. I have a very personal question to ask you."

"Oh Mammy! We're not living together if that's what's bothering you. We decided to wait till—"

"It's not *your* living arrangements I'm concerned with, it's your father's." She pitched her voice so as to be just audible to Eilis, though she felt like screaming for the entire parish to hear. "That was Eugene Banaghan on the phone during dinner. He rang to tell me that you and he were together in a restaurant in Galway and that you saw your father there with another woman. Holding hands. Julia, he said her name was." Though she already knew the answer from Eilis's expression, she asked the question anyway. "Is this true?"

"So what are you going to do?" Eilis spoke in the resigned tone of one accustomed to disaster.

"Why didn't you tell me?"

"Mammy! What would *you* have done if you were in my

shoes?"

Bridget felt the tears coming on but refused to allow them control. "I don't think I can live with him after this. Dear God, why did You do this to me?" Then she surrendered to her emotions and let her daughter hold her.

A knock at the door disturbed her grieving. "Jamesie wants to know when will you be ready, Eilis?" Niamh shouted.

"Five minutes. And don't disturb me again, Niamh."

Bridget dried her eyes with a tissue from her sleeve. "Sorry. I hate being the weak woman crying."

Eilis stroked her hair. "You were never a weak woman, Mammy, and I doubt if you ever will be." They both had to smile at that. "Don't be too hard on Daddy. Just tie him up in the cattle shed with a chain and feed him silage for the next six months."

Bridget couldn't smile this time. "I don't know what I'll do yet. But don't you go telling him anything tonight, do you hear?"

"No, Mammy, I won't."

After her guests had left, she told Terry to take charge of the cleaning-up, returned to her bedroom without saying a word to Frank, and locked the door. She wasn't long in bed before he was trying to get in. "Bridget? The door is locked."

"Go sleep somewhere else. I need to be alone."

She didn't get up in the morning till she knew the children were all away. Frank was sitting at the table cracking the top off a boiled egg when she came into the kitchen. "What was that all about last night?" he asked without looking up from his task.

"You'll know soon enough." She poured a cup of tea

from the pot on the stove, sat across from him, put in sugar and milk, stirred with the sugar spoon—a breach of etiquette for which she had often rebuked her children—and sipped slowly and deliberately. She didn't so much as glance at him, though she could feel his eyes on her as he scraped the eggshell and buttered slices of brown bread. After drinking half the cup she said, "That was Eugene Banaghan on the phone last night during dinner."

"Was it indeed? Inviting us over for tea, no doubt."

"He told me about Julia."

"Who's Julia?" The tone of an honestly puzzled man.

"Don't, Frank." It was all she could do not to throw the remainder of her tea in his face. "I got it out of Eilis, too." The clock on the shelf over the stove ticked loudly, a sound she hadn't noticed for years. "Why did you do it?" Her voice even, she was determined to avoid histrionics. When minutes went by and he didn't reply she added, "Wasn't I enough for you? Wasn't it enough to have your family and your farm and all your cursed money, that you had to go and do this?"

"The things you have are never enough." He said it in the tone of a man communing with himself. "Sure even you must feel that now and again."

"No, I do not feel that. I have learned to be content with what I have and not to go scavenging for what I shouldn't have."

"We're all different, I suppose. Some of us *do* need something else."

The touch of grievance in his voice brought a rush of anger that she barely suppressed. "So you went and got it."

"Listen," he said, in the wheedling tone she knew so

well. "We all have a need for what we can't have. It's part of our nature, for God's sake. Forbid us something and we'll do it. It's always been the way in human history. Look at Adam and Eve even; and you can't go back farther than that."

"I suppose in a minute you'll be telling me that what you did was positively virtuous?"

"I won't go that far, no. But let me ask you this: didn't you ever feel the urge to wander a bit yourself? I'm serious. There have been times when honest to God I wished you would. 'Twould have done you a world of good, instead of always being the perfect wife and mother whose goodness no one can match."

The infinite gall of the man! She got up from the table and walked to the back door lest she throw her cup at him. She opened the door and stood staring unseeing out across fields turned newly green, not moving when she heard his footsteps behind her.

"I'm sorry now I did it." The spurious contrition of the recidivist in his tone. "For all the world I wouldn't want to harm you and the children."

She turned and faced him. "You only want what you can't have? Is that the way it is with you? Well, now you *can* have her. So let's see how long you'll want her." She took in a deep breath and closed her eyes. "I'm going into Ballinamore now to do some shopping. Be out of the house by the time I come back."

When she returned, Marie and Niamh were home from school. "Where's Daddy?" her youngest asked.

"He's gone to Galway and he won't be back for a while." She put away the groceries and then rang Michael Heaney.

"I'll be in Galway for the weekend," she told that delighted man. "And I was hoping you might be free."

It was lunchtime at Kildawree National School. Children were shouting and running and playing basketball in the playground. Aisling Banaghan was heating homemade soup in the microwave in the administration room when the phone rang. "This is Frank O'Connor," the voice at the other end said. Her instinctive reaction was to hang up. But he immediately added, "I've got something important to tell you." There was an edge to his tone that suggested she better listen.

"Yes?" The pent-up bitterness of the past eight months compressed into a single word.

"Your husband has just done to me the dirtiest, foulest thing that one man can do to another." The anger and the self-pity came clearly across the phone line.

"Good. I'm glad. You'll get no sympathy from me." Keeping her voice low because her two fellow teachers were in the room.

"Well I thought you might like to know this: your saintly Eugene is the father of my grandchild. So put that in your pipe and smoke it." Frank O'Connor laughed harshly and hung up.

Maybe the shock would come later, but at that moment she felt hardly anything. The suspicion had long since entered her mind. She retrieved her soup from the microwave and began to eat. It all made sense: Eugene's wild reaction to the prospect of Joe denying paternity in court, and his obvious relief when the fellow didn't. His rejection of her suggestion that they appeal and have tests made to determine if Joe were really the father. 'Twould do no good at all, he claimed, only involve them in more expense and hurt to themselves.

She ought to be devastated at this confirmation of her suspicion, for she had no doubt that Frank O'Connor was telling the truth. However, her pain was for the moment subsumed by the positive possibilities that Eugene's infidelity had opened up. Best thing for her to do was see Branagh. Straight away, before she even talked to Eugene. She didn't like the solicitor, but he knew the case. She finished her soup and when the others left the room she rang and made an appointment to see him at four.

"We surely have grounds for appeal now, haven't we?" she put to Con Branagh, after suffering the acute embarrassment of telling him what Frank O'Connor had said.

The solicitor leaned back in his chair and joined his hands over his bloated belly. "I doubt very much, Mrs. Banaghan, if we'll even need to appeal." He smiled at her. "We've now got what the Yanks call the smoking gun. And by God we'll use it."

She was halfway home before she remembered that she had yet to confront Eugene for cheating on her. The proposal Branagh had made was so simple and so devastating that it had literally taken her breath away. She was going to get her baby after all. For this she might even forgive her rotten stinking husband. But only after she had put him through the wringer of contrition and remorse.

When Eilis told her mother she wasn't living with her fiancé she implied that she was refraining from sex. She had no intention of abstaining, however. Ever since promising to marry Jamesie she had been lambasting herself for her less-than-enthusiastic response to his proposal, and she had been trying to make up for that failure with warm displays of affection every time they got together. But it wasn't till after the engagement party that she plucked up the courage to suggest making love. Jamesie, for his part, seemed so happy with her attention that he not only never pressed her on that issue, but neither by word or act did he even hint at consummation. Which reticence itself served to fuel Eilis's already smoldering desires. So when on Friday night after they'd been to a movie and picked up Mary Kate from Mrs. McDonough on the way home and she'd invited him in for a cup of tea and managed to get her daughter to sleep without too much trouble, she felt in the mood for more than kissing.

"I love you, Jamesie O'Malley," she told him as they smooched on the sofa.

"Me, too." He was nibbling her lower lip. "I mean," corrected the lawyer, "I too love you."

"I especially love your earlobe." At which point she bit that rather useless appendage. From there she proceeded to chew on his chin, undo his red tie—the ever-correct solicitor had gone to the pictures wearing a suit—loosen his collar, remove his jacket, and unbutton his shirt. Next she untucked his undershirt, ran her hands up his torso, pushed the man down on the sofa, straddled his hips, licked his nipples, and tugged playfully with her teeth at the hair on his chest. Then she pulled the sleeves of his shirt till his arms came out, got the undershirt over his head, and triumphantly kissed him, her tongue caressing his.

"You're something else," he gasped when she at length pulled back.

"I haven't started yet." She slid off the sofa and knelt on the floor, removed his shoes and socks, unzipped his fly, yanked off pants and briefs, gently grasped his erected phallus and covered it with her mouth. Professor O'Flaherty had tutored her well.

"Ohmygod!" Jamesie's moans kept pace with the pleasure. "You better stop or it's going to be all over." He pulled himself up and quickly, with her help, removed her clothes. "Are we safe?" he queried as she slid beneath him.

Sanity intervened. "Oh my God, no!" Though she could hardly bear to wait, neither did she want another baby yet. "In my purse. Give me my purse, will you, quick."

He leaned sideways and grabbed it off the floor. She delved long and impatiently from flat on her back, before finding the packet of condoms. When he seemed inexpert at putting the thing on she took it from him and slid it into place. After that she remembered only the waves of pleasure that passed all understanding.

They scarcely had time to talk Monday morning, other than about business matters. Preparatory work on two lawsuits, the finalizing of a couple of wills, review of a contract to renovate a church in Connemara kept them both busy. Sometime after eleven Jamesie stopped at her door to chat. "I rang Mammy last night and told her the good news."

"You mean about Friday night? Did you give her all the delicious details?"

"No, silly." He cupped her face in his hands and kissed her. "About our engagement."

"And?" Eileen O'Malley had been cool to her as Jamesie's friend even before the notoriety of the court case. So what glacial response would she make to her son's *engagement* to this disreputable woman?

"She wasn't exactly thrilled, I have to tell you that. But I told her firmly that this is the way it's going to be and that she might as well accept it. Do you know, it was the first time I've ever seriously stood up to Mammy."

"Good man yourself."

The phone rang. Mr. Branagh, to speak with Mr. O'Malley. She put the call through to his office. Solicitors were forever talking to each other: yesterday's adversary was today's advisor. But when Jamesie returned to her doorway a couple of minutes later with the solemn face of the bad-news bearer, her heart gave an extra thump.

"Is there something wrong?"

"He wants to meet with us. You and me and the Banaghans and himself. Something new has come up, he said."

She closed her eyes. "Will we ever be done with this? Are they going to appeal, do you think?"

"Branagh was tight as a miser's fist, which means he has something up his sleeve. All he'd say was it'll be in our best interest to come to his office tomorrow at ten."

She worried all day, fretted all evening, and slept poorly that night. In the morning they left Eyre Square at a quarter past nine and at three minutes after ten found a parking spot just a few doors from Con Branagh's office in Glebe Street, Ballinamore. The Banaghans were there before them. Eugene didn't even look up, but Aisling's stiff nod seemed to Eilis fraught with the foreboding of triumph.

"There's been a new development." Branagh from behind his desk surveyed his audience with all the élan of a frog on a lily pad.

"That's why we're here, I gather," Jamesie acknowledged dryly.

"That it is. We have just learned the identity of Mary Kate's father."

Eilis's heart began pumping on the double, but her mind refused to function. Only vaguely was she aware of Branagh's stare. She heard Jamesie say, "That's hardly news, Con: a man called Joe Mahony already confessed to it in court, if you remember."

"Well, it wasn't him." Branagh came to sudden life, as if the frog had spotted a dragonfly. "It was *him!*" Pointing dramatically at Eugene, who sat motionless with shoulders hunched and head cast down.

"Nice try, Con." Jamesie seemed unfazed; Eilis clung to the arms of her chair against the terrible urge to get up and run. "But if Eilis says it was Joe and Joe says it was Joe, you don't have too much to go on, do you?"

"Eugene Banaghan is ready to give blood to prove his paternity. As you well know, Jamesie, there are such things nowadays as DNA tests that can settle the issue. Issue? Ha, ha! So is your Joe Mahony willing to do the same?"

She had to hand it to her fiancé: unflappable in the face of checkmate. "Let's suppose for a moment—mind you, we're not admitting a thing—but just let us imagine that due to some preposterous error of juxtaposed test tubes it was decided that Eugene Banaghan and not Joe Mahony was the father of Mary Kate. Do you think that piece of information would make the slightest difference to the judgment delivered? Look at the facts: Eilis O'Connor was proven to be a fit mother and was given custody of her child on that basis, whereas the best that can be said for Eugene Banaghan now is that he is an adulterous father who failed to acknowledge his paternity at the trial when he had every opportunity to do so. You wouldn't even get leave to appeal on those grounds."

Eilis searched Branagh's face for signs of discomfiture, but found none. All the while Jamesie was speaking he retained his half-smile, suggestive of hidden resources to which *they* weren't yet privy. "I don't quite agree with you. Though it might be a close call, I do think we'd have a fair shot at winning. However," settling back in his chair and joining hands as if in prayer, "for other reasons, which I'll outline for you now, you may decide that you don't want to let the case go that far."

No more, please. *Gran, I hope you're listening to all this. You troublemaker.*

"We're all agog," Jamesie said.

"One fallout from this new evidence is that we can now prove Joe Mahony committed perjury." He switched his frog-stare to Eilis. "Which means your very good friend will end up in jail, sharing an overcrowded cell with murderers and crackheads. Which is too bad indeed: he seems such a nice refined fellow. Good-looking, too; just the kind that some of those Mountjoy perverts would love to get their hands on." His smile set her teeth on edge. "And all because he tried to help *you*."

She looked at Jamesie. Was Branagh bluffing, just trying to frighten her? She found no comfort in her fiancé's solemn mien. "All pure speculation, Con," Jamesie said. But she missed the confident tone of his earlier arguments. "Even if you did prove perjury it would *not* be likely to affect the final judgment. You know that as well as I do."

Branagh waved a hand as if brushing off a fly. "Not the issue anymore, Jamesie. Not the issue. The real question now is whether Eilis O'Connor is willing to let Joe Mahony go to jail. That's what we're talking about here." He gave Eilis the frog's eye again. "Would you have your best friend wind up in Mountjoy?"

"Don't answer that," Jamesie said.

Branagh supported his chin in his hands. "The position of the plaintiffs is the following: if you sign adoption papers for Mary Kate they'll refrain from revealing Joe Mahony's crime. Conversely, if you don't sign adoption papers they *will* expose his perjury."

Her hands held dead-man's grip on the chair. She must not show emotion: the matter was too serious for tears or histrionics. But there had to be a way out. If only her brain would function. Jamesie got to his feet. "We'll take your remarks under advisement, Mr. Branagh, and give you our answer in due course."

"Right. But don't take too long." Branagh glanced up at

Eilis. "The plaintiffs are agreeable to wait one week for your reply, but not a minute longer."

"What am I going to do?" Her paralyzed brain was coming to life again as they drove through Kildawree on the way back to Galway.

"I'd suggest that we not even talk about it yet. Let's just do our work and let it percolate for a few hours."

"For God's sake, Jamesie. Do you think I'll be able to concentrate on a single other thing for the rest of the day? Or the next week, for that matter?" She looked crossly at him. "Do you even care?"

His left hand dropped from the wheel and took hers. "You have no idea how much I care, my love. For you *and* Mary Kate. But I've learned a bit over the years from clients who are hit with dilemmas that involve the emotions. They can't even begin to discuss them until they've had time to let the problem sink in."

At five o'clock he walked into her office. "How about Paddy Burke's?"

"Paddy Burke's what?" Cantankerous, her mind exhausted, her emotions drained.

"Restaurant, of course. What better place for some good grub? And then we can discuss our problem."

"I suppose." Although hungry—she had skipped lunch in her misery—she didn't feel much like eating; it would take a miracle, not food, to ease the gnawing in her stomach. "I'll have to see if Mrs. McDonagh can mind Mary Kate, and then I'll have to go and feed her." The baby cried when she walked in the door. "Yes, you missed your mammy, my precious." She had to restrain her tears in the presence of stolid Dearbhla McDonagh. She nursed Mary Kate in the small parlor, then held her tightly and rocked her and sang to her and cried softly as the child wriggled and twisted on her lap.

Jamesie picked her up at seven. They sat in Paddy Burke's bar—she had a mineral, he a large whiskey—and examined the menu slowly and studiously till their table was ready. Their conversation was casual, desultory, and without mention of the morning's bombshell. After a plate of oysters she started to thaw just a bit. With the salad the pain became somewhat muted. The beef entrée and a glass of wine helped to lighten her depression. Dessert and coffee left her feeling that just maybe she'd survive.

"Okay," he said, draining his after-dinner cognac. "Shoot."

"Shoot who?" She had become so unused to alcohol that the wine made her feel giddy.

"What do you want to do?"

The horror came flooding back, over the euphoric dikes of dinner and Cabernet. "I've thought about nothing else all day, but I'm still no closer to an answer."

He squeezed her hand. "Here's a technique I've found often works: describe your options and the consequences of taking each one."

She thought for a bit. "Well, I can thumb my nose at them and say go to hell. Of course then Joe will go to jail. I don't know if I could live with that."

"That's one option."

"The only other one I can think of is to give up Mary Kate. I can't do that either."

"Tell me *why* you can't."

"Didn't we go into all that for the court case?"

"Why do I think you didn't tell everything then?" His adoring gaze held just a trace of Bridget O'Connor's inquisitiveness.

She'd been too embarrassed to tell him about Gran—his logical mind would have scorned her story of a voice from the grave. But he had to know about Gran's wishes now in order to help resolve this dilemma. So she told him about the letter and her conversations with her dead grandmother. All the while he held her hand across the table, giving no hint whatever of belief or disbelief in her preposterous story. "But what I said in court is also true," she said in conclusion.

"I believe you."

"So what should I do?"

He squeezed her hand tighter. "I can't advise you what to do. You understand the issues. *You* must make the decision." That night in bed the feeling came to her that he'd prefer she relinquished her child.

"You want my opinion?" Mairead said the following evening when Eilis rang her.

"You're the wisest woman I know, Ms. Conneely. What does your crystal ball say?"

"I know you like Joe a lot—and what's not to like: if he had different sexual preferences I might have gone after him myself. However, that's neither here nor there. When it comes to choosing between Joe and your child I don't see that there can be any contest. You didn't *ask* him to commit perjury. That was his choice. So you don't owe it to him to give up your child to save him from the consequences of his own free act."

Her father rang ten minutes later. "You sound terrible, Daddy." He was sporting that sad-sack tone of despair he adopted whenever he caught the flu. "Are you all right?"

"I'm not all right; I'll never be all right again."

Oh God! Was it cancer? His heart? The liver? She always did say he drank too much. "What's the matter?"

"Your mother found out, that's what's the matter. And do you know who did it to me?" Despair giving way to fury. "Fecking blasted Eugene. He rang her the night you were down for dinner. So she threw me out." A sound suspiciously like a sob emanated from the other end.

She considered retorting *you can't say you didn't deserve it.* Instead she asked, "So what are you going to do?" He was silent so long she thought the line had gone dead. "Are you still there, Daddy?"

"She laid down some terrible conditions for taking me back." The petulant tone of a boy complaining he had been grounded.

She wanted to laugh, despite her own misery. "You're lucky she's taking you back at all."

"I can't see Julia anymore."

"Well, that sounds perfectly reasonable."

"And I'm not to be allowed to go anywhere by myself, she says."

"You'll be like a dog on a leash, won't you? And she'll choke you if you take two steps ahead of her. Maybe she'll learn to trust you eventually. In ten or twenty years or so."

"She said I owe it to Michael Heaney that she's taking me back at all. Do you have any idea what she meant by that?"

"I think I do, but I'm not going to tell you."

"God blast that lousy bastard anyway."

"Daddy! Michael Heaney has done nothing to you. On the contrary…"

"I'm talking about fecking Eugene Banaghan. I just hope his wife does the same thing to him."

A suspicion so stupefying as to curl her toes invaded Eilis's brain. "Daddy, you didn't…? Oh sainted mother of God!"

"Didn't what?"

"Someone told Aisling about Eugene and me. It was you, wasn't it?"

"Ah now Eilis, you don't think…" But the wheedling tone gave him away.

"Thank you very much, Daddy. Because of you I'm about to lose my baby." She rang off and cried.

RESOLUTION

Saturday morning was bleak and wet. Eilis put on her galoshes and raincoat, dressed Mary Kate in winter garb, grabbed her big black umbrella, and drove down to Kildawree. The clouds hung low, a dense mist swept over the stone-walled fields, the wind sighed in the tall perimeter trees; it was a setting worthy of *Kitty the Hare*. She stood before the grave, holding her child. Sharp-edged lettering stood out on the new black marble headstone:

MARY McGREEVY
KILDUFF, KILDAWREE
1916-1997
TEACHTA DALA, 1972-1984
MINISTER OF STATE, 1976-1982

KITTY TARRAGH
KILDUFF, KILDAWREE
1909-1997

R.I.P.

"Do you hear me, Gran?" she shouted, after looking around to make sure there was no one else in the graveyard.

I've made a right horse's collar of it for you, haven't I, a gradh?

"For such a nice woman, you can certainly create terrible turmoil." Remembering the Gran stories she had grown up hearing: Gran having her baby out of wedlock, Gran dressing down the Archbishop in church, Gran kneeling for a week in the rain at the Feericks' door until Grandma Rita forgave her for seducing Grandpa Wattie. "I'm sorry, Gran. Sorry. I shouldn't speak to you like that."

But 'tis true for you, a stor. I've never made life easy for my friends.

"What am I going to do at all? I have to keep my baby, and I can't let Joe go to jail."

I suppose I could make do with Aisling and Eugene. After all, they are relations. I think that would please Wattie, too, wherever he is.

"What about me? How do you think I'd feel about giving up my beautiful Mary Kate?"

I'm so terribly sorry, a stor. If I had foreseen all this at the beginning… Unfortunately, I don't have any better vision in my present state than in the last one.

"So you want me to give Mary Kate to the Banaghans?"

What I want to do, a gradh, is release you from your obligation to me. And I do. Joe is a decent lad; I liked him the few times we met. So you make up your mind now without worrying about your Gran.

Eilis cried. Mary Kate whimpered. "I love you, Gran. I'll never give you up."

Don't say never, a stor. I learned from my years in politics that you can compromise on almost anything when you have to. I often said that to you, too, if you remember?

"*You* make the decision," Jamesie had said. And she'd

have to. Anyway, it would be unfair to involve him. It was an impossible choice. Who did she love more, her baby or Joe? She'd have to choose her child, of course. But then, was she asking the right question? Shouldn't it be: *who would suffer more*? Shouldn't the comparison be *Joe in jail* versus *Mary Kate with the Banaghans and Eilis bereft*? Mary Kate herself would cry for a bit, but she'd get used to Aisling and Eugene, and they'd certainly take the very best care of her. In which case the issue came down to *Joe in jail* versus *Eilis bereft*. So who do you love more, yourself or Joe? How could you give up your baby? How could you let Joe go to jail?

In desperation she rang Joe: maybe he could suggest some way out. When she had spoken to him on the phone the day after the trial to thank him for what he had done on her behalf, he brushed off the deed with a light-hearted *what are friends for*. This time he sounded awfully depressed.

"What's the matter?" The mother reaching out to comfort her baby.

"Ger's leaving me. He's packing his stuff right now."

"Oh Joe, I'm so sorry. What happened? I thought you two were…"

"He believes what I said in court. I can't convince him it's not true."

Was there no end to the misery her good deed had wrought? "Let me come over and talk to him. Maybe I can change his mind?"

"Would you?" The cry of a despairing child.

The rain had stopped and the clouds had lifted. Five minutes' driving took her to the flat in Salthill. She found a spot for her car fifty yards down the street. As she approached the house, carrying Mary Kate, Ger came out the door carrying a lamp with a large orange shade. He put it into the back of a panel van parked in front of the gate.

"Hello, Ger."

He swung around, glared at her, then without a word strode quickly back into the house and slammed the door. She had to ring the bell three times before Joe appeared. "Sorry, very sorry." He made a brave attempt at a smile. "We're having some problems, but come on in anyway."

She wanted to go away and leave them to their squabble, until she reminded herself that she was its cause. Mary Kate was squawking and trying to wriggle out of her arms as they followed Joe down the hall. He had to use his key to get in the door of the flat. As they walked into the parlor, Ger was coming out of another room, carrying a pile of books. He made to brush past but Eilis, holding on to Mary Kate, stepped in front of him. "I've something to tell you, Ger."

He made to go around her. "I don't want to hear it." All gloom and phlegm and barely controlled anger.

"You will when I tell you." She moved into his path again.

He stopped, head down, not looking at her. "Go on so, but be quick."

"Not only is Joe *not* Mary Kate's father, but he's in danger of going to jail for perjuring himself about it."

"Says who?"

"Sit down and I'll tell you." He stood for a minute, tapping his foot on the floor, then put down his books and took three reluctant steps to a chair. Eilis placed Mary Kate on the carpet, joined Joe on the sofa, and told them what had occurred in the solicitor's office.

When she finished, Ger looked up, indecision in his face.

"You're not taking me for a ride, are you?"

Eilis grimaced. "I'll have to give up my baby to keep Joe out of jail. Does that sound like I'm telling you lies?" She got up and retrieved Mary Kate from under a lamp table.

"No you won't!" Joe shouted. He jumped to his feet. "I'll *go* to jail. It's my fault. I was only trying to help you. Ah shit." He slumped back onto the sofa.

"I'm such a fecking eejit," Ger said. He bent forward in his chair as if in pain with duodenal gas.

"I'll leave you to it then." Eilis struggled to hold on to her protesting child. She had to get away before she herself started screaming.

When she got home she rang Aisling Banaghan. "Could we meet somewhere to talk? Just the two of us?"

"I don't think so, no." Aisling's tone was glacial. "Anything I have to say to you I'll say through my solicitor."

"Please, Aisling. It'll be good news for you. Please? We were best friends once."

There was the longest pause at the other end. Eilis waited. Eventually, in a voice that quavered, Aisling asked, "Did you say—did I hear you say it would be good news?" The last two words came out as a sort of cracked whisper.

"That's what I said."

"Eugene would want to be present, of course."

"No." No way could she handle the two of them at this point. "Just yourself, Aisling. Please."

Another long pause. "All right then. When?"

"Tomorrow, if you can manage it."

"Eugene is going to a football match in the afternoon. We could get together then. Will you be coming here?"

"I thought we might meet somewhere in between." They agreed on a pub about a mile from Headford on the Galway road. At three o'clock on Sunday afternoon.

The crowd at the bar was noisy, drinking and watching a football match on the telly. The two cousins sat at a corner table by the window. Other than a perfunctory greeting they said nothing until their drinks arrived. Aisling had a sherry, Eilis a glass of white wine. "I'll want to be able to visit her," Eilis said after she had a sip.

Aisling stared across at the television as if not comprehending. Then she put down her glass and, bending over, gripped the edge of the low table with both hands. Her breathing was audible over the din. "Can I trust you this time?" she asked, without raising her head.

"I'm so sorry about all I've put you through." Eilis hadn't been able to decide whether she should or should not apologize, but now, in the presence of her anguished cousin, it seemed not only right but necessary.

Aisling, still gripping the table and with her head still bent, persisted, in a tiny voice, "You're going to sign the papers and give her to us?"

"Yes." An explosion of sound at the bar when a goal was scored drowned both Eilis's anguished wail and Aisling's suppressed half-screech.

"You're absolutely sure this time?"

"As long as you agree to let me visit her—say once a week." She felt as if she were reciting lines, as she had done years ago in convent school plays, and that in a minute she'd walk off-stage and be herself again.

"Didn't we always tell you that you could do that?"

"I'm sorry. So sorry."

"I don't know what came over you at all." Aisling put her hands on top of her head, as if to keep it from exploding. "You, of all people. There's no one I'd have trusted more in the whole entire world."

"I had to do it." She had been undecided about acknowledging Gran's part in the business, but now she told her cousin of the letter, and of Gran's voice from beyond the grave. Aisling ran a finger around the rim of her glass all through the telling. When Eilis finished she put the glass down.

"If you told me that story about anyone else I'd say you were either a terrible liar or you should be committed." There were tears in her eyes as she looked at Eilis, though they were accompanied by an incongruous hint of a smile that wouldn't stay suppressed. "But when it comes to Granny McGreevy, there's nothing I wouldn't put past the woman, dead or alive."

They sipped in silence. The game played on. The crowd at the bar shouted and chortled and groaned in despair. Did it always have to be that one must lose for another to win? Eilis drained the last of her wine.

Acknowledgments

My special thanks to Mary Lyndon Shanley, whose elegant paper on surrogate motherhood inspired this novel.

I am very grateful to my agent, Regina Ryan, for her many helpful suggestions, and for her continued faith in me.

My thanks to the Taconic Writers, my wife Patricia, and Carolyn Palmer for reading the manuscript at various stages. I owe them more than I can say.